TWO SIDES

TO

EVERY COIN

Acknowledgements

Thanks to Rick, Barry, and John
for keeping my writing honest.

Contents

Prologue

Emily Holden, age 28, sits at the window of her room, in Canaan, New Hampshire, looking out at the hillside on the other side of the valley. The sun is going down and lights are just beginning to come on in the houses she can see from her second story room. She holds an envelope and letter in her left fist which now, after two hours, is crinkled up almost into a ball. Her eyes are red and her cheeks show she has been crying.

Like most young women and girls, Emily has fallen in love with a young man who was called off to war in the spring of 1944. Her lover, Francois Beechen, 31, was drafted and recently shipped overseas to Europe as part of the second wave after D-Day.

Like many of those same young women and girls, Emily decided to give herself to her lover before he left for war, hoping that would seal their love for each other, and give each other something to hold onto during the many long and lonely nights to come.

Now, more than six months after discovering that she is pregnant with François' child, and more than a month and a half since she left her hometown of Boston and the comfort of her parent's house, she has moved in with her lover's brother and wife, Pierre and Louise Beechen in Canaan. It is mid-summer and her pregnancy is obvious to anyone that sees her. She is not the only woman in New Hampshire that will have a child by someone who will not be returning from the war, someone to whom she is not married. Like so many children born during the war, this child will never know its father.

She rubs her right hand over her belly and remembers how Francois would rub his hands on her shoulders whenever they sat looking out at Boston Harbor.

She opens her left hand and the envelope sits there in her palm, a lifeless ball of paper. She takes it in both hands, flattening and straightening it out on the table in front of her. She reads the return address first:

PFC Dominic Fontella – 324508733

HQ Co - Medical Center

London, Eng.

c/o APO 625 , NY, NY.

She sees the censor examiner's stamp on the envelope and the 6 cent postage stamp showing a red bomber in the air. She stares at the postmark: Aug 23, 1944.

She reads the address:

> Miss Emily Holden
> 16 High St.
> Canaan, New Hampshire, USA

She unfolds the triangular flap on the back of the envelope and removes the letter, slowly opening it again and praying it will read something different this time. She lays it flat on the table in front of her and in the dimming light reads:

> *Dear Emily,*
>
> *My name is Dominic Fontella, and I served with François. As you know, I cannot say where we served together nor when, but I can tell you we became fast buddies. You do that over here because you don't really have time to do otherwise.*
>
> *I am writing you because François asked me to, should anything happen to him. Well, I am so sorry to tell you this, but the worst did happen to him, and all I can tell you is that I was with him when it happened and I held his hand so he wouldn't be alone at the end.*
>
> *I was also hit that day and am recovering here in England. I don't know yet how well I will recover or whether I will be allowed to go back to the front.*
>
> *I do know this, though, François loved you very much and was looking forward to seeing that baby of yours when he returned.*
>
> *I know you will miss him, and I will, too. We became very close here in the few months we knew each other.*
>
> *I just wanted to let you know, you were the last person he thought of before he died, and that he loved you very much.*
>
> *I hope you are in someway comforted by that thought.*
>
> *With great respect and sorrow,*
> *Dominic Fontella*

She pushes the letter away and lets a tear fall on the table. She is almost all cried out now. She wonders why Pierre has not yet received any notice of François' death from the Army Department. Maybe they are having trouble notifying people due to the large number of deaths occurring overseas.

She hears a knock on her bedroom door. It is Louise asking her if she is alright. She gets up, letter in hand, and goes to the door. Opening it, she hands the letter to Louise who reads it, and they both stand there crying and holding on to each other.

It is then that Emily decides she will not keep this baby. She will have it, but keeping it around her will only cause her pain for the rest of her life. She will bear the child and she will ensure immediately after birth it will be given to and raised by a loving family, but she will not keep it. The next day, she takes a bus south where she visits a couple of adoption agencies in Manchester, New Hampshire, to find out the particulars of adoption and how to go about it.

A little more than two months later, she gives birth.

Don Winston stares over his drink at the well-worn mahogany bar top. You don't see many of these anymore, he says to himself. Most bar tops are now made of some kind of laminate or butcher block. This one has a long list of stories to share if only he can urge them out of the wood. This one has a thick wood bar rail, polished smooth by maybe 100 years of elbows resting on it. It doesn't even need varnish to protect it; the oil from human forearms has penetrated the surface years ago providing better protection than any varnish, shellac, or polyurethane could ever hope to provide.

This is a "man's" bar. This is where tall tails are told, politics discussed, friendships solidified. This is also where secrets are shared and fortunes lost by loose lips. Plans for life are made here, and bets move dollars from one hand to another. This is somewhere you go to hide on a dark rainy night or share in the joy of a winning ballgame on a Saturday afternoon.

There aren't many of these bars left anymore. Not too many places left where an old man can spend his afternoons nursing a cheap beer while trying to keep from being lonely. Places where you can walk through the door at 5:30 at night and half the bar acknowledges your entrance.

There used to be a couple of these types of bars in almost every town, but not anymore. Don instinctively "knew" this bar and he hopes he will get to know it better because he wants to know those stories buried deep in the grains of the mahogany.

Don's brother, Tom, sits a few feet away at the corner of the bar. Tom has a habit of separating himself from Don whenever they first enter a bar together. He always wants to survey a room for any unattached females that he might be able to approach. Tom never needs a "wingman" and has more confidence than any one man should be allowed to have. As soon as the brothers walked into the bar tonight, Tom spied a 30 something brunette sitting alone at the end of the bar playing with the straw in her drink, immediately determining she would be the quest for the night. Tom wastes no time in making conversation with the brunette, and soon she is laughing at things he says.

There are not too many people in the bar tonight. Other than Don, Tom, and the brunette, there is a couple at a table in a corner and one other man in his fifties at the bar. It is still early, so maybe people haven't come out for the night yet, Don thinks. Then again, maybe Tuesday night isn't a night for bar flies in this town.

At one end of the bar, a big plate glass window looks over the lake. Looking through the window one sees little since there are no lights on the lake to reflect. Because of the reflections on the window, all you see with clarity are the patrons at the bar, the bottles of liquor behind the bar, and a few of the tables. The moon has just started to rise so there is only the faintest reflection visible on the surface of the water showing through the window. To the right of the window, a door leads to an outside eating area with some wooden Adirondack chairs circling a small Adirondack style table.

Don picks up his drink and casually walks to the door. Opening it, he smells the pine scent of the trees surrounding the lake. He walks out on the porch and closes the door behind him taking in what view there is of the lake. Choosing a chair away from the glare of the inside light, he settles down into it and stares up at the sky. So many stars, he thinks. This is just what he needs right now. This is everything his home in the city is not. His mind will clear up here, and maybe he can think of a new story for the book he is about to begin writing.

This will be the third book in a series about Jeffrey Stamford, the main character in his last two books. JS, as he always refers to him, is in many ways an aggregate of him and his brother, Tom. Tom, a 47-year-old retired police detective with a lot of rough edges and a very cynical view of the world is one aspect of JS. Don, a 36-year-old carpenter turned writer, has a more trusting view of life. Therefore, JS is a very untrusting character who is constantly at odds with himself about not trusting people more easily. He is consistently kind to people, yet expects nothing from them.

This allows Don great freedom when writing about JS as it is never really clear how JS sees any situation he encounters. You can always guarantee that JS will do something, but you're never sure what that is going to be.

The last two novels were mysteries and Don feels he had two

or three more left in him for JS, but no ideas have come to him in the last couple of months. He figured getting out of town might let him find a story somewhere, so he called Tom and suggested a road trip to nowhere in hopes of having the literary fire lit inside him.

After a few days rambling the back roads of New York, Connecticut, and now Vermont, they end up in this town on a lake in Vermont, about five miles from the Canadian border. It is both a typical lake town catering to tourists as well as local folks, yet non-descript in its own way. There is a grain storage and processing facility almost in the center of the town, a set of railroad tracks runs through it, and across the street from it, a fancy restaurant with a marina that has both fifteen-foot aluminum fishing boats as well as forty foot cabin cruisers tied to floating wooden docks.

Downtown consists of fifteen or twenty small businesses housed in old brick buildings. There are no fast food places in town, save for Claire's Pizza. The only gas station in town doesn't even have a min-mart attached to it. Once you get outside of downtown there is a Pizza Hut, a supermarket, the Dexter Liquor Outlet and a Subways shop. After that, houses fade fast into nothing but fields and pastures. It's hard to imagine people make a living here.

Don looks out over the lake wondering what secrets this town hides. Towns like this always have secrets, you just have to search and dig deep for them. There are always people that know those secrets, but they are even harder to find. Maybe tomorrow he'll take some time to talk with the folks over at the town hall. He hopes they have stories to tell that will kindle his imagination.

He gets up and walks back into the bar. Tom is still chatting up the brunette and Don sees the couple at the table have left. No one else is coming in tonight, Don thinks, as he walks over to his brother.

"Tom – I'm turning in for the night. I'll leave the car here for you, and I'll walk back to the motel. It's a nice night out and I can use the walk."

Tom turns to him and nods as Don hands him the keys. The brunette says nothing, but her hand is on Tom's thigh so Don bets he won't see Tom till morning. Don pats Tom on the shoulder, smiles, and turns to leave. "Later," he says with a smile.

Once outside, the short walk to the motel allows him time to wonder what stories he'll hear tomorrow when he stops by the town hall. There's got to be a few scandals and mysteries in this old town, especially being this close to the Canadian border. Surely, there must have been rum-running on this lake during prohibition, and somebody must have made a lot of money doing that – and made a lot of enemies as well.

Thirty minutes later, Don is sound asleep in his motel room.

2

Don wakes to the sound of Tom's key in the door. He immediately remembers he forgot to pull the shades down last night before bed, and now the early morning sunlight pours into the room blinding him as he opens his eyes.

The door opens, and a sheepishly smiling Tom walks into the room. "Sorry old buddy," he says.

"What time is it?" Don asks.

"Around 6:30, I think," Tom replies. "Did you sleep well?"

"The better question is," Don asks his brother, "did you even get any sleep?"

Tom closes the door behind him. "Not much," he smiles.

"Uhhh! Don't rub it in. You'll probably want to sleep all day now, won't you?"

"Well, I could use a few hours."

"I guess that will work out for me," Don lifts himself up to rest on an elbow. "I have a few things I want to explore in town so I'm going to need the car. You just end up sitting in the damn thing anyway when I'm researching things. You might as well catch some sleep here in a comfortable bed, I guess."

Tom throws the car keys on the dresser and walks toward the bathroom. "I'm going to shower and then go to bed."

"OK! I'll shower when you're done and then leave you to your dreams."

Tom turns to him. "You know, she works at the local supermarket and she seems to know a lot of people. You might want to talk with her. She might be useful to you," Tom lowers his head and furrows his brow, "research-wise, that is."

Don shakes his head at his brother, and snickers. He throws off the covers, and spins onto the side of the bed, placing his feet on the carpet. Probably get some kind of foot fungus from the carpet, he muses and quickly lifts his feet back up to the edge of the bed. He throws the covers on the floor and places his feet back down.

Soon, Tom emerges from the bathroom and motions Don to go ahead. Don finds his shoes and slips them on his feet and heads to the bathroom.

It's going to be a long day, Don thinks as he closes the bathroom door behind him. When he comes out, Tom is already under the covers and asleep. At least today's research time won't be infringed upon by Tom's restlessness from being stuck in a car in a parking lot all day.

Don dresses and heads out for a little breakfast before his long day of searching for a story begins.

There is a small restaurant a half mile away, The Chicken and Cow, and the parking lot in back is almost filled with trucks and a few cars. Don turns in and finds a space half way around the side of the small building. He looks at all the pickups parked there and wonders who the folks are that own them. I'll find out in a couple of minutes, he says to himself.

Entering the restaurant he finds space at the counter between a burly man in his late forties who sports a graying beard and a "Best Bass Boats" ball cap, and a man in his thirties who is clean-shaven with long hair pulled back in a ponytail and wearing a salt and pepper sports coat. Each of the men is more than halfway through his breakfast and talk animatedly with others at their sides.

One of the waitresses behind the counter places a cup of coffee in front of a man at the end of the counter, turns and sees Don and walks toward him.

Stopping in front of Don, she asks, "What can I get ya, honey?"

"Let's start with some coffee," he sees her name tag, "Laura. Then a couple of eggs over easy, toast, and maybe a glass of OJ."

She smiles at him, writes down his order, and walks to the kitchen window. She says something to the cook and places the slip of paper with his order on it on a metal clip over the window. She grabs a glass off the back shelf, pours some orange juice into it and brings it over to Don, setting it in front of him. She hardly stops as she continues on to the coffee pot and pours his coffee. She sets the coffee in front of Don and from under the counter pulls up a small shiny metal pitcher full of milk and sets it next to the coffee. A bell rings and she smiles at him and turns to pick up someone's order.

Don puts a little of the milk into his cup, stirs it and smells the aroma of the coffee. At least it isn't burned, he thinks and takes a sip. The coffee tastes as good as it smells; good coffee always promises a good day.

He takes a writer's eye look around this little restaurant. The folks in here have the look of a real cross section of who lives in this town. He makes mental notes of these people which he will use when he creates the characters in the story he is going to start writing soon.

The man with the beard accidently bumps his arm against Don's elbow causing Don to spill a little of his coffee on the counter.

"Oh! Geeze, man. I'm sorry," he says.

Don smiles and shakes his head, "That's ok. It's kinda tight here at the counter and it's hard not to bump elbows."

"True enough," the man says. "I don't think I've seen you in here before. You new in town?"

"Yeah! My brother and I are on a little vacation. Right now, he's sleeping off a little too much good cheer from last night."

"I know the feeling. The older I get, the less I party, and the more I feel it when I do," he laughs. "You plan on staying in town long?"

"I don't know. Depends on if there are interesting things to do here. I see the marina, but I don't have a boat. And there doesn't look like there is much else to do around here. Any places of interest I should see or any strange places to visit? Any haunted houses or spooky cemeteries?

"In some of these small towns there is a storyteller that knows everything about everybody, and I love to talk with them when I can find them. Anyone around here like that? They always have a lot of history to share."

"You a history buff," the beard asks.

"Kinda," Don says. "I love hearing not only historical stuff but regular stories about, well, I guess you might call it gossip, for lack of a better term.

"I love all those stories about who had done what to whom, and about all the skeletons hiding in closets, the stories people were never sure about whether they were true or not. Sometimes, small towns have strange disappearances or even crimes that have gone unsolved for years, even decades. I find all that stuff fascinating.

"My name is Don," and he holds out his hand.

The man turns toward Don and extends his hand, "Billy Shavers. I work at the grain and feed plant. They run that place 24/7. I work the midnight to eight shift.

"What do you do for a living, Don?"

Don always has to be careful how he replies to this question. Once people know you write for a living, they have a tendency to become extremely closed-mouthed. That doesn't help Don get the information he wants and needs. "Mostly carpentry, small home construction, and remodeling. I freelance, so that lets me take off as much time as I want. I work till I can afford to take time off, then I take time off," Don laughs.

"My brother is retired so we get to take road trips whenever we want, with no strings holding us back. It's a good life so far."

"Sounds like it," Billy says. "Wish I could do that, but I'm married with two kids, a boy 16, and a girl 14, and of course a wife," he laughs. "Kinda keeps you settled down."

Don nods understandably.

"So, you're looking for town history or town secrets, are you? There's a guy lives just outside of town. He's lived here his whole life and knows just about everyone. He's an older fellow, maybe 80, and I've heard him tell stories from when he was a kid when there weren't a lot of paved roads around here, and when the only outsiders that came through town were usually lost," he laughs.

"I'm pretty friendly with him, and I drive past his place on the way home. I'll stop in and see if he wouldn't mind you stopping out there and talking with him.

"Where you staying, at the motel?"

"Yeah, Room 27. Don Winston."

"OK then, Don. I'll do that on the way home and if he says

OK, I'll give the motel a call and leave you a message and directions to his place. His name is Benjamin Harper, but everyone calls him Benny."

Just then, Don's eggs and toast are placed in front of him. "Can I get you anything else right now, honey?" Laura asks.

Don shakes his head and smiles at her. She returns to serving others at the counter.

"I want to thank you, Billy. It's kind of you to do this." Don offers his hand again and Billy shakes it.

Billy gets up and pulls out his wallet, removing a five-dollar bill and places it under his coffee cup saucer. "Hey Laura," and he points to the cup; she looks at him and nods.

"Talk to you later," Billy says as he turns to leave.

Don looks down at his eggs and toast, then grabs his cup and sips some more coffee. Yeah, it's going to be a good day, he smiles to himself.

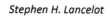

3

Don finishes his breakfast and Laura brings him his check. He hands Laura six dollars, telling her to keep the change. She smiles, says thanks, takes his empty plate placing it in a sink below the counter, and walks back to the cash register to ring up his bill.

Don sits there taking the last few sips of coffee, thinking about this guy Benjamin that Billy is going to talk with this morning. Benjamin sounds like the perfect guy to help Don get the creative juices flowing again.

He stands, and seeing that Laura is looking at him, nods and smiles, then walks out of the restaurant and back to his car. He pulls out of the lot and turns in the direction of the town hall. Should be open by now, he thinks. I can get some background on the town before I see Benjamin. That way I can have some idea of places he references when I speak with him.

As he pulls up to the town hall, he sees that the historical society is located in the same building. One stop shopping , he says to himself. Now, I don't have to go trekking all over town looking for folks to talk with about this town. Things really are looking up.

He parks the car in a space in front of the building and walks up the five granite steps that lead to the front door. The building must be 120 years old, he guesses, but they have tried to modernize it with glass entry doors and vinyl windows. The updates do the building a disservice, though, even if the changes probably provide better insulating properties. He pulls open the glass entry door and feels the cooler air inside the building. Air conditioning. Probably why they updated the doors and windows.

He decides to start at the Historical Society before going into the main part of the town hall. Let's see what the town can tell me before I start digging into its soul, he says under his breath. He opens the door and walks in.

"Good morning, Gertrude," he says to the clerk behind the desk situated off to the side of the entrance. *Gertrude Revere* is engraved on the brass plate glued to the green triangular piece of marble sitting on Gertrude's desk. "How are you this fine day," Don says with a great big smile.

Gertrude looks up from her reading and smiles back at him. "Well, I am just fine today. How about you?" Gertrude has that famous Vermont accent and Don feels immediately comfortable.

"Couldn't be better," Don answers.

"So what can I do for you?" Gertrude asks.

"To tell you the truth, Gertrude, I am not sure. This is my first day in town and I would love to know all about Dexter, Vermont. Whenever I am in a new town, I like to learn about how it started, hear any famous stories about it, discover who its famous sons or daughters are, and what makes it so special. You can enjoy someplace much more if you know its history.

"I can see what this place is now, but how did it get here, what made it what it is today. That's the fun part, that's where the interest lies for me."

"Well, do you want a book or two? I could recommend some town history books for you."

"I bet you know as much about this town as any book in this place. It doesn't look like you are really busy right now, so perhaps you could give me the highlights and then we can figure out what books I might want to read to know more about what you're going to tell me." Don looks around the room at the two bookcases of books hoping she'll take the time to do what he has suggested.

"Yes, I do. I have lived here my whole life and I have forgotten more stuff about this town than most people have known. Why don't you drag that chair over there," she points to an old oak jury chair, one of four along the wall, "and sit down here near me. I'll give you an overview of Dexter and then we can figure out what you want to know more about. Then I can help you select the right books for any follow-up information you want to know."

"That sounds great, Gertrude," Don says as he drags one of the chairs over to the side of her desk. "I can't wait for you to get started."

"OK!" Gertrude smiles. "I'll give you a snapshot of what makes Dexter what she is. We refer to the town as her – seems fitting for some reason, although I can't right say why." Gertrude chuckles.

"The town of Dexter is the second smallest town by population in Vermont. It was once the County seat, but that was changed way back in 1879.

"Dexter has been lucky in that not much fighting has ever taken place around here. Not during the Revolutionary war, nor the French and Indian Wars, nor the War of 1812, or even the Civil War. We have never been sucked in like so many of the other New England towns, although further south in Vermont there was plenty of fighting going on in almost every conflict. One time, though, following an attack on Saint-Francis, Quebec in 1759, Rogers' Rangers were forced to retreat through the County and passed right through town.

"Dexter was settled in 1793, but it wasn't called that then. Its original name was Confluence Junction because two lakes meet here. In 1803, a bridge was built crossing the narrowest point of the river downtown and the town was renamed Bridgetown. In 1889, Bridgetown settlement was incorporated and took the name Dexter, named for the leading landowner of the town at that time, Johnathan Dexter.

"In 1868, the railroad reached the village, connecting it with Bennington and soon after that, Quebec. The railroad operated under many different owners until the mid-1950s. One line operated until 1970 as a passenger and freight line but was then converted into just a freight line. The other one, the Quebec line, operated as a passenger line until 1982 when the right of way was sold to the state and Canada, and the tracks pulled. A multi-use bike and hike trail was developed in 1990 and now you can bike or hike from here straight up to Quebec.

"We were really lucky during the Civil War that no fighting ever made it this far north, but Dexter sent many men off to fight in that war as part of the Vermont Regulators. The town lost 54 men to that conflict, and while that doesn't sound like a lot, there were only a little more than 100 families in the town at the time, so almost half of the families lost someone.

"Dexter's two main industries during the latter part of the 19th century were lumbering and dairy farming. We had two big lumber outfits from the 1890s; one went out of business just after the

Second World War, and the other lasted until the 1980s.

"During the 1920s the area began drawing a great number of tourists mainly because of the lake. The first paved road in the area was Main Street and that was in 1926. We still only have three traffic lights in town and two of those are on either side of the bridge. The first one was in the middle of town in 1939, the other two were installed in 1951 because the traffic on the bridge was getting so bad we started having accidents caused by out of town drivers.

"Another big business in town was started by Ernest and Mary Prescott, who owned a farm outside of town. It was Ernest, really, who started the business in the mid-1930s as the depression began to end. He began processing grain for the local farmers in the barn at his farm. Then so many farmers started going to him for their grain processing he opened a small grain processing plant in town. Before long farmers from all over the County, then all over northern Vermont and even into Canada, started using his processing plant to process their grain. Ernest ran that plant until he died in 1966, when his son, Emerson, 22, took over. Emerson has two sons, Emerson Prescott, Jr., the eldest, and John Prescott, a Doctor in Boston.

"A very sad thing happened to Emerson's family in 1986 when Lily, his wife, died in the same car accident that almost killed Emerson. He was thrown from the car and suffered a severe concussion causing him to have partial amnesia. He was very lucky that all he ended up having were a few cuts and bruises. Everyone was amazed, including the doctors, that Emerson not only didn't die in the accident, but he didn't break anything either. He actually walked away from the accident. It took almost a year for Emerson to regain a semblance of memory, though, and be able to return to work at the factory. Emerson, Jr. assumed the day to day operations of the company then while his dad was convalescing, and Junior, that's what everyone calls him, continues even now. Emerson's memory and health continued to improve for a few years, but then he had a setback of sorts around 1990. Seems he blacked out and fell, hitting his head on the fender of his car. No great injury other than a little cut on his head, but after that, his memory seemed to falter again. He tried to return to work but there was so much he couldn't remember about his work he really wasn't much use up there. He still goes to work a little each week since then, but its more for show than anything else.

"Emerson is probably the richest man in town at this point. He is well respected by most folks in town and his company has always treated their workers with great respect. His company was one of the first in the area to offer health care and retirement benefits to their workers. There are some folks in town that worked only for the grain plant, retiring from there."

Gertrude stopped talking and looked at Don. "Is that what you wanted to know?"

"Gertrude, it was fascinating. You really do know everything about this town don't you?"

"Ayah! And I know stuff that isn't in the official records, too." She laughs. "Small towns are just full of gossip and stories that either can't be told, or would ruin people's lives if they were told, and then found out to be wrong.

"They all make their way to me sooner or later."

Now this is what I want to hear about Don thinks to himself. "Like, uh, what kind of stories, Gertrude?" Don prods.

Gertrude gives a nervous laugh. "Oh, Drat! I really can't say. I probably shouldn't have even mentioned anything like that to you," she laughs nervously. "Sometimes I am nothing more than a rambling old woman." She smiles and laughs, tapping Don on his forearm. "So – what part of what I have told you are you interested in following up on?"

"Well, you mentioned this guy Emerson something, who owns the grain company. That's kind of recent and you did say he was the richest man in town. They always seem to have something hiding in their past that is interesting."

Don looks her in the eye with a small smile on his face. "You said that the grain company in town is his, right?"

"Yes, it is. But as I said, you rarely see him there any more. His son runs the day to day operation of the place. Emerson is a little older than me, and you get to be our age you don't run around as much as you used to when you were young. He does own that big boat in the marina, though, and he loves to take it out and go fishing, although why he needs such a big boat just to fish is beyond me. I know he sails way up to the northern part of the lake with it, and he'd probably sail it all the way up to Quebec if it wasn't for the dams just north of the lake."

"So, have you ever heard any interesting stories about Emerson or his family?" Don asks.

"Nope. Not really. They have always lived a normal life. No scandals, no drunks in the family, no dirty dealings. Just normal good old Vermonters, willing to lend a helping hand when needed and charitable beyond all get out."

"So, there is nothing strange about them. No, shall we say, stories told behind their back?"

Gertrude raises her eyebrows a little and scrunches up her lips a bit. "Well, tell the truth, after Emerson's second 'accident' Emerson never seemed himself again when I see him. He and I were always pretty close since we grew up together. I know he had all those problems with his memory and everything, but he and I always seemed to do alright, even after the car accident. Sure, he couldn't recall some things, but he always knew who I was and he usually asked after my folks, even though dad died right around the time of his accident, and mom died three years later.

"Then one time, right after that second accident, I saw him on the street, which in and of itself was a little odd, walking around downtown, and he walked right by me. Not a bit of recognition. Even after I stopped right there and said hello to him. He just kept walking. I had to shout his name three or four times before he turned and looked at me.

"Emerson, I said, again, and he raised his eyebrows in surprise. Emerson, it's me, Gertrude. He kept looking at me as if he didn't know me. It's Gertrude Revere, Emerson. What's the matter with you?

"Finally, he grabbed my hand and said, 'Oh, Gertrude, how are you?' He was talking, but I had the vague idea he still didn't know who I was.

"We made small talk about the weather, but whenever I asked him about anything personal in his life, he just sort of shrugged his shoulders or nodded his head. I had the feeling he didn't want to talk with me that day.

"For the next few months every time I saw him anywhere, while he recognized me, we didn't seem to have much to talk about, but as I said, we had always had plenty to talk about before. I wasn't the only one in town noticed his demeanor had changed. Most everyone that knew him mentioned it at one time or the other.

"In a few months, like I said, things seemed to return to normal, although with me, still to this day, he doesn't seem to remember things we use to talk about. I have chalked it up to that amnesia thing getting worse. Maybe he is even getting a little of the Alzheimer's, I don't know." Gertrude shrugs her shoulders a little, "Maybe it's me getting old. Maybe I'm forgetting things."

"I don't think it's you, Gertrude. You're pretty darned sharp if you ask me," Don offers. "Has his doctor said anything, that you know of, about his worsening memory? Do you talk with his son about it."

"Yes. I spoke with Junior about it, and he said Senior's mind is as sharp as ever, except for the partial amnesia. Prior to that day on the street I mentioned to you, Emerson didn't have any trouble remembering things from the years since the car accident, just trouble with the years before then. He even lost most of the memory of his wife, poor thing. But it seems after the second accident, he lost the memories of the years since the first accident as well, but, as I said, his recollection of things since then are pretty good."

Don stood up and took Gertrude's hand in his. "I want to thank you for spending time with me, telling me all about Dexter. You are a great ambassador for this town."

"Why thank you, young man. You be sure to stop in again before you go. It's been fun talking with you." Gertrude grasped Don's hand with both of hers.

"I'll do that." He lets go of her hand, drags the chair back against the wall with the others, waves at her, and exits the historical society office.

Whew! That was entertaining, he thought as he walks out into the lobby of the building. He stops to look at the directory board of the town hall.

Tax Office – room 6, 1st floor

Vital Records – room 8, 1st floor

Which one should he go to next? The tax office he decides. He can see how the land is divided up. It is always good to know the average size of property that people own. It gives you a sense of who has money, and how successful they are. He really wants to see how big Emerson Prescott's holdings are, and what they are valued at. If Prescott owns not only a farm but the land that the grain processing plant stands on, then as Gertrude said, he has to be one of the wealthiest men in town, if not the richest.

He turns and strolls down to the tax office in room 6 on the first floor. This is turning out to be a great day.

4

The door to the tax office is wide open. There is only one clerk sitting at the desk opposite the entryway. The clerk sits in front of a computer screen, a stack of papers to her right, a cup of coffee to her left. When Don walks in, she looks up from her work and smiles. Everyone here is so darned friendly, he notes.

"Good morning. May I help you," the clerk asks.

"Hi," Don replies. "I hope so."

Don once again explains he is just passing through on vacation and is sort of a history buff, and he wonders, could he possibly look at some tax maps to get an idea of how property around town is divided up. He tells her he has a theory towns develop according to how people buy land and designate borders.

The clerk looks at him quizzically, not having the slightest idea what he is talking about. She asks him if there is a particular section he is interested in seeing, and he says, downtown would be a good place to start.

She nods and walks him to a section of the room that has old cabinets with thin drawers, which, when she opens one, he sees contain maps of the properties in town.

"We haven't computerized the tax maps yet. In Vermont, each county is responsible for digitizing their own tax maps and money hasn't been set aside for that yet. They are supposed to start doing that in the next year or so, but none of us are holding our breath for that to happen." She pulls out a large cardboard folio containing five large maps. From the edges of the maps he can see, they all look very old and almost ready to fall apart from use.

"Luckily, properties don't change hands much around here, so we rarely have to take these maps out to update them. They are pretty fragile, so please use care in using them. I'll place them over here on the map table for you." She walks about twenty steps to a large oak table, setting the maps down with care. "No coffee or drinks, and of course, no smoking is allowed. Do not bend or crease or mark the maps. As you go through the maps, just set them to one side. There's plenty of room on this table so you won't have to lift them up or anything; just slide them to the side. When you are finished I'll put them back in their portfolio, and put them away. Any questions?

"If there is anything I can do for you, let me know."

"Thank you very much. You are very kind," Don says. They smile at each other and she returns to her desk. Don opens the portfolio and looks at the first map. It maps the east side of the town and shows three blocks of Main Street and two blocks on either side of it. Every building has a lot number on it as well as the street address, the Owner of Record, and a tax designation:

R for Residential   C for Commercial
G for Government   F for House of Faith
H for Health   P for Public.

Don scours the addresses, taking notes on a sheet of paper he gets from the clerk. "Only pencil, please!" she states emphatically.

Don spends the next couple of hours looking over fifty or more maps. He finds the grain company property downtown almost immediately, but spends the remainder of the time searching for the property marked "Emerson Prescott". He sees that the farm is made up of at least four separate adjoining pieces of property. The properties add up to more than 150 acres about ten miles outside of town. Must have bought the properties as they came up for sale. Smart man, Don thinks. He notes all the tax map information for the farm, adding it to the information he copies off the grain processing plant tax map.

Don walks to the desk and hands the pencil to the clerk, thanking her for all her help. She smiles, takes the pencil and asks if he is finished with the maps. Don tells her he found all the information he needs, smiles at her and thanks her again, then leaves the office.

Don checks his watch and realizes it is afternoon already. He wonders if Tom will still be sleeping, and decides he will be.

He gets in the car and returns to the motel to see if Billy Shavers called and left a message for him. Fifteen minutes later he stands in front of the motel clerk asking if there are any messages for him.

"Yeah! Billy Shavers called around 9 or so...message is around here somewhere," the clerk says as he looks around behind the counter. "Yeah! Here it is. Something about old Benny on the other side of town." The clerk slips him a folded piece of paper.

9:10 – for Don Winston. Ben said to stop by this afternoon. Take Abenaki Trail Rd. south out of town to the second road on the right just past Farrell's concrete and gravel plant, that's Freedom Road, the first driveway on the left is Ben's place.

Billy.

Don looks at his watch. It is almost 1 PM. He thanks the clerk and walks over to his room. He enters to find Tom sitting in bed watching the TV news.

Tom looks up at Don. "Hi, Bro. How's everything going?"

"It's almost 1 and you still aren't up yet," Don says.

"Almost only counts in horseshoes." Tom jumps out of bed. "Now I am officially up before 1."

"Put some clothes on. We'll get something to eat and then we're taking a ride. I am going to meet an old man named Benny who may have some really interesting stuff to tell me."

Tom puts on his pants and grabs his shirt from the chair next to the bed. "Oh, yeah? What kind of stuff?"

"Well, while you were sleeping the day away I met Mr. Billy Shavers, who told me that old Ben was someone that knew a little about everything in this town, so I figure he is the guy to talk with to find out where any of the skeleton's are buried.

"Then, I went over to the historical society and met Gertrude Revere who let it slip that a man named Emerson Prescott, a lifelong resident and big business owner around here, has been acting strange for quite a few years and although she didn't come right out and say, she indicated she thought something was wrong about him.

"Then I went to the tax office to find where Prescott lives. He's pretty well heeled and owns that big grain plant we saw when we first drove through town. I want to see what old Ben has to say about Prescott. Maybe there's a story there I can use for the book.

"If you are really nice, I may let you sit in on that

conversation. You know, I value that cop intuition you have, and you often see things I don't when I am putting storylines together. You always ask me questions about lapses in my storyline and reasoning, and you make me dig deeper into thinking rationally.

"So, having you there when I start questioning Ben about the town and about Prescott, you'll hear important things I miss in his answers. You'll have a new question or two for the next time, questions that I don't realize I should have asked this time. Just don't ask them in front of Ben. I don't want him to look at us as interrogators or anything, just as inquisitive history buffs on vacation, and you always sound like a police detective when you start asking questions.

"Maybe for the next book, I'll give you credit as a researcher and contributor."

"I would rather you give me half the profit on the book. That would be a much nicer way of saying 'Thank you' don't you think?." Tom finishes tying his shoes. "Can we get something to eat first, I'm famished. You know I haven't eaten anything since last night."

'Yeah…come on. Let's go." Don opens the door and motions for Tom to follow.

They drive into town and stop at the Chicken and Cow where Don ate breakfast. Laura is still there and she smiles at Don as he and Tom take seats at a table. "Couldn't wait to come back, huh, hon," she says. "What can I get ya?"

"Let's start with some coffee," Tom says. "Then we'll take a look at your lovely menu."

Laura looks at him, nods her head, and runs off to the counter to get two coffees. Don looks at Tom, "Be nice, Tom. I want them to be friends, not think we're making fun of them."

'Sorry," Tom says, just before Laura returns and places the cups in front of them, then she goes back to the counter for the creamer.

Placing the creamer on the table, she asks them what they would like.

"I think I'll have a tuna on rye toast," Tom says.

"Me, too," says Don.

"You want fries with that," asks Laura. They shake their heads, no, and she walks to the kitchen window to place their order.

"So, you gonna fill me in on what we're looking for when we get to old Ben's place? Sounds like you have some sort of idea fermenting in your head and you hope old Ben will sort it all out for you," Tom says as he sips his coffee. "By the way, this is great coffee, isn't it? I'll have to remember this place tomorrow morning."

"Yeah! I think there's a story here about this Prescott guy and I'm betting that Ben knows all about it, even if he doesn't really know that he knows," Don says.

As they sit and eat their lunch, Don fills him in on what Gertrude told him about Emerson Prescott. Don talks in hushed terms so other folks in the restaurant won't hear him. He knows if word gets out that he is zeroing in on one specific subject, like a person or an incident, people tend to hold back from telling him what he wants to know. It is better to have folks think you are just a nosey tourist than someone looking to use their town as a backdrop for a book.

They finish their lunch and Don signals Laura to bring them the check. The three of them have a little light conversation about the day and the food before Don pays the bill. Tom and Don rise from the table and say goodbye to Laura, then head out to the car to drive on down the road to Ben's place.

About ten minutes later, just past Farrell's concrete and gravel plant, they turn off Abenaki Trail Rd. onto Freedom Road, and then make a left into Benjamin Harper's driveway.

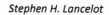

Stephen H. Lancelot

5

Benjamin's house is a typical farmhouse from the turn of the century: white clapboard siding that needs painting, a porch that could use some work with the railings, and three front steps that are cupped from years of water falling on them with no protective paint covering them. Two ladder-back rocking chairs sit on the porch with a small beat-up looking table separating them.

The lawn seems to be well kept although the grass seems a little long to be called manicured. The few bushes around the edge of the house are neatly cut, and there are areas with rose bushes that have been tended carefully and still have a few roses left on the shoots. From the driveway, you can see a small raised bed vegetable garden out back.

To the left of the house is a two car garage separated from the house by about forty feet. Way in the back of the yard is a large two story barn painted red with white trim. It looks to be in better shape than the house and seems to have been painted recently.

A yellow 2003 Ford pickup sits in front of the garage and a 55-gallon oil barrel sits sideways in the bed of the truck. The license on the truck reads CBENGO.

Don pulls the car up close to the house and turns the motor off. He and Tom get out of the car and walk up to the front door, but before they can get to the porch the screen door pops open and Ben walks out to greet them.

"You the guy Billy said wanted to talk to me," Ben asks in his deep Vermont accented voice.

Benjamin Harper, 86, is a slightly eccentric and immensely independent man who at one time had one of the largest farms in the area. When the farm becomes too much for him in his early 50s, he sells most of the acreage to Emerson Prescott, a neighbor down the road who has a small dairy farm, and the owner of the grain processing plant in town. Benjamin keeps five acres that his house and barn sit on, and retires. He is a close friend of Emerson for most of his life until Emerson has his second accident a few years after the accident that kills Lily, Emerson's wife. After that, Emerson becomes standoffish from Ben, and Ben no longer pursues an active friendship with him, even though they live next door to each other.

Don walks up the steps followed by Tom. "Yep, that's me alright," Don says with a smile on his face and stretches out his hand toward Ben. "And this is my brother, Tom.

"You must be Benjamin Harper, right? Thanks for letting me come up here to talk with you; I appreciate it."

Ben reaches for Don's hand, and surprised Don with a handshake much firmer and stronger than Don expects from this old man. "I like Billy. He's a straight shooter, so if he says you're OK, well, then, I'm OK with talking with you. Would you like to sit inside or out here in the nice weather?"

"Out here's fine," Don says. With only two chairs on the porch, Tom sits down on the edge of the porch on the stairway.

"Sorry, Tom," Ben says. "Don't ever have much need for more than two chairs out here. You look like a strong young man, though, so I don't think it'll kill ya to sit there for a while," Ben chuckles.

"No, I think I'll survive," Tom smiles back.

Don lets Ben pick which chair he wants to sit in and then settles into the other one. The air is warm with a very slight breeze and Don is instantly comfortable as he rocks back and forth a little.

"Days like this make you want to rock in this old chair all day long. Just seems like the right thing to do, don't you think," asks Ben.

"It sure does," Don answers.

"So, Don, Billy tells me you are kind of a history buff. That you like small towns and the history behind them. That true?"

"Yep. You can only get so much history from books. I found the best way to find out about someplace is to sit and talk with people that have been there a long time. People like you and Gertrude Revere at the historical society office in town."

Ben nods his head. "So you've met Gertrude? She's a fine woman and she knows a lot about this town. I've known her all her life and she's as honest as the day is long. If she tells ya something, you can take it to the bank."

"Yes – she seems that way. She is a lovely woman and she was very helpful."

"So, what do you want to know about Dexter that Gertrude hasn't already told you?"

"Gertrude mentioned something about Emerson Prescott," Don starts. "He sounds like an interesting guy, especially since he seems to employ so many people around here at the grain plant. Were you and he good friends? You know him pretty well, right?"

"Yeah, I guess so.

"I sold him most of my farm about 30 or 40 years ago. This house, the barn, and five acres are all I kept. His property borders right up alongside mine. You can just about see his house from my back yard." Ben points over his shoulder in the direction of his back yard.

"Gertrude told me about how he lost his wife back in the '80s," Don continues, "and how he lost most of his memory, partial amnesia is what she called it. She said he took a long while to recover. Then a few years later he had another small accident and seemed to have a relapse of his amnesia.

"After the second accident, Gertrude said he hardly knew her. Did that type of thing happen to you, too? Do you speak to him much these days? Did you notice the same thing that Gertrude noticed?

"Why do you want to know so much about whether he and I are still good friends?" Ben looks at him with suspicion. "You some kind of a lawyer or something? You working for Junior?"

"No, no, no. Nothing like that," Don says. "I just found it odd that Gertrude said she found it strange that he one day stopped knowing her and couldn't even recall things they talked about a few months before the second accident. She said otherwise he seemed, well, pretty normal.

"I've heard about partial amnesia, where people forget things that happen just before an accident. The brain seems to lock out the horrific events of the accident; it helps them cope with the tragedy they just experienced.

"I can even understand the almost total amnesia of life before the accident. It's been known to happen quite often. Thing is, people usually forget everything before a certain point in time when that happens. Usually, though, the amnesia doesn't seem to be selective, although I guess it is possible. Medicine sure doesn't know everything about the human brain, does it?

"So, I was just wondering if you noticed the same thing with Emerson. Was he one way before the second accident and another after? Could you feel a difference in him, too?"

Ben studies Don. Ben's face expresses puzzlement as to what Don's angle is. What does Don really want to know, he wonders?

"I guess I would go along with what Gertrude told you about Emerson. It seemed he was just starting to get back to remembering things when he had that second bonk on the head. Doctors said he must have smacked the same part of his brain as the first time. According to Junior, they were surprised that his more recent memory faded along with his memories of the distant past.

"As I think I said, I don't talk with him much anymore. We just don't have a lot to talk about now. I keep up on him through Junior, but then again, I don't see Junior very often either anymore. We don't run in the same circle. Hell, I don't even have a circle anymore," Ben laughs.

"So, when Emerson had the second accident, was he driving or what?" Don needs to be careful what questions he asks, as he doesn't want Ben to shut down on him.

"No. Nothing serious like that," Ben answers. "Emerson apparently was standing in front of his car and when he turned to get back into it, he slipped and fell, and hit his head on the car, at least that's what he told Junior when Junior found him. Luckily, he was in his yard, but there was no one home at the time so he laid there for a couple of hours before anyone found him.

"When Junior got home, Emerson was sitting on the ground leaning against the car. Junior asked him if he was alright and Emerson said yeah. Junior helped Emerson up off the ground and insisted on taking Emerson to the hospital, but Emerson was just as insistent that he was fine. Junior insisted again, but Emerson yelled at him saying kids should listen to their father and not always argue, and they went into the house. Apparently, once they were inside the house, Emerson asked who Junior was, and Junior told him. Emerson just answered yeah, he just forgot for a minute. Junior sat Emerson down in a chair and then called Doc Harrison in town, who came right out.

"Other than the scratch on Emerson's head, there was nothing else wrong with him, the doc said. The doc told Junior not to worry about the confusion of Emerson not knowing who he was, that it would go away in a day or so.

"Thing is, it didn't go away, and soon after that accident, I guess it was a few months actually before he and I stopped talking. It was almost as if he wanted nothing to do with me anymore. I don't go where I'm not wanted, so I let the friendship lag."

"That sounds sad for you. I'm sorry to hear that," Don says.

"Well, it is what it is, I guess. That was a long time ago now, and other than seeing Emerson when I go into town, or when Junior stops by here and Emerson is in the car with him, I never know what Emerson is up to." Ben shakes his head. "You know, at my age, most of my friends are out in the cemetery, and I don't mean they are visiting. So, losing a friend I've known most of my life is a sad thing, whether it is to death or to something like what happened between me and Emerson."

Don follows up on some of the other things Gertrude told him about Dexter, so Ben doesn't think his only interest is in Emerson Prescott. Thing is, Emerson Prescott *IS* the only thing he is interested in here in Dexter. Something seems a little odd about old Emerson Prescott and Don wants to talk with Tom to get his take.

Don and Ben spend another half hour or so talking about Dexter, and about some other folks in town before Don stands and offers his hand to Ben, thanking him for his time and for the great stories. He asks Ben if he can come back again and hear some more about Dexter, and Ben says sure, anytime.

Tom stands and nods goodbye to Ben and the brothers walk quietly back to the car, waving again as they get in the car. Don backs the car down the driveway onto Freedom Road, then out to Abenaki Trail Rd. When they get to the corner of Ben's street, Don looks at

Tom and asks, "So – what's your take on all that?"

"Well, that amnesia stuff sounds a little far fetched, especially the part about the second time the guy hits his head. How do you forget some things and not everything? I guess it's possible, but not really probable. We have to remember, the only physician that looked at Emerson after the second accident was an old country doctor, not a psychiatrist or a neurosurgeon. I wonder why they felt they didn't need to have him go to the hospital. That's something you need to check into.

"I saw a sign with an 'H' on it on the way to the restaurant this afternoon. You know one of those signs that direct you to a hospital, so there must be one nearby. Doesn't seem like anyone thought he needed to go. I guess if he seemed unhurt in any other way and didn't want to go, that might be the reason." Tom rolls down the window. "Sure smells nice out, doesn't it?

"Seems odd, though, that Junior didn't insist on Emerson going to the hospital. If it were Dad, I would have insisted. Maybe folks are just different out here." Tom breathes in the air again.

"Want to go get a drink?" Don asks Tom.

"I thought you'd never ask," Tom replies.

Fifteen minutes later they sit in front of the same mahogany bar they were at last night, each nursing a scotch and soda.

They try not to talk about what they heard that afternoon and instead focus on the beautiful lake out back, and on how everyone in this town just seems so darned, nice.

6

They decide to have dinner at the bar, and afterward, have a couple of drinks with people that filter in after 5 PM. Most of the patrons work at the grain processing plant, one works at the local post office, one is an attorney, one is a real estate salesperson, and a few work at the supermarket. The girl Tom spent the night with doesn't come in that night, and Tom is a little disappointed.

Around 7:30, Don suggests they leave. He wants to talk with Tom about Ben, and what Ben told them, but he wants to do it in the privacy of their motel room.

The door to the motel room is hardly closed when Don flops down on his bed and shakes his head. "So what do you make of everything the old man said today?"

"Well, he sure knows a lot about that Prescott guy. Sounds like they were very close friends until the second accident. I wonder what the tiff was about?" Tom sits on the bed opposite Don's and rests his elbows on his knees.

"Maybe it all had to do with Prescott's memory issues. Maybe he just didn't feel close to him anymore. It meshes with Gertrude's story. Prescott seems to treat her the same way."

"I think Gertrude told me one of Prescott's sons is a physician. I would love to hear his take on that memory thing." Don pushes himself up onto the pillows resting against the headboard of the bed. "I have a funny feeling, though, there is just so much more to it than just a concussion and a loss of memory.

"Tomorrow, we should try to find some more folks that know Prescott well and see how they feel about this amnesia story. What do you think?"

"I know a doctor down in the city that works in the emergency room. I'll give him a call and see what kind of information he can provide relating to partial amnesia." He removes his phone from his pocket, taps the face of the phone a few times, and dials the doctor.

"Doctor Boissard? Detective Tom Winston….Yeah, how are you?"

Tom nods a little and continues. "Yes…I did retire recently….yes it beats working all to hell…

"Listen , you once told me I could get in touch with you anytime, and I have a couple of questions I thought you might be able to answer. They have to do with concussions and resultant partial amnesia….no, it isn't part of an investigation. I sometimes do a little research for my brother, the writer. Remember, I told you about him? Well, he tricks me into working for him for almost nothing when he is writing a book, and he's writing another book.

"Yeah…well, I can't tell you about it, because he never tells me anything; he only asks me questions. Being his brother doesn't get me any special treatment.

"So can you help me out?" Tom nods his head in Don's direction. "That's great, doc," Toms says.

Tom asks Dr. Boissard questions relating to how Ben and Gertrude describe Prescott's behavior. He takes notes as the Dr. speaks, and every once in a while asks specific questions. After more than twenty-five minutes on the phone, he thanks the doctor for his time and promises to send him a copy of Don's new book when it is published.

"Whew! Now that was an education," Tom says to Don.

"So, tell me everything. Can we assume Prescott has real amnesia," Don asks?

"It sounds like it, but one thing sticks in my craw a little. That has to do with the second time he hurt himself, but first, let me tell you what the doctor told me about the amnesia symptoms. Then you can make up your mind whether there is anything fishy about the stories you've heard.

"First thing, the doctor says there should have been some kind of physical exam and tests conducted, such as an MRI, a magnetic resonance imaging scan which creates a detailed image of the brain to determine if there is any physical damage to his brain or if there is any kind of brain abnormality. If not an MRI scan, at least a CT scan, which is a computerized tomography scan, at least I think that's what he called it, a, uh," Tom looks down at his notes again, "medical imaging procedure using x-rays to generate two-dimensional images of the brain.

"You'll have to check this out better," Tom says. "I was writing so fast I know I missed things.

"Also an EEG, electroencephalogram should have been used while the patient performs a cognitive task. That provides an image of the brain for a task that requires thinking. It allows the doctor to locate any brain activity involved in several types of cognitive functions.

"The doctor said this should have been done as soon as possible after a patient is conscious even if there is no amnesia presenting itself. I wonder if any of that was done, and I don't recall hearing Ben mention it and I don't think you indicated that Gertrude said if it happened."

"Maybe that's something I can ask Ben the next time I see him," Don says. "I think Ben is the better person to be asking questions of than Gertrude. I think Gertrude may have a tendency to talk to folks a little more than Ben does.

"Now, how about the partial amnesia stuff? What did the doctor say about that?"

"He said there are many types of amnesia, and as he started to tell me about all of them, I asked him specifically about the things Ben and Gertrude said. He then limited it down to three I think it was," Tom looks at his notes. "Nope – make that four possibilities.

"The first is ... anterograde amnesia. We'll work on the pronunciation and spelling later. It's when the patient cannot remember new information. Stuff that happens recently, that should be stored into short-term memory, well, that information just disappears. He said that usually happens because of a brain trauma, like a blow to the head. Usually, though, someone that has this type of amnesia remembers stuff that happens before the injury.

"The second type is retrograde amnesia. Almost the opposite of anterograde amnesia. They cannot remember anything before the trauma, but they remember things after the incident.

"The third thing is transient global amnesia - a temporary loss of all memory. They find it hard to form new memories – basically severe anterograde amnesia. The loss of past memories is milder, and they might remember some things from their past with time. This is a very rare form of amnesia. Interestingly, though, transient global amnesia people tend to be older. Maybe that is a factor with Prescott.

"The last thing is traumatic amnesia - memory loss caused by a hard blow to the head. People who lose their memory as the result of a car accident are an example. They may experience a brief loss of consciousness or even go into a coma. Usually, though, this is temporary, although how long it lasts usually depends on how severe the injury is.

"The doctor said something interesting though about hypnosis. He said it can be an effective way of recalling forgotten memories. I wonder if anything like that was tried on Prescott."

"Tom, you are amazing," Don said to his brother. "That is great information.

"Put on your detective's cap and tell me, how can we use what we've learned from the good doctor? What's the next step of this investigation?"

"There are a few things you need to do. The first would be to talk with either Gertrude or Ben and find out how much of Prescott's memory really returned before the second incident, and how much was lost after the second accident. Then, I would try to talk with the son to see if he ever noticed anything strange about his father other than the loss of memory.

"Tell me something, though, what is it you expect to find out about Prescott that has you so interested. So far he sounds like a guy that worked hard all his life, had an accident that caused him to lose his memory, and then he was unlucky enough to have a second accident a few years later. That happens to a lot of folks; there's nothing really strange about all that."

Don thought for a moment. Tom saying this makes sense. Why does he feel something is wrong with the picture he is getting of Emerson Prescott? Couldn't Prescott just be someone that had more hardship in his life than he should have to shoulder? The only thing he can think of to support that feeling is something both Gertrude and Ben have mentioned to him: one day Emerson Prescott just seemed to not want to talk to two of his oldest friends anymore. It was almost as if he either didn't want them around him anymore or they suspected something he didn't want them to reveal.

Don wasn't sure which it was, but he wanted to find out. Plus, all this intrigue would be good fodder for a new book. He could already feel the pages of that book taking shape in his mind. If nothing else, continuing to follow-up on this Prescott thing would get the creative juices flowing, and after all, isn't that why he was in Dexter in the first place?

When Don and Tom wake the next morning they decide to drive down to the Chicken and Cow for breakfast. A little after 8 o'clock, Billy Shavers walks into the restaurant and sees Don. Don waves him over to their table and asks Billy to join them. He introduces Tom, and Billy pulls over a chair from the table next to them and sits down.

"Good to meet you," Billy says to Tom, and Tom nods.

Billy looks at Don and asks, "Did you get out to see Ben yesterday?"

"Yes I did, and thanks so much for speaking with him about me. He's a really knowledgeable guy about this town and the people in it," replies Don. "How well do you know folks around here? You've lived here a long time and you work in town, so I bet you know almost everyone, right?"

"Yeah – I know almost everyone. Lived here all of my life and my family has been here for almost 100 years. This is the kind of town that when you get here, you like it so much you never want to leave." Billy says that with a big grin on his face. "A lot of us wish the town would grow more, but most of us really like it just the way it is. Keeps us out of the fray that way."

"I can appreciate that," Don says.

"I spoke with Gertrude over at the historical society yesterday and she filled me in on the history of this place. She's quite the knowledgeable person, too. Between her and Ben, they told me so much stuff that now I have a hundred more questions to ask people," Don laughs. "Do you mind if I ask you some stuff?"

Laura stops at the table to ask Billy what he wants, and he tells her the regular. She nods and leaves.

"I get the same thing every day, not exciting, but its breakfast, right?

"So what can I tell you that Ben and Gertrude didn't?"

"Both of them mentioned Emerson Prescott a lot," Don starts. "He seems to be a pretty interesting character around here.

One of the things both of them mentioned are the two accidents he had. Do you know much about them?"

"Yeah, he is a character. I don't know him really well. I know Junior better than the old man. I was pretty young when Senior had the car accident where his wife was killed. I guess I was around 17 or 18, I think it was right after I graduated from High School, so I must have been 17. Anyway," Billy pauses "most of what I know is from what I read in the paper after the accident. He ran off the road, hit a tree or a guardrail, he flew out of the car, his wife flew into the windshield; she died and he didn't.

"That's about it. I know it took him some time to get back to where he could even come to work, and that Junior took over for his dad then. What else can I tell you?"

"I heard he had a second accident a couple of years later. He fell and hit his head on his car, right?"

"That's what I heard," Billy says. "Funny thing is, he wasn't seriously injured in either of those accidents, but he got amnesia from the first accident, and just about the time he started getting some of his memory back, he had the second accident, and that screwed him up in a more permanent way, from what I hear."

"In what way did it screw him up?"

"Seems that most people that knew him well started talking about how he not only didn't know who they were, but that he began to not even talk to them anymore. And these were people he had known his whole life. People said it was more than just him not knowing them, it was distinctly evident he just didn't want to talk with them anymore.

"My wife's father, Pete, has known Emerson for more than 50 years and they hung out together a lot when they were younger. Even after the first accident, even though it took some time, Pete, and Emerson would spend time together. I remember Pete saying that he thought Emerson's memory was coming back because they would sometimes talk about things that happened when they were younger. Then, after the second accident, Pete said that Emerson acted as if he didn't even know him, and couldn't even recall anything prior to the second accident. Nothing at all. Pete said he finally gave up trying to be friends with Emerson after Emerson told him to leave him alone one day.

"I asked Pete why, and he said that he had been talking with Emerson about something when Emerson mentioned how he had done something in New Hampshire a few years earlier, and Pete said Emerson couldn't have been in New Hampshire then because he was still recovering from the first accident. Emerson got all nasty and everything and stormed away. After that, Emerson avoided Pete whenever he saw Pete coming his way. Finally, Pete said he just stopped trying to be Emerson's friend anymore."

"Wow!" Don wondered aloud. "I wonder what was said in that conversation that would cause Emerson to give up a lifelong friendship on the spur of the moment?"

"Pete has always wondered that as well. He said it was almost as if Emerson had been caught in a lie or something, and decided to not put himself in that spot again."

"I wonder what Emerson said he had done" Don said, "that Pete knew he couldn't have done. Why would Emerson be so cold to an old friend? Doesn't make much sense, does it?

"Could you ask Pete what that was? I am really curious. It doesn't sound like Emerson had a problem with his memory during that conversation, but Pete would know. That's an odd thing to do if you've lost your memory, saying you did something, somewhere, when you supposedly shouldn't have a memory of that."

"You know, you're right. I never thought of that and I bet Pete didn't either. I'll ask him about that incident and see what he says," Billy replies.

Don decides not to pursue asking Billy any more questions this morning; he doesn't want to spook him. This is interesting information, though, and Don thinks maybe Gertrude might even know what happened between Emerson and Pete. Right after breakfast, he and Tom are going to have to pay her a little visit.

The three of them finish eating and Billy gets his check, pays Laura, and pushes himself away from the table. "I guess I'll see you guys tomorrow for breakfast. I'll let you know then what Pete says. Have a great day."

"You too, Billy. Thanks again for everything," Don says.

Once Billy is out of earshot Tom says, "I guess we'll be going over to see Gertrude after breakfast huh, Don? You have that look on your face like you are about ready to set the hounds free. I know you have the scent and you're dying to follow it.

"Do I get to sit in again with you," Tom asks.

"Absolutely, you do," Don laughs. He signals for the check, and as soon as Laura takes his money for breakfast, Don and Tom leave the Chicken and Cow, and walk over to the historical society to speak with Gertrude.

"Nice old building," says Tom as they approach the town hall. "Is this where the historical society is?"

"Yep," says Don. "You're going to love Gertrude. She's such a sweet old gal."

They walk up the steps and go through the glass doors of the town hall, and walk straight into the historical society's office, where Gertrude sits reading a newspaper.

She puts the paper down when she hears them come in and her face lights up when she sees it is Don.

"You came back, young man. It's so nice to see ya again. Did you have a good time yesterday, riding around town, seeing the sights?"

"Yes I did, Gertrude," Don smiles, "and I wanted my brother, Tom, to meet you. I told him all about you, and how you know everything about Dexter."

"Well, almost everything," she laughs.

"Hello, Gertrude. It is truly a pleasure to meet you." Tom extends his hand across the desk and Gertrude grabs it with both hands.

"Well, it's a pleasure to meet you, too, young man. Your mother must be so proud of you two boys; you both have such nice manners and all.

"Both of you, grab a chair and sit down," Gertrude motions toward the row of chairs against the wall. "What can I do for you today," Gertrude smiles, "or did you just stop by to spend the morning with me."

"A little of both, I guess, Gertrude." Don and Tom settle into their chairs.

"I met Billy Shavers at the coffee shop yesterday morning while I was having breakfast and we got talking about who knew the most about this town and Billy suggested I talk with Ben Harper, who I am sure you know."

"Yes, I know Ben very well," Gertrude says.

"So, after I left you yesterday I had the opportunity to drive out to his place, and we had a lovely conversation about Dexter and some of the folks that live here. One name came up a couple of times, the name of someone you know well: Emerson Prescott. Seems Ben had an experience much like yours, with Emerson, and he too has not spoken with the man in quite a while.

"Then this morning at breakfast I saw Billy again, and we started talking about what I did yesterday, and the subject of Emerson came up. Billy then told me that his father in law, Pete, also another old friend of Emerson's, did the same thing to him.

"Now, my curiosity is up as to why Emerson would cut loose three of his oldest friends in town for no apparent reason. It just seems really odd to me."

"Well, I guess getting bumped on the head a few times might change people," Gertrude replies. "I have read a lot of things about how bumps on the head can injure brains. Why, I've heard of people that after getting a brain injury can no longer speak their native tongue, but can speak a foreign language they had no knowledge of before the accident. Or people could all of a sudden play a musical instrument, when before they didn't.

"It's my guess that some brain injuries can change personalities, too, and I have always thought that maybe that's what happened to Emerson."

"I guess that could be it. But Billy said Pete's issue, the one that caused the relationship to end, had to do with something that Emerson said he did. Seems Pete knew it had been impossible for Emerson to do what he said he did because he knew Emerson was here during that timeframe, and not where Emerson said he had been. Pete said Emerson got so mad after that discussion, Emerson hardly spoke to him anymore, as if Emerson didn't want him around.

"Three townsfolk that had been Emerson's lifelong friends all cut out of his life. Yet, he seems to know a lot of folks here in town, so it's not like he cut everyone out of his life one day. And all of this happened after the second accident, not after the first."

Don watches Gertrude's face to see if he is treading on a touchy subject, but she has more of a questioning look on her face than one of anger or insult. Don knows from experience that people get very touchy when you start talking about their personal lives.

"I never thought of it that way. It all did seem to start after the second accident, but not immediately after the accident. He was fine for a lot of months then he started to get, well, we call it squirrely, up here in Vermont.

"Made me wonder too, what happened to him, and why he changed like that. He's never been nice to me again and to tell the truth, I miss the old Emerson." Gertrude stares at Don as if he has an explanation for why Emerson has acted this way.

"I think it may all hinge on what he and Pete were talking about. Billy said he would ask Pete tonight, and tell me tomorrow at breakfast what Pete says. Maybe Billy got it wrong and it was just an argument between Pete and Emerson, and you know how those things can sometimes escalate far beyond whatever the argument was about." Don once again has to hold back about what he is really thinking, for fear of having Gertrude begin to not want to share any more information about this.

"I'll see what Billy has to say tomorrow and let you know." Don smiles at her. "On another subject, tell me more about the lake and the dams up at the northern end of the lake. That part of the lake is in Canada, right? How's that work out for immigration and border crossings, and stuff like that?"

Don wants to act the history buff again hoping Gertrude would just continue treating him as a nosey tourist. Inside, though, Don just wants to grill her for more information. This is turning into a great story and he can't wait to see what was going on here in Dexter. He feels he has found a few bones, now he has to figure out where the rest of the skeleton is buried and by whom.

8

Don and Tom spend the rest of the morning talking with Gertrude about the lake and the tourists, about the high school football team (there were so few kids in the high school that many of the kids on the team played both offense and defense) and of course the stories of the Future Farmers of America and of the competitions held each year at the county and state fairs.

Tom runs out at lunchtime to pick up some sandwiches for the three of them, and when they finish eating, Don and Tom tell Gertrude they want to ride around the lake, maybe even go up into Canada. Gertrude reminds them to make sure they have their passports. "You can't cross the border anymore without one. So many people forget," she reminds them.

They say good by, promising to stop in once they speak with Billy tomorrow.

They walk back to the Chicken and Cow parking lot where they have left the car, then head north out of town, following the Lake Road on the west side of the lake. In twenty minutes, they come to a dead end at the Canadian border.

"Now what," Tom laughs. "How the hell do we get to Canada from here?"

He turns the car around and heads back to town. Stopping at the first store they see, Don runs in and asks how to get to the border crossing. The clerk tells him the nearest crossing is the North Troy/Highwater Border Crossing, about fifteen miles north up route 105. Don thanks him and returns to the car.

"Get on 105, go north for about fifteen miles, and we'll get to the crossing. After that, we'll have to ask for more directions to get to the lake again."

For most of the ride, they speak about the countryside, the lake, the houses along the road, avoiding any talk about Emerson Prescott.

When they get to the Canadian border crossing, there is a

crossing gate and a one-room building, little more than a shed actually, where a bored Canadian border crossing guard sits reading a newspaper. When he sees the car stop at the gate, he puts the paper down, grabs his cap and places it on his head, and walks out to the car. Walking over to Tom, who is driving, he crosses the front of the car taking a quick look at the license plate, then as he gets to the driver's side of the car, peeks into the car checking out the back seat, and says, "Good afternoon gentleman. Where are you headed?"

"We're staying down in Dexter and thought we'd take a ride around the lake," Tom says.

"Well, it's a beautiful day for it, isn't it," the guard says. "I'll need to see your passports or your valid enhanced state ID for border crossings."

Don hands the passports to Tom, who passes them on to the guard. "So which of you is Don?" he asks. Don waves at him.

"Where were you born, Don?"

"A place called Parkchester, in the Bronx. Both of us were," Don replies. "We're brothers. He was born there, too."

"Is that like Westchester, NY?"

"No," Don says. "Westchester is north of the city. Parkchester is in the Bronx, part of New York City."

"So you are…" he asks Tom.

"I'm Tom Winston, the smarter brother," Tom laughs.

The guard doesn't laugh, he just peers at Tom as if Tom had just said something bad.

"Ok, then," he says as he finishes inspecting the passports. Handing them back to Tom he says, "Have a nice trip. The dams at the northern end of the lake are kinda interesting to see. There are a couple of towns just a little farther north of them that have some decent restaurants you might try if you are up there around dinner time."

He gives a little two finger salute from the brim of his cap and walks around the back of the car on his way to the guard building. He goes inside, presses a button, and the crossing gate raises as he waves them through. Tom nods and drives forward.

"Wow! That's sure easier than crossing the Mexican border isn't it," he laughs. Forty-five minutes later they arrive at the northernmost part of the lake, stopping at a bar-restaurant right on the lake. Once they are seated, and each has a beer in front of them, the conversation finally turns to Emerson Prescott and the three people who had once been his friends.

"I hope Pete can shed some light on his apparent termination of his friendship with Emerson," Don says. "Seems like Ben, Gertrude, and Pete were just jettisoned from Emerson's life for no reason, at least no reason they have alluded to yet.

"The chances of someone ending relationships with three lifelong friends, all in a matter of months, seems a little more than odd, don't you think?"

Tom nods in agreement. "It makes no sense. If this was a case I was working on, my first guess would be Emerson was trying to keep people away from him, as if he was trying to hide a part of his life from those that know him best. You know, your best friends, especially those that have known you for a very long time, can usually tell when you start to bullshit them. All three of them indicated that Emerson acted as if he didn't know them, even though he had previously recovered from the first accident enough to reintroduce them to his current memory. He even vaguely recognized them as friends after the second accident, but then treated them as if he didn't know them.

"It sounds, in Pete's case anyway, that Emerson had no trouble being friends with Pete again after the second accident until Emerson said something that Pete knew couldn't be true. Then, it was as if Pete had caught him in a lie. We need to find out what that was because I think there's a gigantic clue there as to what's going on with Emerson."

"I wish we didn't have to wait until tomorrow to hear what Pete had to say." Don sips his beer. "Do you think we should go back to Ben today and let him know about what Billy told us? Do you think that might jog Ben's memory about what Emerson said to him before ending the relationship with him?"

"If we get back to town early enough, it might be worth a trip out there to talk with Ben. We might try to talk with some folks who have become friendly with Emerson since the second accident. It would be interesting to see how he relates to new friends. Maybe, he tells them things that wouldn't jibe with what Gertrude, Pete, and Ben know about Emerson. I bet Billy can tell us who Emerson's new friends might be." Tom raises an eyebrow of wonder at the thought. "The best way to make sure you know what's really going on is to know the truth, and then ask someone about that subject to see if they will tell you the truth. In this case, we can compare the 'old' Emerson with what the 'new' Emerson tells people about his life."

"That's worth a try," Don says. "Let's finish up the beer and ride up to that town the guard told us about, just to see what's there. Then we'll head back to Dexter, and if we can, go over to Ben's place for a while."

They leave the bar and drive to Sherbrooke, Quebec, alongside the Magog river until it reaches the Saint-François River. They explore the town for a while before turning back south toward the lake, and ultimately the border at Beebe Plain Crossing in Vermont.

Beebe Plain Crossing is an even smaller crossing than the one they used to enter into Canada, with a one-room brick building, a carport sort of roofed area where you stop your car, and a stop sign. There isn't even a crossing gate.

This crossing is a little unique in that it is bisected by Canusa Street, a street that runs along the Canada–United States border for almost a half-mile, before running right between the Canadian border station to the north and the Unites States border station to the south. If you live on the south side of the street, you live in the US; live on the north side, you are in Canada. By law, residents are prohibited from visiting each other across the center line of the street without first going to the appropriate border station for permission, but the guards know everyone that lives on the street and residents rarely, if ever, check in with either border stations when visiting one another.

Entering into the United States is very easy at this border crossing. The guard walks up to the car, asks for their passports, verifies Tom and Don are who they say they are, and then waves them on into the country. It took all of about 30 seconds.

Following the east side of the lake as much as they can, the trip into Dexter takes less than 30 minutes of leisurely driving.

When they cross over the bridge in Dexter they make a left turn and drive out to Ben Harper's place. It is almost 4 PM, and what might pass for traffic in Dexter is heading into town, probably to the processing plant for the four to midnight shift.

They pass Farrell's concrete and gravel plant and turn onto Ben's road, then into Ben's driveway, stopping just short of his front steps. Ben hears them and is at the door by the time they reach the bottoms step to his porch.

"Didn't think I'd see you gents again so soon," Ben says as the door closes behind him. "Am I that good company?"

"Well, yes you are, Ben. Mind if we sit and talk for a while," Don asks.

"Set yourself down over here," Ben says as he walks to his chair. "Can I get you anything to drink first?"

"No, thanks, Ben. I think we're OK."

"Good," Ben says as he sits down. "What ya boys been up to today?"

""We took a little drive up to the northern part of the lake, and then on up to Sherbrooke. Pretty country up there, and Sherbrooke is a nice little town." Don again takes the chair as Tom sits down on the top step again.

"Guess I should get another chair out here for Tom," Ben says, "so he has someplace to sit, next time you come visiting."

"Ah! This is fine, Ben," Toms says. "No sense going to any trouble for me."

Ben shrugs. "So, boys, what can I do for you today?"

"Well, Ben, to be honest, I've gotten interested in this guy Emerson. I saw Billy this morning at breakfast and he told me that his father in law, Pete, was also an old friend of Emerson's. Billy said that Emerson killed his relationship with Pete much the same way he ended both yours and Gertrude's friendship. Quickly and with no apparent reason. Just one day it seems he no longer needed or wanted your friendship.

"Now, why would someone end life long friendships like that? Even if he had lost some of his memory, he had been able to regain knowledge of all three of you after the first accident, and by everyone's account, even started remembering things about your relationships from before the first accident.

"Then, after the second accident, he again began to remember who you were, but suddenly just cut all of you out of his life.

"In talking with Gertrude, and you , and of course Billy, there seems to be something that doesn't appear clear to me about all that. Did you and Emerson have a falling out over anything?" Don hoped he didn't sound like he was prying into Ben's life.

"Nope. No really." Ben answers. "I guess when we would talk about relatively recent events since his first accident, he would sometimes get confused about the timeline, thinking he was doing something somewhere when I knew all along he was here and couldn't have been doing what he said he was doing someplace else.

"Once in a while, I tried to correct him and he would get all mad at me, telling me I was wrong, and then he'd go on his way, and I wouldn't see or hear from him for a while. But soon, we'd see each other somewhere and stop and talk. I could tell, though, that he was only repeating things back to me that I had told him before. There wasn't any real substance behind his words. It was as if the only memories he had of us were from what I had told him. Before the second accident, he was able to start conversations about things we both knew; after the second accident, not so much, if at all."

"From what Billy told me, that was pretty much what he did with Pete, too." Don sits thinking for a moment. "I know this was probably a long time ago, but do you remember what it was he said that you disagreed with?"

Ben scratches his forehead a little and crinkles up his lips, trying to recall Emerson's words. "Seems to me he mentioned something about when he was a boy working at a supermarket, and I told him, you never worked at no supermarket when you were a kid. When he was a kid the closest supermarket was over in St. Albans, about fifty miles from here. Dexter didn't have a supermarket; all we had was a small country store with a gas pump outside. Carried bread, milk, eggs, canned goods...you know... day to day stuff.

"Hell, this was farm country when he was a kid. People raised their own livestock, hunted in the winter for deer, had chickens for eggs, cows for milk; even Emerson hunted when he was a kid. His dad taught him. Emerson would have had to drive to that supermarket to be able to work there and I know for a fact, he never did, certainly not when he was a kid. Hell, he wouldn't have had a license then, no way he could have gotten over to St. Albans."

"So that was what you argued about? And shortly after that, he began to back away from you," Don asks.

"Yeah. As I remember it anyway," Ben says.

"That sounds a lot like what happened to Pete," Don says.

"Well, that was a long time ago, and Emerson and me, well, we haven't talked much, if at all, recently. I miss the guy...we had some good conversations when we were younger, before the first accident." Ben shook his head.. "Yep, that was a long time ago now."

"By the way," Don asks, "do you know if any tests were performed on Emerson after the first or the second accident? I hear it is quite common to have some if there are head injuries."

"Don't know," Ben says. "Only thing I know is that he didn't go to the hospital for either of the accidents, although the paramedics did check him out at the scene of the accident. People up here can be like that; if they feel ok, they figure they don't even need a doctor, let alone go to a hospital."

9

Don sits on Ben's porch a while longer, talking about where he and Tom have driven, about how pretty the lake is, and how cute all the towns around Dexter are, until he notices that Ben is starting to get bored with his small talk. Not wanting to overstay his welcome, he motions to Tom to get up, and Tom says something about how they really need to get going.

Don gets up from his chair and shakes Ben's hand, and again thanks him for the information. He also asks if he can come back to see him again.

"Sure," Ben says. "We're getting to be old friends now."

Don nods and turns to leave when Ben grabs his arm and stops him. "Be sure to let me know what Pete tells you. You got me interested now as to why Emerson stopped being friends with Pete."

"Will do, Ben. See you soon."

Tom waves goodbye to Ben, then slides into the driver's seat this time after leading Don to the car. "You were pushing it there for a while," Tom says as Don closes the door. "Even I could tell you were talking just to talk. I think he knew it, too."

"Yeah," Don says. "Ben may be old but he is still pretty observant. Did you get that last thing he said about telling him what Pete says?

"I think he has a suspicion we are after more than just town history, and he doesn't want to be left out of anything."

"I think you're right," Tom says as he backs out of the drive. "What do you think our next move is after you hear what Pete has to say?"

"Somehow, we have to talk with Junior about his dad," Don says. "We can ask to speak with Junior about his company and how he came to run it. You think that will get us a meeting with him?"

"I never knew any company head that didn't like talking about himself," Tom answers. "They all seem to have pretty big egos.

Let's sit down after dinner and work out a bunch of questions to ask him. Then we can sort of segue into questions about his dad."

Don shakes his head in agreement and opens the window as Tom drives them back to their motel room.

After dinner at the bar, they take a little walk around the marina and ask about Emerson's boat. They aren't surprised when the dock boy points them in the direction of the biggest boat in the marina. When they get next to it, they notice it has an abundance of fishing gear sitting out in the open on the deck of the cockpit, which is in contrast to the fact that the boat is a pleasure boat, not a fishing boat. There are buckets, rags, and fish scaling boards lying around, and the boat has a slight odor of fish.

"This baby cost a lot of money," Tom says. "You'd think he'd keep it in better shape and certainly keep it cleaner."

"Gertrude said he uses it as a fishing boat," Don says.

"Yeah, maybe; but this is ridiculous. This must be a $250,000 boat and he treats it like it's a gigantic bass boat. I wonder why."

Don walks over to one of the portholes and peers into the cabin. Whistling softly, he nods his head at Tom to take a look.

"Leather chairs, a full galley, he even has a small wine rack full of wine, and of course, there's another fish scaling board by the sink. And look, near the door to the stateroom…a pair of rubber hip boots with mud all over the feet. What a waste of a beautiful boat." Don shakes his head in disgust.

"Let's find that dock boy and see what he knows about Emerson and his boat." They both turn and walk back to the small dock house at the beginning of the dock, where the dock boy sits listening to the radio.

"Hi there," Don says to him. "That's some boat Emerson has. Looks like he doesn't take too good care of it, though."

The kid looks at him. "He uses it mostly for fishing. I've only seen him take people out on it maybe four or five times in the last three years I've been here. He's only taken his kid out on it once that I know of. That's his kid's boat over there," the kid points to a 32 footer at another dock. "Tell you the truth, I am not even sure he likes his kid. You never see them together unless the kid is driving him somewhere. According to most folks, though, they were once really close and Emerson would have done anything for Junior, that's what everyone calls him, Junior."

"What changed that," Tom asks.

"You mean them hanging out together? Don't rightly know. Guess things changed a lot between them after Emerson's second accident. I don't remember, cause I wasn't even born when that happened, but my dad knows Junior real well since they went to school together, and he said the old man and Junior were almost inseparable before the second accident." The kid adjusts his cap. "Ya know, the old man don't even tip me most times when I help him dock his boat. Cheap bastard. He only tips me when he wants me to clean his boat, which he hasn't done for a while this summer. It is dirty as hell, and by the time he asks me to clean it, its gonna take me a couple of days of hard work to get it spiffy again."

"Sounds like you aren't a big fan of his," Don says.

"Let's just say he ain't like Junior. Junior's a real gentleman, and always treats you with respect, but not the old man. He acts as if he owns you. Well, he don't own me. I take my time cleaning that boat and at fifteen dollars an hour, you can bet I take me sweet ass time doing it."

"Thanks for the info. You take care," Don says.

"See ya around," the kid says.

As they walk back to their car, Tom says, "Emerson sure seems to have burned a lot of bridges around here, including with his son. If we get a chance to talk with Junior, I bet we're going to find out a lot more about the old man than we can ever guess."

"I'm beginning to see a pattern here and it all seems to turn around that second accident," Don replies. "Let's get back to our room and start thinking of questions we want to ask Junior."

They spend a couple of hours going over questions to ask Junior, figuring out how to phrase them to get the most information without seeming to pry too much. Tom is good at this sort of thing since he has done it hundreds of times with suspects. They decide that maybe Tom should handle most of the interrogation when they meet with Junior. Don will just interject questions when he wants more follow up on something.

"I'm looking forward to hearing what Pete tells Billy. That's going to tell us a lot," Don says as he pulls back the covers to his bed. "Should be an interesting day tomorrow."

The next morning they sit waiting for Billy Shavers to enter the Chicken and Cow for his daily breakfast. By now Laura starts treating them like regulars and just automatically brings them coffee with the menu.

"How are you gent's this morning," she asks.

"We're doing fine, Laura," Tom says. "How are you doing today?"

"You waiting for Billy? He should be in any minute now. Seems like the three of you are getting to be pretty friendly."

"Yes, we are. He's a nice guy and he's been really helpful telling us about the town and who to talk with, too. We've met quite a few people through him."

"Yeah! He's a sweetie," she says. "His wife and kids are just as nice as he is, too. Oh look, here he comes now."

The door opens and Billy walks in, proceeding straight to Don's table. "Morning, Laura. Can I get some coffee?" He pulls up a chair and sits down.

"Sure thing, honey," she answers and walks to the counter.

"Good morning gents. I got some interesting information for you. Pete was more than willing to tell me all about what caused the fuss between him and Emerson, and I guess it was more than just a little disagreement they had. According to Pete, they almost came to blows with Emerson even threatening Pete at one point."

"Really," Don says. "What was the argument over?"

"I'll tell you everything, but the highlight is that Emerson told him he had worked for a while as a mate on a lobster boat out of Portsmouth, New Hampshire when he was a teenager, and Pete told him he was full of shit, that Emerson had never worked on a boat in New Hampshire as a teenager.

"Pete was willing to let it go since Emerson was still recuperating from that second accident and his memory was shaky on a lot of things, but it seems Emerson got really agitated that Pete was calling him a liar, didn't want to let it go.

"When Pete reminded Emerson that at the time he said he was working on the boat, they were both in high school here and working at his father's processing plant. He said Emerson just shut up, gave him a dirty look, turned and walked away.

"Pete said next time he saw him, Emerson was cold and distant and after that Emerson always treated him differently, not at all like the friends they had been, and it went downhill from there."

"Hmmm! Was that all Pete said," Don asks.

"No. There's more," Billy says.

"Ok Hon, what will you guys have for breakfast today," Laura asks as she walks up to their table.

After giving Laura their order, Billy waits till she is out of earshot before resuming his story about what Pete has told him.

"Pete also told me that a year or so later, after Emerson had begun to be functional again, Emerson bought that big boat in the marina. Have you seen it yet? It's pretty much the biggest thing on this side of the lake. Anyway, he bought the boat and for the first couple of summers he took out a few friends and some family for little outings. He even hosted a couple of day trips for folks from the plant as a sort of bonus for good work.

"By about the third or fourth year, though, those types of outings became fewer, and then they just stopped. Pete said it seemed like one summer everything was fine and the next summer Emerson didn't want anything to do with anyone in town anymore.

"Around the fourth or fifth year, Emerson started taking the boat out all by himself, anchoring or docking up at the north end of the lake for days, and sometimes weeks at a time. The fishing is better up there because the lake is deeper, and Emerson had developed a real fondness for fishing.

"Since that end of the lake is on the Canadian side of the border, local folks around here don't get up there much. About the only reason, any of us down here even cross the border, is to go to Sherbrooke for the shopping. They have a few really good stores up there and when the exchange rates are favorable, it is cheaper to buy things there."

"We were in Sherbrooke yesterday," Tom says. "Nice little town and not too far a drive."

"Yeah, it's close, but there is always that damned border crossing stuff, and you can't drink anything and then drive across the border. Either side will nail you for that," Billy replies.

"So, Emerson starts taking these little trips where he disappears for days and sometimes weeks at a time. When he started doing that, Junior would take his boat up the north end of the lake to see if he could find Emerson, just to make sure he was OK. He always was, so by the end of that summer, I guess he figured Emerson could take care of himself and he didn't bother anymore.

"There are a few young guys around here that still go up to the north end of the lake to a couple of bars up there, and they have seen Emerson quite a few times. They don't talk with him cause they know he doesn't like most people here in town anymore.

"Pete said he heard that Emerson is fairly well known up there, but mostly by the boating crowd, and that he socializes more up there than he ever did down here."

"That really seems odd," Don says. "It kind of backs up the story about Emerson not wanting to have anything to do with people from around here. I wonder why he is so sociable up there and so anti-social down here."

"Pete thinks it is because people up there only know him as he is now, or maybe he just doesn't like the folks in town anymore, for some reason." Billy shrugs his shoulders. "Maybe Emerson got tired of everyone treating him like a mental cripple after he got that amnesia stuff. Maybe they accept him up there as he is, memory lapses and all."

"Could be the reason, but it's still strange. If he likes it up there so much, he could just move there, couldn't he? Certainly, he could afford a second home up there," Don says.

Billy nods in agreement. "And now, since he doesn't really do much of anything at the plant, he has no need to stay down this end of the lake. He's become a bit of a strange bird I guess."

Don decides this is a good time to ask Billy if he thinks there is a chance that Junior would meet with them to talk about Emerson a little more, and Billy says he knows him well enough that he could introduce them to Junior if they want him to.

"Yeah. That would be great. You know, the more I learn about Emerson, the more I want to know. Don't you feel the same way, Billy."

""Well, as a matter of fact, you've made me interested in what his story is," Billy laughs. "I didn't give a shit before, but you have made it interesting."

"Good. Do you think you could get us in to see Junior today?"

"I think so. He has an open door policy with his employees; he is really good that way. As soon as we finish breakfast, we can go over to the plant and see if he is in yet, and if he is, we'll go talk to him."

Just before 10 AM, all three of them walk into the Prescott Grain Processing Corporation corporate office area, which was little more than a fifty-year-old concrete block building separated from the main plant by a parking lot. Inside the entrance door sat Millie Beckett, who over the years has become Junior's "right-hand man" and secretary. Millie handles all incoming communications for Junior, as his secretary, office manager, and human resources officer.

"Billy Shavers. What the hell are doing here? Isn't your shift over?" Millie smiles up at Billy as he walks into the office. Her eyes look behind him to see two other men she does not recognize.

"I see you got some people behind you; you do something bad," she laughs.

"No, nothing like that Millie. These men are friends of mine and I wanted them to meet Junior," Billy says. "I saw his car outside so I assume he's here, right?"

Millie nods. "He's always here by 7:30, you know that. He's having his third cup of morning coffee and going over some scheduling plans, but I am sure he'd make time to see you. Just wait here a second." She gets up and walks into Junior's office, and within ten seconds walks back out. "Go on in. He said he always has time for you."

"Thank you, Millie." He starts to walk into Junior's office but stops just outside the door, turning to Millie. "Where are my manner's Millie? This is Don," and Billy points first to Don, "and his brother Tom," and then to Tom. "They're a couple of new friends of mine who are just itching to meet Junior, but I'm sure they are just as eager to meet you as well."

Both of the brothers smile at Millie, and walk over to her desk to shake her hand.

"Come on boys," Billy says and proceeds into Junior's office.

Sitting behind a large, cluttered oak desk, Junior stands to greet Billy with an extended hand. "Billy Shavers. How the heck are you? What brings you in to see me today?" Junior is a tall, thin man, with a full head of salt and pepper hair, who looks every bit the successful head of a company, but with none of the false accoutrements often associated with people who are trying to impress other people with their wealth. He wears a button down blue Oxford shirt, open at the collar, and a pair of dark blue chino pants.

"How are you, Junior? We haven't had a chance to see other too much recently. Good to see you." Billy walks over to Junior and takes his hand in his. "These are two friends of mine that I wanted you to meet." He introduces Don and Tom, and each brother reaches out to shake Junior's hand. "They are a couple of tourists that I met at the Chicken and Cow the other day, and we keep bumping into each other at breakfast.

"Don is a history buff and loves to learn everything he can about every place he visits. From what I understand, he drags Tom around to keep him company." Billy lays a hand on Junior's shoulder.

"How can anyone get an idea of what this town is all about if you and your dad are not included in the conversation," Billy continues. "If it weren't for you and your dad, and this plant, Dexter would be hardly more than a dot on the map of Vermont."

"Thank you, Billy, that's very kind of you to say that." Junior turns to Don. "I always think it is the opposite. What would the Prescott's be without the town of Dexter and all the support it gives to our company. I like to think we have the best workers in Vermont, and dad thinks that as well."

Pointing to the chairs in front of the desk, Junior motions for them to sit down. "Can I have Millie get you some coffee," he asks.

"No thanks," Don replies. "We just finished breakfast over at the Chicken and Cow. They give you enough food and coffee to fill you up for the whole day."

"That they do," Junior says. "So what can I tell you about Dexter and the plant? Do you want a tour? I'm sure Billy could show you around. He knows this place as well as anyone."

"Actually, we want to talk with you. I'm fascinated by how successful your company is, tucked way up here in the corner of Vermont. Before driving into Dexter I would never have thought such an important company, doing what you do, would be located here."

"Well, that's due to my dad, and his dad. My grandfather, Ernie, owned a dairy farm just south of town back in the 1920s and 30s. He used to grow most all of his feed for the cows, but he never grew enough to make it through the winter, so he was always forced to buy some. During the depression, a lot of farmers couldn't afford to keep their dairy farms operating, and ended up selling off their livestock. Ernie had saved a few bucks and every now and then he bought up some of the cows, but feeding them was a bit of a problem because he couldn't grow enough for them.

"He figured he could help to keep the farmers on their land if he convinced the farmers to start growing corn and other feed products. He was successful at doing that, but even for him, there was a limit as to how much feed he could buy and use, and there started to be a surplus which the local folks had no way of selling.

"He thought that if he could start a sort of cooperative for the local grain and feed growers, that he might be able to sell it to the feed distributors in the northeast. He made some contacts and before long he was buying and storing all the feed the County could produce.

"Then 1941 came along, and there was a need for alcohol for all sorts of governmental uses. Grandpa saw another opportunity and built one of the first industrial alcohol plants supplying alcohol for the World War II synthetic rubber program right there in town.

"Soon, farms all over the state of Vermont, New Hampshire, even Massachusetts and New York, were sending their grain over here to process for the program. The train ran right through Dexter so the finished product could be shipped directly from here, making it very efficient to transport.

"It wasn't long before Grandpa had to stop being a farmer and concentrate on running what had become the largest grain processing center in the northeast. We were turning out tank cars of alcohol every day, and producing feed as well. By the end of the war, Ernie was employing almost everyone in town. Around March 1944, the government asked Ernie to go to Manchester, New Hampshire, to work with the government on a special project that had to do with refining grain alcohol. Instead of it being just for a few weeks, Ernie ended up moving my Grandmother, Mary, down there with him.

They ended up staying there until well after D-day in 1944.

"Ernie hated leaving the plant alone for all that time, but he chose some good folks to run it while he was away, and every month or so he returned just to check up on things.

"While they were in Manchester, Mary got pregnant with Dad, and he was born October 14, 1944. Ernie, Mary, and Dad were able to return to Dexter in February of 1945, and Grandpa returned to running the plant.

"After the war, the demand for grain alcohol diminished greatly and grandpa had to concentrate on the feed side of the business. It was about then that the first genetically altered grains were being tested and distributed and grain production in New England shot through the roof. Grandpa, always the businessman, was prepared to capitalize on the boom and transitioned from producing alcohol back to feed and seed processing.

"We still produce some alcohol, mostly for local paint companies and such, but nowhere near what our capacity was during WWII.

"We now employ about 120 folks, maybe a little more, and most of them are local folks, and we're proud of that. Billy can tell you, we have so many folks that have not only worked here for forty and even fifty years, but we have two and three generations working together.

"I think that says something about the town's commitment to us and our commitment to the town. The success of this company is due as much to the hard work of this town, as it is to my family.

"We feel it is a partnership that has worked out beautifully for everyone.

"That's the history of this company in a nutshell," Junior says. "Is that what you wanted to know? Do you want a tour of the place now? I'm sure Billy would be happy to show you around."

Don and Tom had been taking notes during the presentation of the history of the company. Don was the first to speak up.

"So, how did your dad come to be the head of this place, and of course, how did you come to succeed him," Don asks.

"In 1966, when my dad, Emerson, was about 22, Ernie died.

I think he had a heart attack or a stroke. Dad had always worked in some capacity at the plant and knew almost everything there was to know about how to run the physical aspects of the place, but he didn't have the business knowledge that Ernie had. Still, Ernie left him the place and dad had to learn all the logistics of running a company.

"He took a few courses at the local community college and learned enough to understand how to keep books and such. He was always a natural salesman, so he was able to use that skill to grow the company. Dad was a conscientious objector during the Viet Nam war and did not have to serve in the military, so it was pure luck that he was available to devote his life to continuing the business.

"He ran it until 1986 when my mom died in a car accident that also injured him. After that I became sort of the go-to guy to run the company."

"I am sorry to hear that about your mom. It must have been tough," Don says. "You must have been young when that happened. When were you born," Don asks.

"Just out of high school, actually. Mom and dad got married in 1967, and I came along pretty quickly after that. My brother John, who is a doctor in Boston now, came along about a year later. We were both devastated by the loss of our mom. Dad somehow survived the car accident with only some minor bruising and a case of partial amnesia. It took him almost a year to start getting back memories of his life, and other than having seen pictures of mom, he really doesn't remember her much at all."

"You dad is well liked in this town from what I hear," Don says.

"I think he was better liked years ago, when he was still vibrant and alive and involved. He had lots of friends then, until his second accident. Since then he has kept pretty much to himself."

"Really," Don says. "He had another car accident?" Don doesn't want to let on that he knows more about Emerson and about how people really felt about him now.

"I don't think I'd describe it that way, but yeah, he fell and hit his head on the bumper of his car, and I think it reactivated his memory loss. My brother is pretty sure that's what caused him to lose

67

more of his memory than he lost from the first accident.

"I found dad one afternoon on the ground, leaning against his car, a small cut over his forehead, bleeding, disoriented and not knowing who I was. It was like after the first accident, only dad never quite recovered this time. He is only able to recall things that have happened since that second accident.

"Every once in a while, he mentions something that he did as a kid, but it never makes any sense to me or my brother because it is usually something we know he never did. My brother says that can happen with amnesia. People can sometimes assume things they hear as being part of their life, and they repeat it as if it really happened to them or that they had really done it.

"He may never get completely well again. Hell, he's almost in his mid-70s now, and for the most part enjoys himself, so that's really all that's important I guess. He comes into the office every once in a while, but since the second accident he really has no working knowledge of what happens here."

"I guess you're right," Don says. "As long as he's happy and healthy that's really what's important.

"So you run this place now? And your brother lives in Boston and is a doctor. Your mom would be very proud of both of you, I'm sure."

"We both like to think that." Junior stands and offers his hand to Don. "I hope I didn't bore you with the short history of the company.

"Billy, why don't you give these fellows a tour of the place, and put yourself on the clock while you're doing that, and thank you for bringing them in."

Don grabs Junior's hand and shakes it, thanking him for his time, then Tom does the same. Don and Tom walk out of the office while Billy thanks Junior for his time. They all walk passed Millie on the way out and say goodbye.

Once outside Tom turns to Don and says, "Wow. A lot of information there. Even he seems to notice the inconsistent stories that Emerson tells. That inconsistency seems to be more consistent than you would expect. Something happened to Emerson during his life and even with this amnesia thing, it seems to slip out every once in a while. I wonder if he's trying to hide something, or the mixed up stories are all just attributable to the amnesia."

"I don't know. But we're going to try to find out." Don turns and walks toward the plant. "Billy," he yells to Shavers, "let's have that tour of the place we were promised. Then, since it is getting near lunch time, I think I need to buy you a nice lunch over at the marina's restaurant."

After lunch with Billy, Don and Tom return to their room to discuss everything they learned from Junior. They determine it is time for Tom to do what he does best, some old fashioned foot detective work. Tom wants to follow up on why Emerson spends so much time at the northern end of the lake. Don wants to make some phone calls to try to track down what kind of work Emerson's dad, Ernie, did for the government during the war while he was in New Hampshire.

"Don't you also find it curious that Emerson was born in Manchester, New Hampshire," Don says to Tom, "and never went back there again according to Junior, but he remembers sailing out of Portsmouth on a lobster boat when he was a teen? Maybe there is a connection there between his dad working in the area and Emerson thinking he worked on a lobster boat out of there.

"Maybe the key to all this lies in New Hampshire."

"Maybe we'll know more after I get back from Canada. I don't think I'll get back tonight, so do you want me to take you anywhere before I leave?" Tom stands and walks into the bathroom to get his shaving kit for the trip. "I wish we had two cars up here. We never thought we would need separate transportation, did we?" Returning to the bed he places the kit into his overnight bag containing clothes he has not yet unpacked.

"I'll be OK. I'll make some calls and then I think I'll start putting what we know down on paper and see if it talks to me at all." Don picks up his notepad and begins writing. "If you find out anything interesting today, give me a call on my cell."

Tom picks up his bag and opens the door to the parking lot. "You sure you don't need anything before I go?"

"I'll be fine. I can walk to the restaurant from here and I do have quite a lot of work to do. I can also get on the laptop and hit the net if I need something I can't find out on the phone.

"I might even run a check on Emerson to see what the net has on him. You never know what you can find on the net. Make sure you have your passport and your cell phone, in case I need to get in touch with you."

Tom pats his shirt pocket and nods at Don. He then walks out of the room and closes the door behind him.

Don looks down at the pad on his lap:

Ernest Prescott

- Portsmouth, New Hampshire

- 1944

- Prescott Grain Processing Corporation

Emerson Prescott

- Conscientious objector, 1960s

- Lobster boat

- Accidents

- 1986, loss of memory; regains it

- 1990, loss of memory; does not regain it

Gertrude Revere

Ben Harper

Pete

How the hell do these all fit together? There must be a common thread somewhere. Don stares at the page waiting for something to jump up at him, but nothing does. The words seem to have no relationship other than they all relate to Prescott.

Don picks up his phone and dials a number in Washington, D.C. A voice on the other end of the call answers. "Department of Defense, Intelligence Division. How may I direct your call?"

"Capt. Norman Johnson, War Records section, please."

"Please hold," the voice says.

"Captain Johnson, War Records. How may I help you?"

"Hey, Norm, this is Don Winston. How are you?"

"Don, you old son of a gun. Good to hear from you. How the hell are you? Are you in D.C.?"

"No, I am in Vermont, trying to figure out how to get a story started for my next book, and, well, Norm, I need your help on something."

"You're not going to ask for any state secrets are you, cause if you are, you know I have to report you." The Captain chuckles at his joke.

"Well," Don says, "I don't think it will be a state secret, but I guess you will find out once I ask you the favor."

"Oh, boy! What is it, Don?"

Don proceeds to tell Norm that he wants to know what Ernest Prescott from Dexter, Vermont, might have been working on for the government in 1944, in New Hampshire.

"Prescott owned a grain alcohol processing plant during the war and his major buyer was the government, that much I know. What I don't know is why the government would request his assistance on a project in New Hampshire that would take him away from his home for almost nine months, from March 1944 until February 1945.

"I thought you might be able to tell me why he had to be in Manchester, New Hampshire for that length of time. I spoke with his grandson and he said the old man never even told his son, or anyone in his town for that matter, why he was there during the war other than to say it was requested by the government.

"Think you can find out for me? I would really appreciate it if you could. It's worth a really good steak dinner at your choice of restaurant in Washington, next time I am down there."

"Yeah, yeah! You never come down here. You hate it here, but I'll do it for you anyway if I can. When do you need the information?"

"Uh, well, as soon as you could get it to me would be fine."

"I figured as much. Give me all that info again and I'll run it through the computer to see what I can find; give me your phone number, too. And don't think I'll forget about the steak dinner. I'll get you down here one day if I have to have you arrested for something."

"Norm, you're a saint." Don gives him the information again along with his cell number. "Thank you so much, Norm. Take care." Don hears the phone click and hits the disconnect button on his cell.

Norm has been a help to him so many times clarifying any military information he needs to know for his books. He cherishes Norm as only a very old friend is cherished. They know each other since high school, and though their careers take them in different directions, their friendship remains solid.

Don opens his laptop, finds the motel's network, and logs on. He runs a search for Ernest Prescott and only finds what he has been told by Junior. There is no mention of his time working for the government in New Hampshire, which Don finds odd, but there is a lot about his processing corporation during the war. He even finds some personal information about Ernest and his wife, and there is a mention of Emerson as well. None of the info is earth shattering, though, and most of it, he already knows.

Don searches for Emerson, and the search returns more than Ernest's search returns. For the next hour, Don reads page after page of information mentioning Emerson, from his history with the company to donations to the town of Dexter, and many stories about the car accident in which he was injured and his wife died.

There are a few follow-up stories about his amnesia and recovery from the first accident, but nothing at all about his second accident where he injured his head again.

Don assumes that because it didn't require any police or medical involvement, it never made the papers. Those types of stories don't usually make headlines.

He does find a story on Emerson's boat, though. It was a big deal in town when it was delivered by rail since it was too big to be shipped on the highway. That was early in the spring of 1994. That meant that boat had been on the lake for more than 20 years. Emerson must have taken great care of it for a lot of years because it sure doesn't look that old, Don thinks to himself. Even now, it may be dirty, but otherwise, it looks in almost perfect shape.

Searching on Manchester, New Hampshire, and Emerson Prescott returns nothing. He decides to do a record check on Emerson, checking birth certificates, driving records, education records, and other public records that are kept on everyone these days.

He opens the record checking website he subscribes to, logs in, enters Emerson's name and presses the "Submit" button. A message flashes that reads "Searching......", and it keeps flashing for a couple of minutes until the message window changes to read "Done. Pick up your report."

He clicks the report button and a message displays asking if he wants to download it or read the report online. He presses the download button and an arrow begins moving to the bottom of the screen with a message reading "Downloading". After almost a minute, a message states the files are downloaded and stored in his default directory. He logs out of the website, closes the browser and locates the desktop shortcut to the file and clicks on it.

The screen opens to a directory where there are more than ten subdirectories under Emerson Prescott. Don clicks on the first one, "Birth Information", opening the directory showing three more files:

1.   New Hampshire Birth Certificate

2.   Baptismal Certificate

3.   Hospital Record of Birth

He clicks on the New Hampshire Birth Certificate file, and it opens to what appears to be a photo-static copy of the original birth certificate with Ernest and Mary Prescott's names, their age at time of Emerson's birth, their hometown, the hospital name and location where Emerson was born, date and time of birth, weight and length, sex, hair color, eye color, number of live births this pregnancy, attending physician, and local address for Ernest and Mary.

Just under the words "Birth Certificate – State of New Hampshire" are the Italicized words, "*Amended Birth Certificate*", which means that the record was amended sometime after the original issuance of the birth certificate.

I wonder what that's about, Don says to himself. I wonder how I can find out what was amended?

He goes back to the directory and clicks the file "Baptismal Certificate" and the baptismal certificate from Dexter Unitarian church opens. It contains much of the same information that is on the birth certificate, except on this document there are two little footprints inked onto the bottom of the certificate. It is dated March 23, 1945, and signed by the Rev. Mark Hammersmith.

Returning to the directory, he clicks on the file "Hospital Record of Birth" and the Manchester General Hospital birth record opens on the screen. It contains the same information that is on the birth certificate, except under the space "live births this delivery" something has been crossed out and the number one inserted. Don guesses that must be why the birth certificate is an amended one; but why is the hospital record amended too? Usually, hospital records are permanent legal medical records, and if something is changed on it, the old information is just crossed out with a single line and initialed by whoever makes the change, not blotted out completely. This is something to follow up on, and Don makes a note on his legal pad under Emerson.

Don closes the windows and begins to look through the other directories:

Driving Records	Former Addresses
Education Records	Financial Judgements
Marriage/Divorce Records	Relatives
Social Media Connections	Arrest Records

Nothing else stands out from anything he heard about Emerson. There was a better police description of the car accident that had killed Lily, Emerson's wife, but no blame was attached to Emerson. There had been a nail in the road and it caused the tire to blow. Emerson lost control of the car, and it ran into a tree causing Lily to fly headfirst into the dashboard and then the window of the car. The car hit the tree on Lily's side, spun around 180 degrees and slammed into another tree, causing Emerson's door to fly open, ejecting him into a pile of hay and leaves on the side of the road.

Emerson hadn't been wearing his seat belt, and the report indicates that if he had, he probably would have suffered a severe case of whiplash and maybe even broken his neck. On the other hand, Lily had been wearing her seat belt which protected her from the initial head-on crash, but the secondary crash caused her body to turn sideways and that's when she hit the dashboard and ultimately the windshield.

Don takes notes as he goes through all the records, adding questions along the way. He closes his laptop and decides to take a walk down to the marina and have another look at Emerson's boat, and maybe have another conversation with the dock boy.

12

Tom passes through customs in Canada and drives to the northern part of the lake. He begins his search for marinas as well as any bars or restaurants near the lake. If Emerson boats to the northern part of the lake and stays somewhere, he either anchors or docks at a marina. Tom bets that Emerson is the kind of man that docks at a marina if he is going to stay anywhere for any length of time.

Tom drives along the eastern shore of the lake initially not seeing any marinas or even a restaurant or bar. Private houses occupy the shoreline for the first ten miles or so before he finally sees what appear to be private marinas, but none of them appear to be associated with public access, and there are no bars or restaurants nearby, so he ignores them.

He turns a corner into a point of land and sees a sign indicating there is a restaurant and a marina down a small dirt road. He turns in and almost immediately sees a large clapboard house with a wrap around porch housing an eating area with ten tables overlooking the marina. He gets out and walks into the restaurant.

Once inside, he walks over to the bar and orders a beer from the young lady working behind the bar. She places a bottle of Molson's in front of him and walks back to the magazine she was reading when Tom entered the bar.

Tom looks around the bar and restaurant, which at 2:45 in the afternoon is empty except for him and the barkeep. It isn't a fancy place. It has light pine wainscoting in the dining room, and fifteen or twenty tables sit on an old oak floor that needs refinishing. Red and white checkered tablecloths cover the tables, and little glass cups hold small votive candles, probably for "atmosphere" at night, Tom assumes. Two sets of French doors open to the porch seating area, and there is a half-wall separating the bar from the dining area.

Tom can see the marina slips through the French doors. Three fingers protrude out into the lake with boats moored on either side of the docks. He counts more than thirty boats tied up, with a few slips vacant, probably for visitors coming in off the lake.

"Excuse me," he says to the waitress. She puts the magazine down and walks over to him.

"Yes. What can I do for you?" She has a slight French-Canadian accent which doesn't surprise Tom since this is Quebec, and people in Quebec like to talk French rather than English.

"Do you get a lot of boaters up here from the states?"

"We get our share. Mostly fisherman. The fishing is good in this area."

"Do you rent overnight slips?"

"Yes, we do. I didn't see you pull in on a boat; why do you ask?"

"Oh! I am staying down in Dexter at the southern end of the lake, and someone I met down there said renting a boat and motoring up here to fish would be worthwhile. I hate to do that just for the day, though, so I was looking to maybe stay on the boat overnight or if there was lodging near a marina, rent a room for the night."

"Yes. We rent slips for the night, and we even have a couple of rooms to rent upstairs, but the rooms usually need a reservation. Not so much the slips. They are usually available.

"May I ask who recommended us to you?"

"Emerson Prescott. Do you know him?"

The barkeep wrinkles her nose a little bit and thinks for a second. "The name doesn't ring a bell. What does he look like?"

"He's in his late 60s, early 70s, and owns 38-foot cruiser. I am sure you would know the boat if you saw it. It's registered in Dexter, VT, and that's on the stern of the boat. I forget the name of the darned thing."

"We have many large boats on the lake, but I don't get to see the names on them from here. Maybe the night man knows your Emerson friend. He comes on in about an hour."

"Maybe I'll hang around till then and ask him. Thank you."

She smiles at him and returns to the other end of the bar to resume reading her magazine.

About forty-five minutes later a man walks in and shouts out a hello to Cheryl, the barkeep. She smiles at him and then walks over to the cash register to begin checking out. This must be the night man.

Without turning around to him, Cheryl tells him Tom wants to speak with him. The man walks over to where Tom sits, and Tom turns to face him. "Hi! My name is Tom. As I mentioned to Cheryl, I might be sailing up here for a visit. The place was recommended to me by a friend down in Dexter and Cheryl said you might know him. His name is Emerson Prescott, and he has a big 38-foot cruiser."

"The name sounds familiar, and so does the boat, but I seem to associate the boat with another name. There's a guy named Antoine that has a big boat like you mention. Well, he says it's his friend's boat actually.

"He's up here a couple of times a summer. Stays overnight and then heads further up the lake. He is an avid fisherman, and sometimes he brings his catch in for us to cook for him. We do that for the folks.

"Every once in a while Antoine comes up with his friend, but his friend never seems to leave the boat. I asked him about that once, and he said his friend was kind of anti-social."

"No – I don't think it's the same guy," Tom says.

"Yeah, maybe not. There are a lot of big boats up here. Some are even bigger than that one. They probably shouldn't even be on the lake cause they are so big, but some folks use them as a summer home, so I guess it makes sense."

"Well, thanks anyway. At least this seems like the place he mentioned to me, so you may see me again before the summer is out."

"You're always welcomed here." He smiles and walks around to the back of the bar. He and Cheryl talk, then Cheryl takes her tips, says goodbye to the night man, and waves goodbye to Tom.

Tom opens his little notebook and writes down what the barkeep has told him, along with the name of the restaurant and marina. At least Emerson has been up here a couple of times, so the trip isn't a waste, Tom says to himself. Who is this Antoine guy though? He sounds as if he must be a good friend of Emerson's if Emerson lends him that fancy boat. That's not something you let just anyone use.

Tom decides he can stop in one or two more places before the night's out so he pays for the beer, says goodbye to the barkeep, and continues on with his drive north along the lake.

He locates three more marinas that have bars or restaurants associated with them and goes through the same routine with each bartender.

One place has no recollection of anyone named Emerson or Antoine, but two of the places do, and the bartender in the Saint Bernard Yacht Club just south of Magog, the northernmost town on the lake, says that Antoine is almost a regular.

"Yeah. Antoine is up here eight or nine times a summer," the barman tells Tom. "Sometimes, he stays here at the yacht club for a week. We've even gone up to Sherbrooke a few times for dinner and drinks.

"He's a real nice older guy. Quite often he picks up the check. I figure he must have money, after all, he has a friend that owns that big boat and even lets him take it out whenever he wants.

"The guy, Emerson I think his name is, comes up with Antoine a few times every summer, but he always stays on the boat. Antoine says he doesn't really like people, but he and Antoine go way back, and I guess Antoine is one of very few friends the guy has."

"It sounds as if you know him well," Tom says.

"I guess as well as anyone around here. As I said, we've even driven up to Sherbrooke a few times."

"He ever say where he lives? Does he live down in Dexter, near his friend?"

"I don't think so. I think he lives somewhere in New Hampshire. From the way he described it, I think it is a little town somewhere just over the Vermont border, about an hour or so south of the Canadian border."

"Did he ever say what he does for a living or how he knows Emerson?"

"I think he was a laborer when he was younger, and I think when I first met him, oh that would be maybe fifteen years ago or somewhere thereabout, I always had the impression he was a salesman of some sort. But he's got to be in his late 60s now, at least, so I think he is probably retired. He must have a lot of time on his hands and doesn't just show up on weekends, so he must be free to do whatever he wants, whenever he wants.

"If I recall, I think he said he had worked on a lobster boat when he was a kid. He once told me his folks moved to Maine when he was in high school, I think it was Damariscotta. Always remembered that name cause it is such a strange name. I think that was where he worked on the lobster boat during the summer."

"A lobster boat, huh? I wonder how he ever met that guy Prescott. Doesn't sound like the have a lot in common."

"Maybe he was a sales contact, that is if Antoine was a salesman. That might explain how they met. Antoine never talked about what kind of business he was in, so I am just guessing here."

"Did he ever tell you how long they had known each other?"

"I met Antoine in the late '90s and he had already been coming up here with his friend by then. I think he told me they met around '92 or so, but never told me how."

"Have you seen him much this summer?"

"Truth be told, he hasn't been up this way much the last couple of years, and then both times this summer he had his friend with him. Maybe it's getting too much for him to handle the boat all by himself as he gets older."

"Yeah. That's a big boat to handle by yourself. I bet you need some serious seamanship skills to maneuver that baby around."

"You're almost finished with that beer," the barman says. "Can I get you another one?"

Tom nods, and when the man comes back with the beer, asks him about a place to stay.

"Well, about a quarter mile down the road there's a Country Suite Motel. It's clean and relatively cheap, and if you drink too much you can walk there. If you want, you could call and have them hold a room for you."

"Let's do that. I don't want to be driving up here and get caught for drinking."

"That, my friend, is a very good idea. I'll get you the phone."

13

Tom spends the rest of the evening at the Yacht Club, first eating dinner, and then having a few more beers with Frank, the bartender. For most of the evening, Tom keeps away from the subject of Emerson Prescott and the mysterious Antoine, Emerson's long time friend. But every once in a while he subtly delves into the history of Emerson's friend, Antoine.

"Hey, Frank. Were you ever on board that boat Antoine used," Tom asks. "I bet it is beautiful inside."

"To tell you the truth, Antoine never invited me on board, which isn't odd since his friend is so shy and probably doesn't want strangers on board when he is there."

"Did you ever see the two of them together, I mean they must have sat out on the deck drinking together sometime."

"Nope. Never did. Never saw that guy Emerson leave the boat either."

"You said Antoine was from New Hampshire, right?"

"Yeah, somewhere down there. I know he mentioned the town once, but..." Frank looks off into the distance like he was searching for the name of the town in the air in front of him, "Darn, I can almost see the name. I know it was near some lake, Moose Lake, or something like that."

"Well, I guess the two of them knowing each other is no odder than you and I knowing each other. People sometimes just seem to run into each other and become friends."

"Ain't that the truth?"

Tom and Frank keep talking until around 11 PM when Tom decides he should get to his motel room before they give it away to someone else.

"You be good, Tom," Frank says. "Nice meeting you. If you end up renting a boat, come on up and stay a day or two at the marina. It'd be nice to see you again."

Tom said he would do that, and left for the motel.

He is amazed at how much information Frank gave him. This guy Antoine is a new twist to the whole story of Emerson Prescott. Prescott seems to have very few friends in Dexter, but here he has a friend that he feels close enough to that he lets this friend use his very expensive boat, and not just once in a while, whenever the friend wants to use it. That, by anyone's definition, is a close friend.

As soon as he checks into the motel and gets to his room, he calls Don to let him know what he discovered. Don has some news of his own for Tom.

"Remember my friend, Norm," Don asks Tom.

"Yeah," Tom replies.

"Well, right after you left, I gave him a call to ask him about Ernie's time working for the government in New Hampshire, and it turns out Ernie didn't work for the government for all the time he spent in Manchester.

"Ernie and Mary were in Manchester for almost a year, eleven months, I think, but Ernie only worked for the government for a little more than four months, from March until the end of June or early August. He and Mary stayed there for another seven months, during which time Emerson was born. But they stayed there for four months after Emerson was born. Why wouldn't they have returned home with the baby soon after it was born? That seems like the obvious thing to do, bring your baby home, right?

"Yeah, I guess. Maybe the baby was sick or something and needed to stay in Manchester because there was a hospital there," Tom suggests.

"Yeah, I guess that could be the reason, but I think Junior would have known that, don't you?"

"Well, I know we would have known that about dad, that's for sure."

"Another thing I found out was that Emerson has an Amended Birth Certificate. I tried to find out why it was amended but the clerk at the New Hampshire Records bureau said there was no way of knowing without the permission of the person listed on the birth certificate authorizing the release of that information. I don't think we'll get Emerson's permission, do you?"

"Probably not in this lifetime."

"I also saw the hospital record of birth, and there was a section that had been blacked out and rewritten, the section listing live births for that delivery, and it was crossed out and then written as one.

"Could there have been a second child born at the same time that died during delivery? I guess that could have been the reason for the amended birth certificate. Maybe Ernie and Mary never told Emerson about that."

"That makes sense. That may be why they stayed down there longer. Maybe something happened to Mary during delivery and she had to stay in the hospital for a while."

"I guess that could be the reason.

"So, who is this Antoine fellow? Seems strange he is such good friends with Emerson, but no one in Dexter ever mentioned him."

"Apparently, they are fishing buddies and have been for a while," Tom says. "No one I've met knows much about Antoine other than he is friends with Emerson. No one even knows his last name.

"I am going to visit a couple more marinas up here and see if anyone else knows this Antoine. Maybe I can find out what his last name is and where he lives. Then we can run a check on him and see what the connection is between him and Emerson.

"Hey, Don. Do me a favor; search the net and see if there is a Moose Lake in New Hampshire, will you? I'm looking for something about fifty miles south of the Canadian border and near the Vermont border."

Don turns on his laptop and searches for Moose Lake, New Hampshire.

"No Moose Lake; but there is a Moose Pond, a Moose Brook, a Moose Hillock Campground, a Moose Alley, a Moose Mountain, A Moose-a-look river, and a Camp Moosilauke. The only other thing I see that is even close to Moose Lake is someplace called

Mooseeum Lake in the eastern part of the state, right on the border of Maine and New Hampshire."

"Are any of them near the Vermont border?"

"Let me see." Don clicks on each one to locate it on a map.

"Three of them are near the Vermont border and one is right on it."

"Which one is on the border?"

"Moose-a-look River, and it looks like the river has been dammed and there is a reservoir behind the dam. Not big enough, I guess, to be called a lake. It is called Little Moose Reservoir."

"How far is that from the Canadian border," Tom Asks.

"According to the map, it looks to be about forty or fifty miles south of the border as the crow flies."

"Is there a little town near there?"

"Yeah. A place called Harmony Corners. Doesn't look like much of anything, though. About the same size as Dexter."

"Well, when I get back, maybe we'll take a ride over that way and check it out. One of the people I met up here said this Antoine guy lives in a small town near someplace called Moose Lake, and it is supposed to be about an hour or so south of the Canadian border. I guess Little Moose Reservoir could be the lake, and Harmony Corners could be the town. It would really help if I knew Antoine's last name."

"Maybe tomorrow you can find someone who will be able to provide that for you. People always pay by credit card these days, so someone has to have sold Antoine something in all these years where he signed his name or used a credit card."

"Maybe one of your old buddies on the police force can get you that credit card information."

"Yeah...never thought of that. I mean, he must have at some time over the years bought gas for that boat up here, or paid for dinner, or a hotel room and paid by credit card. Who doesn't have a credit card these days?"

"OK, Tom. See if you can track him down that way through

your contacts. If you get Antoine's last name, give them a call in the morning and get things started. I'll see you tomorrow, maybe in the afternoon. Good hunting." Don pushes the disconnect button on the phone and sets it down on the nightstand next to the bed. He picks up the notepad from the nightstand next to the bed and adds the information Tom has given him. He is on the second page already and knows there are going to be a lot more pages before they figure this all out.

Once he finishes writing, he puts the notepad next to his phone, shuts off the light, and goes to sleep.

The next morning at breakfast, he sees Billy and asks him if he has ever heard of Antoine.

"I don't know anyone named Antoine in Dexter," Billy says.

When Don tells him that Emerson lets Antoine use his boat almost anytime he wants to, Billy is amazed.

"He never even lets Junior take that boat out alone," Billy says. "Have you asked the guy down at the marina? If Antoine takes the boat out, Emerson must have told the kid it was OK, cause I don't think he would ever let someone not authorized to take the boat out, do that."

"Good idea," Don says. "Tom also told me Antoine may not be from Dexter. He may be from somewhere in New Hampshire. Tom is going to look into that today."

"Wow! This is getting interesting. You are finding out all sorts of things I never knew about Emerson. He is turning into a very complicated guy."

"Remember, I told you that there are always stories hidden in little towns like this that no one knows about. That's why I love looking for them.

"By the way, let's keep this on the down-low for a while until we know more. Once a secret is exposed, it starts to get buried deeper by those that know something about it."

"OK, Don," Billy says. "But you gotta promise me you'll keep me updated, cause now I just gotta know what's going on."

"You're part of it now, Billy. I wouldn't have been able to

find out half of this without your input."

Billy finishes his breakfast and heads home. Don decides to walk over to visit Gertrude to see if she knows anything about Antoine, although Don doubts that anyone in Dexter knows of Antoine.

He picks up some tea for Gertrude before leaving the Chicken and Cow, then walks over to the Historical Society. Along the way, he looks over at the marina and wonders if the dock boy would know anything about Antoine. If he does, that would really move things forward.

"Hi Gertrude," Don says as he walks through the door to the society. "How are you this fine day? Brought you some tea."

"You are such a dear," Gertrude says. "Sit yourself down and tell me what you've been up to since yesterday?"

Don sets the tea down on a yellow tablet sitting on Gertrude's desk and pulls over one of the chairs. Once he settles in the chair, he tells her of meeting Junior and having Junior give him a complete history of the company.

"Junior is very proud of what his family has accomplished with that company," Gertrude says. "He feels a great responsibility to this town since the town has always supported the company. All three of the Prescott men treated the town as part of their family."

"Yes, it seems they are well respected here."

"Always, have been. And Junior keeps up that tradition."

Don decides to ask her if she knows anyone named Antoine that might know Emerson. She thinks for a moment before replying.

"Nope. That sounds like one of them French Canadian names, maybe Cajun or Acadian, or Creole, like the singer "Fats" Domino. He real first name was Antoine, did you know that?. He was really something back in the 50s, but I guess that was a little before your time, wasn't it?"

"Yeah, but I know who he is."

"Anyways, I don't know any Antoine. Never heard of anyone from this town named Antoine either. What's his connection with Emerson?"

"I don't know, I just heard he was a fishing buddy of Emerson's and I thought I might be able to talk to him about Emerson.

"Emerson is turning into a very interesting person for me. There is a lot about him I bet most people don't know. Once I get a true picture of the man, I'll tell you all I have learned, but I found out that telling people only snippets of information on someone presents an incomplete picture a man, and it is so much better to be able to present the complete picture, don't you agree?'

"Well, my boy, I guess you're right. But what more could you possibly tell me about Emerson? I've know him almost all my life."

"That's true, but there are always some things we don't know about someone."

"Guess you're right again. For instance, and I tell you this in confidence so don't go spreading it around, I once went to Boston to audition for a theatrical production scheduled to go to Broadway. I fancied myself a singer and dancer and thought I could make it big.

"They laughed me off that stage after my audition. I was crushed, but they were right; I couldn't sing or dance compared to those that do that for a living. It was just a dream of a farm girl in Vermont." Gertrude's eyes had that faraway look of someone who is remembering a time from their past.

"Well, at least you tried. That's better than most folks do. Most people never try to live their dream."

"At least I have no regrets. But you're right – I do have my secrets."

Don smiles at Gertrude and tries to picture her as a young woman auditioning in Boston. That would have taken a lot of courage to do that.

Don stays for a while just passing the time with Gertrude then decides it is time to have a talk with the dock boy to find out what he knows about Antoine. He replaces the chair to its rightful place and says goodbye to Gertrude, who smiles at him and reminds him to come back and see her soon.

It is a short walk to the marina and Don finds the dock boy sitting in a chair in the dock house doing something on his smartphone. Don knocks on the door frame and the kid looks up at him with one finger raised, then taps the phone a couple of times before turning his attention to Don.

"Yes, sir," the kid says, not moving from his chair. "What can I do for you today?"

"Just a couple of questions," Don says. "You ever see a guy around here by the name of Antoine?"

The kid scrunches his lips together, then rolls his eyes around as if he is searching a card catalog in his head. "Nope. Can't say I ever heard of no Antoine. Should I know him?"

"Oh – I just heard he was a fishing buddy of Prescott's. I thought maybe you'd seen him go out fishing with Prescott over the summer."

"Old Prescott rarely, if ever, takes anyone out on the boat with him anymore and I've worked almost four summers here."

"Has anyone ever taken out Prescott's boat without him on it?"

The kid laughs. "You gotta be kidding me. If I let anyone take that boat out of here, other than the mechanic that works on it every once in a while, he'd probably have me shot. Nobody, and I mean not even Junior, gets to take that boat out."

"Are you here every day during the season? Could someone take the boat out without you knowing it?"

"Well, I'm here from 5 AM until 8 PM unless I'm so sick I can't get out of bed, which happens once or twice a summer. I guess someone could be using the boat at night that I don't know about, but it's always there in the morning unless Prescott has taken it out."

"Thanks," Don says. "Enjoy your day. It looks like another beauty, doesn't it?"

"Ya know, it always seems to be beautiful up here in the summer. I guess we save our crap weather for the winter."

Don laughs and turns away from the kid. So, no one takes the boat out except Emerson, and yet this guy Antoine is seen on it without Emerson quite often How the hell does that happen?

On the walk back to the motel Don gets a call from Tom.

Dons stops and answers the phone, moving off the road to sit on a berm under a tree.

"What's up, Tom?"

"You were right about him having had to purchase something up here by credit card. I just spoke with a guy at the marina who said Antoine purchases gas from him a few times a year. There are only a few places you can buy gas on the lake up here and he is the only one on the eastern side of the lake, so he gets almost everyone's business.

"When I asked about Antoine, the guy didn't even have to look up anything. He said he only knew one Antoine with a boat and that is Antoine Beechen."

"Bingo. we have a name."

"Yep. I'll give my friend a call to see if he can scare up an address for the credit card bills. Can you do a search on this guy Beechen, and see what you can find out about him? Can't be too many of them. Never heard that name before, have you?

"No. That's a new one for me."

"OK. I'm headed back down there, see you in an hour or so."

14

As soon as Don is in his motel room he opens his laptop and does a search for Antoine Beechen. There are no hits on the name at all. Then he tries just Beechen by itself, and that only returns a reference to Beechen Cliffs, a place in England, and a real estate firm in the Midwest.

He then goes to the record checking website, types in Antoine Beechen, and presses the "Submit" button. The message window flashes, and he waits. Finally, the message window tells him his search results are ready. He downloads the report and opens the directory.

The same directories appear:

Birth Records	Driving Records
Former Addresses	Education Records
Financial Judgments	Relatives
Marriage/Divorce Records	Arrest Records
Social Media Connections	

As he did with Emerson's information, he opens the Birth Records directory first, and again three document files display:

1. New Hampshire Birth Certificate

2. Baptismal Certificate

3. Hospital Record of Birth

He opens the Birth Certificate file first, and what appears to be a photostatic copy of the original birth certificate shows on the screen. The first thing he notices is that under the heading "Birth Certificate – State of New Hampshire" are the Italicized words, "*Amended Birth Certificate*", just like Emerson's birth certificate.

That's odd, he thinks. Both of them have an amended certificate. What are the chances of that? He reads the rest of the document. Seems Emerson and Antoine are born in the same hospital and on the same day, too. Maybe their parents met in the hospital and kept in touch over the years and that's how Emerson and Antoine know each other.

He then opens Antoine's Baptismal file. He was baptized at the First Congregational Church of Canaan, New Hampshire, on April 5, 1945. Again, there are two little footprints inked in at the bottom of the page, and it is signed by a Rev. Charles Simpson.

Returning to the directory, he clicks on the file "Hospital Record of Birth" and the Manchester General Hospital birth record opens on the screen. Under the hospital logo appears the words *COPY*. It contains the same type of information that is on the birth certificate:

> Mother: Emily Holden Age at birth: 28
>
> Father: François Beechen Age at birth: 31
>
> Permanent residence: 16 High St., Canaan, N. Hampshire
>
> Location of birth: Manchester General Hospital
>
> Date of Birth: October 15, 1944 Time of Birth: 12:09A
>
> Weight: 6lbs. 3oz. Length:18" Sex: M
>
> Hair color: Br Eye color: Br
>
> Number of live births this pregnancy: ■ 1
>
> Attending Physician: Dr. Raymond Foster
>
> Local address (if applicable): N/A

Like a bolt of lightening the words "Number of live births this pregnancy" jump up at him when he sees the smudged out number in the entry. It looks the same as on Emerson's hospital birth record.

He opens Emerson's records directory, locates the hospital birth record file, and opens it. He looks at the information on Emerson's file:

> Mother: Mary Prescott Age at birth: 21
>
> Father: Ernest Prescott Age at birth: 23
>
> Permanent residence: Abenaki Trail Rd, Dexter VT
>
> Location of birth: Manchester General Hospital
>
> Date of Birth: October 14, 1944 Time of Birth: 11:52P
>
> Weight: 6lbs. 7oz. Length:19" Sex: M
>
> Hair color: Br Eye color: Br

Number of live births this pregnancy: ▉ 1
Attending Physician: Dr. Raymond Foster
Local address (if applicable): Low's Hotel, Manchester, NH

He sets the two files side by side on the screen to compare them. The first thing he sees is that Emerson and Antoine are born in the same hospital in Manchester and only one day apart. Then he sees the time of birth, which is only separated by 17 minutes, and the attending physician is the same. Both have brown hair and brown eyes and are about the same size and weight.

My god, that may be one of the biggest coincidences I've ever seen, Don thinks. Two men born at almost the same time, in the same place, and having similar characteristics. Then they stay in touch with each other for their whole life, and yet no one knows about that except them. And both of their birth certificates are corrected and amended.

Maybe it was a busy night and that's why there were mistakes on the hospital records. Maybe the attending nurse got things a little mixed up and corrected the information right after the births.

Where the hell is Tom, Don thinks. He should be here by now. We've got to think about this differently now, and now we have Antoine's hometown to check on as well. Tom is going to be busy now, this is his line of work.

Don makes more notes on the notepad as he waits for Tom to arrive. It is another forty minutes before the door to the room opens and Tom walks in drinking a soda.

"How ya doing, bro? Find out anything on the internet about Antoine Beechen?"

Don looks up at his brother. "More than you can ever imagine. It's going to make your head explode when I tell you what I discovered." Don opens his laptop and brings up the files on the screen. "Sit down, Tom. You're gonna love what I found out while you were driving around the countryside."

Don goes over everything he learned of the births of Emerson and Antoine, including his thoughts about how the two of them might know each other. Tom sits there looking at the information on the screen, nodding in agreement.

"That certainly would explain their relationship," Tom says. "Now all we have to do is locate Antoine. Did the search return any addresses for Antoine?"

"Oh, geez! I got so excited about the birth certificate stuff I forgot to check the other files." Don clicks on the "Former Addresses" directory and it opens to a file marked "Addresses". Don clicks on the file and it opens revealing a list of maybe twenty-five addresses associated with Antoine Beechen.

"The man gets around doesn't he," says Tom.

At the top of the list is the address where he lived as a kid: 16 High St, Canaan, New Hampshire, and the years he lived there: 1944 -1953. Then 5 Arlen Lane, Damariscotta, Maine, 1953-1962. After that, the list continues with addresses that change every year or two, sometimes even a few times in one year. At the end of the list is an address that looks familiar: 22 Devon Road, Harmony Corners, New Hampshire, 1989 - present.

"Bingo!" Tom slaps Don on the back. "You were right about the town in New Hampshire. Tomorrow, we'll have to take a ride down there to see where he lives. Maybe he'll be home and we can talk to him a little and find out what his relationship is to Emerson."

Don smiles at his brother. "We make quite a team don't we?"

"Yep, we do. And tomorrow you'll be able to tie this all together and maybe even get started on that book of yours."

"That would be nice. This excursion up here has certainly provided all the elements of a good mystery story, and all I have to do is come up with a plot, and the book will write itself."

"Let's go have a few beers and have dinner, then have a few more beers to celebrate," Tom smiles. "I think we deserve it?"

Don and Tom spend a good part of the evening eating, drinking, and celebrating the fact that they have just about solved the riddle of Emerson's and Antoine's friendship. They leave the bar around midnight and drive back to the motel. Soon they are asleep, filled with anticipation of their trip to New Hampshire the next morning.

They are both up and on the road by 6 AM, anticipating a long day of driving and talking with people in Harmony Corners. Driving south out of Dexter they turn south onto I-91 for the almost 60-mile ride to Harmony Corners. Tom drives while Don opens the laptop and lists things he wants to accomplish on the trip:

- Locate Antoine's house

- Locate Antoine and speak with him

- Talk to neighbors re Emerson Prescott

- Check archives of local newspaper

- Get a photo of Antoine

As soon as they leave the interstate five miles outside of Harmony Corners, they stop at a diner for breakfast. Don takes the laptop in with him so they can look at a map of the area and locate Antoine's house. They place their order, then the waitress brings them their coffee and they settle down to talk about the day. Don opens the files containing Antoine's addresses and enters the most recent address, 22 Devon Road, Harmony Corner, New Hampshire, into the mapping program.

The map opens and locates the house on the north shore of Little Moose Reservoir, about a mile west of the dam. The road into the property is a seasonal dirt road with three or four other houses on it. Don is sure that there will be people there since it is the height of the summer season, and that should make it easy to talk with folks about Antoine.

"I think when we get to Antoine's house, we need to have a

good cover story for our reason for being there," Don says. "I'll tell him I am doing a feature on Emerson and his company, for a newspaper. I heard he is a really good friend of Emerson's, so I thought he might have some insight into the man that I may not have gotten from folks in Dexter.

"People love to hear themselves talk about stuff they know, and it is always easy to get information out of them if you tell them it will be in the newspaper and they will be quoted by name."

"That is," Tom says, "unless they have something to hide. Then they clam up like a…well….like a clam."

"I'll just have to take that chance, I guess. Maybe Antoine is talkative."

"According to the people up in Canada, he is a very sociable guy. So, my guess is, he'll give you what you need."

"I hope so. I think once we talk with him, we'll be able to wrap this whole thing up and head back to the city, and I can get started on my book."

Don grabs a napkin and scribbles down the directions to Antoine's house, and also copies the list of things he wants to accomplish while he is in Harmony Corners, then closes the laptop.

Thirty minutes later, they finish breakfast and begin the drive to Antoine's place. In less than fifteen minutes they reach the seasonal road and turn onto it. Passing the well kept seasonal houses, Don notices there are cars in all the driveways, but no one is outside that he can see. It is only a little after 9AM, but Don thinks people would be up and about by now.

They locate 22 Devon Road. The road itself is about 300 feet from the water, and the house sits between the road and the reservoir, as all the houses on Devon Road do. Each house looks to have three or four acres of land containing trees, brush, and large areas of lawn surrounding it, which allows a good deal of privacy between houses. The view of the water from the road is beautiful, and the area is as quiet as a church. It would be since no motor boats or jet skis are allowed on the reservoir, and most likely there is no swimming allowed either. A perfect get-a-way to relax. If this is Antoine's year round home, it would certainly be almost deserted here in the winter.

Tom pulls into the driveway and up to the steps to the house. He notices there is no car on the property and assumes Antoine is not home. Don opens the car door and steps out.

"I'll see if he's here," Don says as he closes the door.

Walking up the two granite steps in front of the door, Don can see inside the picture window. Not much furniture inside, he thinks. All he can see is a chair, a couch, an end table and lamps, and a stone fireplace. He knocks on the door a few times, but no one answers.

He turns to Tom, and raises a finger in Tom's direction, then walks around the side of the house into the back yard. There is a small deck in the back and he climbs it and walks to the back door, knocking on it when the gets to it.

No answer there, either.

He peers into a window and sees the kitchen. A sink, a stove, some wooden cabinets, a pine table with two chairs, a refrigerator, and a door that he presumes leads either to a basement or a pantry.

He knocks once more, but still no answer. He turns and walks off the deck and continues around the other side of the house. He looks in two windows. One is the bedroom which contains a bed, a nightstand with a lamp on it, and a clothes rack with what looks like two sets of clothes hanging on it.

One other window is to the bathroom, which contains only a toilet, an old fashioned sink hung on the wall, and a shower stall. Don looks around to see if there are any other outbuilding on the property and there are none.

He walks back to the car and gets in. "Well, he's not here. That's going to make things difficult, isn't it?"

"Guess we're going to talk with the neighbors, right?" Tom says as he starts the car.

"Maybe he just went to town for something and he'll be back soon."

"True. But until he returns, we could do a little investigating with the neighbors."

"You're right, Tom. And if he returns, we'll know a little

more about him, won't we?"

Tom backs out of Antoine's driveway and drives to the house next door. Don is out of the car and walks to the front door, but before he is halfway there, the door opens and a man who looks to be in his mid-fifties stands behind the screen door, looking at Don suspiciously.

"What can I do for you? I saw you over there at Antoine's house; you looking for him?"

"As a matter of fact I am," Don says. "I'm Don Winston and I am a freelance writer for Down Home Sunday Magazine. I'm doing a small piece on a guy name Emerson Prescott up in Dexter Vermont, and I heard that Antoine is very good friends with him. I was hoping to get some background on Emerson from Antione.

"Have you seen him today?"

"Nope. Matter of fact, haven't seen him for most of the summer. He only comes up here a few days a summer, and he keeps to himself mostly."

"Really? Does he travel a lot? Is that what keeps him away? Or does he live somewhere else?"

"I guess he must live somewhere else now, cause I never see him most summers now."

"How long have you lived up here?"

"Maybe thirty years. I work for the town and have lived here with the wife since we got married."

"Has Antoine lived here that long?"

"Well, he was here when I bought this place, and that must be the late 1980s, I think."

"So he never really lived here full time then?"

"Oh, yeah, he did. Lived here full time until around the early '90s, then he started going away for long periods of time."

"I hate to say it, but we weren't really good neighbors to each other, other than being handy if there was an emergency or something. Ya know, need help digging out of the snow or ya get hurt and need to have someone take you to the doctor. That kind of stuff.

"I don't think either of us ever ate at the other's house. He was never a real friendly guy. He said hi and all that, but I never talked to him about anything personal, and he never asked me nothing personal about my life or family. I don't think anyone else on this road knows much about him either."

"When was the last time you saw him up here?"

"Maybe beginning of the summer. He usually comes up then to make sure the house is opened up, and then we see him for a day or two in the fall, before winter sets in."

"Ever see him in the winter?"

"I've seen smoke coming out of his chimney once or twice, but not in the last five years or so. My best guess is, he lives somewhere else and only keeps the property cause he owns it. He never seems to use it."

"Well, thanks for your time. Sorry to have bothered you on such a nice morning. It sure is pretty up here."

"Ayah, that it is. Quiet, too. And not many visitors either."

"I know what you mean. Have a good day."

"Yeah, you too," the man says as he closes the door.

"Let's go," Don says to Tom as he gets in the car. "I guess you could hear what he told me."

Tom nods as he backs out of the driveway.

"Any need to talk to any of the other folks on this road," Tom asks.

"I don't think so. Once we are off this road let's drive up to the dam to see what that looks like. We can stop there and plan our next move."

Tom accelerates down the road. Five minutes later they sit looking at the reservoir from a space next to the bridge that runs over the dam. There is a clear view of the entire reservoir from this vantage point, although you can't see any of the houses on Devon Road since they are all set back from the water. There are some rowboats on the water, and the silhouettes of a few fishermen with their lines in the water can just about be seen.

"Now what," Tom says, breaking the silence.

"I think we need to go to the post office to see if Antoine receives mail here," Don says, "and if not, where does his mail end up going.

"He must get tax bills sent to him. And he has electric lines to the place so maybe he has electric bills sent somewhere as well.

"Hey – you said you were going to call your friend down in the city to see if he could get some info from the credit card companies. Why not give him a call and see if he got any information yet. There must be an address they send the bills to, right?"

"OK. Maybe he hasn't got the information back yet, but let's see." Tom pulls out his phone and places a call to his former coworker.

"Hey, Jimmy. This is Tom. Did you get that info I asked for?

"Yeah…hold on… let me write that down." Tom pulls out his notepad and begins writing.

"Yeah…PO Box 421, Burlington, VT

"Does it list his home address? Yeah….22 Devon Road, Harmony Corners, New Hampshire. Any phone contact number? No? Any secondary contact information…no, huh? And his bills are paid directly from a bank account with automatic payment? So his bank must have an address for him, right? What? Someone else pays the bill... Who's account did you say?…Emerson Prescott? Did you say, Emerson Prescott? No kidding.

"You're a godsend, Jimmy. I owe you for this…yeah, I know, I still owe you for the last time…this was a big one, though. Thanks a lot. You take care, Jimmy."

Tom closes his phone and looks at Don. "I assume you heard what I said, right?"

"I heard something about the bill is paid by Emerson Prescott."

"Yep," Don says. "Straight from his bank account. No paper trail. Automatic payment every month."

"Boy, they must be really good friends for Emerson to pay his credit account for him. I mean, I love you, but I don't think I would set up an auto-payment from my account for you."

"Gee – thanks, bro."

"No – I am serious. That's just a little strange, don't you think?"

"Yeah, it is. Maybe Antione doesn't have a lot of money, and Emerson feels sorry for him. Everyone said Emerson used to be a very compassionate guy."

"I wish I was Emerson's friend," Don says. "Emerson pays his credit card bill, lends him his boat, and knowing Antoine never even seems to live in his own home anymore, makes you wonder if Emerson also rents him an apartment or something, too."

"And I thought today was going to be an easy day, and we would wrap things up. I guess I was wrong."

"Before we go, Don says, "let's check with the post office to see if he has a P.O. box here. Maybe they will even tell us if he has his mail forwarded somewhere.

"Then, let's see if there is a local paper up here. Even if it is just a weekly, maybe there is some information about Antoine in the archives. Maybe even a photo. Wouldn't that be interesting?"

Tom starts the car and they drive into Harmony Corners in search of the post office. As they enter the town, they see a sign that says Harmony Corners Press, and Don nudges Tom to pull into the parking lot. The building is little more than an old one family house that now houses the local paper.

They park and walk into the office where a man sits in front of a computer, typing copy for an article his is writing for that week's issue. When he hears Tom and Don enter, he looks up from the screen and stands.

"Hi, fellas. What can I do for you?"

"Are you the owner or maybe the editor?" Don looks around the office which must have once been the living room of the old house.

"Both," the man says with a smile. "Peter Wentworth."

"Well, Peter, we're hoping you can give us some information on one of your citizens here in town. Antoine Beechen," Don says.

He looks at Don, then at Tom, and says, "Are you guys cops or something?"

"No, no, nothing like that. Just doing a story on someone that knows Antoine, and we were hoping to get some background on Antoine for the story. Do you know him?"

"I've heard the name, but not in a long, long while. Not sure I can tell you anything."

"Are your back issues on the computer? Any way to search past issues? Maybe there is a story on him, or maybe even a picture.

We don't even know what he looks like.

"We were hoping to find him home today, but it seems he may be on a trip somewhere according to his neighbors. So I was hoping you might have some information on him and this wouldn't have been a wasted trip up here."

"Our computerized archives only go back to around 1998. Before that, you would have to look at our microfilm records. That could take you a very long time to find anything unless you have an idea when whatever you were looking for occurred."

He sits down at the computer and presses a few keys, then looks up at Don. "What did you say the name was again?"

"Antoine Beechen."

The owner types in the name and presses the search key.

"There are three entries for Antoine Beechen. One in 1999, one in 2000, and one in 2004.

"In 1999, he is mentioned in an article about hitting a deer. It's from a police report. We don't get a lot of hard news up here," Peter laughs.

"In the 2000 article," he presses the key again, "he pulled someone out of a ditch in the winter."

He presses the keys again. "And in 2004, he is mentioned in an article about having won the July 4th raffle at the church in town."

"Any pictures with those articles," Don asks.

"Nope. Guess he is like most people in town. He keeps to his own business and stays out of the limelight. Most folks are like that around here. Sometimes makes it hard to write a weekly paper."

"I guess I can use those items in my story," Don tells Peter. "I am sure the readers would be more than interested."

"Sorry, I couldn't be of more help. Maybe our sheriff might know more about Antoine Beechen. Let me give him a call."

Peter dials the sheriff's number. "Hey, there Jonah. This is Pete Wentworth....no, no problem, just a question.....no, there isn't an accident anywhere.

"Listen, do you know anything about Antoine Beechen?

Lives here in town?

"Yeah…uh, huh…ya don't say…when was that," Pete begins writing on a scrap piece of paper on his desk.

"Yeah,…1969…and again in 1976…any jail time…charges dropped. Only know that because you were the arresting officer, huh. That's it, though. Nothing since then...Nope, just a couple of fellows looking to talk with him and they can't seem to find him…yeah they looked out at his house and he wasn't there, and the neighbors think he may be traveling somewhere. No, I don't think it is any kind of emergency…" He looks up at Don and mouths "Is it?" Don shakes his head no.

"No, no emergency….you too, and thanks, Jonah." He puts the phone down and turns to Don.

Peter begins reading from his notes, "1969 he was arrested for using someone's car without their permission. Wasn't really car theft. He borrowed the car of a friend and didn't tell the friend. No charges were filed.

"Then in 1976 he drove off in a car owned by his girlfriend; Jonah said they had been fighting. Sounds like he drove to Manchester and just as he entered town on his trip back to her house, he ran a stop sign and Jonah stopped him. When he ran the car, he discovered it had been reported stolen, so he detained him overnight until the girlfriend could be reached. She declined to press charges.

"Sounds like a lucky guy. Nobody ever presses charges against him," Peter laughs.

"That's it, huh," Don says. "Nothing else?"

"Nope. Sounds like your guy is pretty squeaky clean."

"Well, I appreciate your help. Have a good day."

"You, too," Peter replies. " Hey, if I come across this Antoine guy, should I tell him you were looking for him?

"Nah! I'll have already finished my article and moved on to something new. Thanks, all the same, though."

Don and Tom walk back to their car. "That was a bust. I had hoped there would have been something about him in the paper.

"Let's drive over to the post office and see what we can find out there. Maybe they have a forwarding address for him."

At the post office, they find he has no forwarding address and the postal clerk says she hasn't delivered any first class mail to that address in years. She thought that was odd since tax bills normally go out to the address of record, but some folks do have their tax bills sent to accountants and or other third parties, especially summer folks, so come to think of it, it is not all that odd.

When Don gets back into the car, Tom asks him what he wants to do next.

"Do you feel like taking a drive over to Burlington? Maybe we can get some information from the post office over there. After all, Antoine has some of his mail sent there, so maybe he lives in Burlington for most of the year and we can get an address for him."

"OK," Toms says. "Burlington, here we come."

Two hours later, they sit in front of the Burlington Main post office, a few hundred feet from Lake Champlain.

"That was a little bit of a ride," Tom says. "Thank god we got an early start this morning."

Don nods as he opens the car door. "This shouldn't take too long. They will either have the info handy, or they won't give it to me at all. I should be back in five – ten minutes, at the most."

Don enters the post office which is almost deserted at this time of day and walks up to the clerk at the desk."

"Hello, sir. How may I help you today?"

"Well, I have sort of a small problem. I forget where my friend lives here in Burlington. I hoped you could tell me his address.

"I've been driving around for an hour or so, trying to see if I could recall his neighborhood, but that didn't work. So, I am hoping you'll be able to tell his me his address." Don smiles his best smile at the clerk. "I remember his P.O. box number, so I assume that would help you find his address, right? It is Post Office Box 421."

"The clerks turns and walks a few feet to a set of file cabinets. Each cabinet has thirty small drawers and each drawer face is a little bigger than the size of an index card. She opens one and begins thumbing through it, finally pulling a card out and sets it at 90 degrees to the others, then removes the one in front of it.

She walks back to the desk and looks at him with a small frown on her face. "You did say this was a friend of yours, right?"

"Yes. Antoine Beechen."

"Antoine Beechen is not listed as the owner of this box number."

"No? Must be. I send him stuff here all the time," Don says.

"This box is owned by My Mail Address, Inc."

"Hmmm. Well, maybe he works there. Where are they located? Here in town?"

"Matter of fact, just a few blocks from here, 102 College Street, opposite City Hall Park I think that would be."

"Ahhh, you've been a sweetheart, thank you. It's going to be good to see Antoine…and I can surprise him at work."

Don walks away wondering if Antoine works at My Mail Address, Inc., or maybe it is simply a mail forwarding company.

Back in the car, Don directs Tom to College Street and My Mail Address, Inc. The company is located in an old brick two story building with only two companies listed on the signage on the lawn. He enters the building and sees the office door of My Mail Address, Inc., to the right. He opens the door to see some desks piled with mail, and standing behind each desk, someone sorts the mail into bins. One of them stops sorting mail and walks over to Don.

"Yeah. Looking for someone?"

"Yes I am," Don says. "Antoine Beechen. Is he here?"

"Nobody by that name works here."

"You sure?"

"Yeah. I've worked here for more than ten years, and ain't nobody named Antoine ever worked here. I would remember that name."

"I understand he has his mail sent here, so I assumed he worked here."

"Well, you assumed wrong, I guess."

"Well, why would he have his mail sent here then?"

"I guess it's because that's what we do around here. Receive people's mail and then forward it to them."

"Could you give me his forwarding address then. I am a friend of his and lost his home address. I am trying to find him."

"Can't do it. Company policy. That's why we exist, so people can have private mail addresses. What good would we be, if we just gave out that information to anyone that asked?"

Don sighs. "Guess you're right. Thanks"

"Why not just write him and ask him for his address. Seems simple to me." He turns and walks back to the desk and resumes sorting mail.

Don looks at the floor. A wasted trip; now what?

He turns and walks back outside to the car.

"So, did we get an address?"

"No," Don replies. "Let's go back to Dexter and figure out what we want to do next. This guy Antoine is a shifty sort. We're going to have to be better than this if we want to find him."

"I'm starving. We didn't eat lunch. Let's stop someplace on the way back, OK?"

17

Sitting in their motel room, Don lays out all the information they gathered during their trip. There is a lot of information, but none of it points to finding Antoine.

- Lives in Harmony Corners on Little Moose reservoir
- His neighbors don't know him well
- He only shows up once or twice a year
- Was in minor trouble with the law but never arrested
- Not well known in town
- Doesn't get mail in local post office
- Uses post office box in Burlington, VT, for mail
- That box owned by mail drop company
- Credit card bills go there, maybe all mail goes there
- Credit card bill paid by Emerson Prescott

Above this list is the list of everything else they know about Antoine.

- Antoine Beechen
- Born Manchester, VT, within 15 minutes of Prescott
- Delivered by the same doctor in the same hospital
- He and Emerson have Amended birth certificates
- Antoine uses Emerson's boat whenever he wants to
- Well known in Canada by some folks on the lake
- Never seen with Emerson
- Lived in Maine and was lobsterman as a teenager
- No one has ever seen Antoine in Dexter

"Tom, look at this list. What's missing from it? What ties this in with Emerson other than that they know each other? What are we missing?"

"One thing I see is that we have shifted our focus from Emerson to Antoine. Maybe it is time to refocus on Emerson." Tom's police skills are kicking in. "Is Antoine important to whatever has your interest about Emerson? I'm not sure where we need to be going right now. I mean, all this stuff about Antoine is really interesting, but what is it adding to your thoughts about Emerson?

Don thinks for a minute. "I don't know. I was about to wrap it up and go home today once I got a little background on Antoine, but now…all this…something is going on between Emerson and Antoine, and I want to know what it is.

"We can't leave yet. We're missing a piece of the puzzle, and I think it has to do with when Antoine came back into Emerson's life. Hear me out on this.

"Emerson has an accident in 1986 that causes him to lose most of his memory, but within four years, by all accounts, he seems to have regained most of it. Then, BAM, he has another knock on the head, and this time doesn't even go to the doctors to be checked out.

"After that, everyone we've met seems to agree that he lost his memory again. Then, when he starts to remember things, he only remembers things after the second accident. Nothing from before.

"As his memory returns, he begins to shed all his old friends, people that have always known him. Plus, he sometimes mentions things he did as a young man that he couldn't have possibly done, and when someone catches him on that, he begins to turn them away, ending their long-term friendship.

"Meanwhile, while he is ridding himself of old friends, he somehow meets up with Antoine Beechen, someone that he probably never met, with whom he shares a birthday only minutes apart.

"He never lets anyone, including his son, use his boat, but gives free reign use to Antoine, who is almost a stranger.

"He pays Antoine's credit card bills, and yet no one has ever seen the two of them together, knows of Antoine's existence, or ever even seen Antoine.

"That's where we are now, and the thing is…I don't understand where that is."

"Well, when you put it like that, how could we leave," Tom laughs. "OK. Here's what we need to do. For one thing, we have to find out why those birth certificates were amended. I might understand them both being amended, but two in a row at the same hospital, and within 20 minutes of each other, and the same doctor delivering both babies? What are the odds?

"The second thing is we need to meet Emerson and somehow let him know we know about Antoine, and then see what his reaction is. Maybe he will tell us everything we want to know, and that will be that.

"Third thing – we have to find out how Antoine and Emerson met. If it was by chance, I would say that was a really big chance meeting."

Don looks at his brother. "I guess that's why you became the cop and I became a carpenter. I think you just boiled it all down. Let's relax tonight, watch a little TV, and then get started on all this tomorrow morning."

The next morning, after breakfast with Billy at the Chicken and Cow restaurant, Don and Tom return to their room. Don decides to make some phone calls to learn more about why New Hampshire might issue an amended birth certificate, and Tom begins to construct a time line chart of the information they have gathered over the last week.

As Tom sits writing information on little yellow and green stickie notes and then sticking them on one section of the motel wall, Don opens his laptop and performs a search on New Hampshire Amended Birth Certificates.

One of the sites returned in the search is the New Hampshire Bureau of Records which states that birth certificates can be amended to correct an error or add omitted information, such as a misspelled name, or no name entered on the hospital record. Having a father's name added subsequent to the hospital record being submitted can also be reflected on the amended birth certificate.

The other sites from the search return similar information. Don decides to search for New Hampshire hospital birth record corrections which return only two hits: one from the New Hampshire Department of Health and the other from the Hospital Association of New Hampshire.

Both places stress that medical records are protected by the Health Insurance Portability and Accountability Act (HIPAA) which states that records can only be released with authorization by the owner or guardian of the person in question. Don knows this and is always amazed at the documentation supplied to him by the website he uses for information. When he obtains information that could jeopardize anyone he conducts searches on, he uses care not to disclose that information to anyone else.

Having not found any new definitive information regarding amended birth certificates or hospital birth records, he decides to call Manchester Hospital directly to ask about why they might have a corrected birth record document.

He finds the phone number on the internet and places the call. "Good morning, Manchester General Hospital, how may I help you," a female voice asks.

"Hi. I am not sure. Maybe you can figure out who I need to speak with; maybe your records section."

"If you tell me what it is you would like to do, I can direct you to the correct area."

"Well, my dad's hospital birth record had something crossed out and corrected, and I was wondering if there was a way to find out what that was."

"Is your father still alive?"

"No, he died a few years ago. He didn't know why there was a correction on the birth record either."

"OK. I think I will refer you to the records department. They may be able to assist you. Please hold…"

The is a short pause as music plays in the background.

"Hello – Records Department."

"Yes, hello. I was wondering if there is a way I can find out why some information was changed at your hospital on my father's original birth record?"

"Sir, your father would have to make that request."

"My dad died a while back. I am simply trying to find out what might have been changed on his birth record and why."

"Sir, we are prevented by HIPAA from releasing that type of information to anyone other than the owner of that information or their legal guardian or executor, in which case they would need to file a formal request to us with proof of who they are. We would then search the records, and if we found anything, we would provide the records to the requestor."

"I see," Don says. He thinks a minute, then asks "Could you at least tell me if that is a common occurrence to change a birth record after it is issued?"

"No, sir, it is not now a common occurrence."

"I heard you say, 'not now'. Was it once allowable."

"From what I understand, the policy regarding not changing an existing birth record has been in effect since right after World War Two. During the war, many women had children that were born while the father was overseas and women sometimes waited to see if they returned before assigning a father's name to the record.

"Also, many times the hospitals were greatly understaffed since so many people were called off to serve in the military, and that of course included doctors and nurses, as well as support staff. Every once in a while, there might only be one doctor available to deliver babies and if more than one woman came in to deliver, the poor doctor might have to rush from one delivery to the next. It wasn't uncommon, so I've been told, to have three deliveries going on at the same time, especially here at the main hospital.

"My mom was a nurse here during the war and told me that she would fill out the birth records from scribbled notes the doctor would provide. Not very legal by today's standards, but that was then and some things just happened because that was the only way they could work then.

"She said that many records would be hand changed later that day or even the next day before the information was sent to the state for issuance of a state birth certificate.

"Now, what I have told you is in no way official, so please do not use it or quote me on this, as I will deny telling you any of it."

"Understood. So, I guess even if I told you precisely what I was looking for, you would not be able to assist me, correct?"

"Not without a formal request being made. Would you like me to send you the form, or you could download it from the internet on our Request Forms section."

"I'll download it, and thank you, you have been very helpful." Don disconnected the call.

"Well, that didn't get me anywhere. I have to be a relative or something to have any information released to me." Don looks at his brother, then at the wall, which is now plastered with little squares of yellow and green paper.

"I need some string or colored yarn to connect the data," Tom says. " We need to make a run to the local crafts store, or maybe a drug store.

"What did you find out about the birth records?"

Don repeats the story the woman in the Records Department told him, then adds, "So it seems the corrections were just that. Probably caused by people being in a rush, especially since the two births occurred so close together. Some information was just incorrectly entered, and then at a later time, corrected.

"Let's move on to the next thing - talking to Emerson, I guess we first need to talk with Junior and have him get us up to the house to talk to the old man."

"Let's go ahead and get the stuff you need for your little project there, and then stop by the plant to see Junior."

After Tom picks up his colored string they drive over to the plant and go straight to Junior's office.

"Hi there, Millie," Don says to the secretary/office manager/overall assistant. "Is Junior in? I wanted to ask him a couple of things."

"Yes he is, but please let me check with him first, ok?"

"Sure, and thank you." Don and Tom wait at Millie's desk for her return.

"Go ahead in. He's only got about five minutes before his next meeting, so please be as brief as possible."

"We will be. Thanks again."

Junior is already standing when they enter his office.

"Hello again, Don and Tom, right," Junior says, extending his hand out to them.

They each shake his hand as Don thanks him for seeing them.

"Millie said you have a couple of questions you want to ask me," Junior sits back in his chair and indicates they should each take a seat.

"This won't take long," Don says. "After everything you've told us about your dad, he sounds like a really interesting guy, and I thought if it was possible, could we meet him? It would be an honor to talk with him and get his perspective on Dexter and this company, even though I understand it would be limited in scope due to the accidents."

Junior thinks for a minute, then says, "Sure. Why not? It would be good for him to meet some new folks. Let me just check with him and see if he has any objections, then I'll let you know.

"Where are you boys staying? Down at the motel, right?"

"Yes. You can contact us there."

"Is there anything else I can do for you today?"

Don stands and extends his hand to Junior. "No. That was it. We really appreciate this."

Junior stands and shakes each of their hands. "Just leave the Motel number for Millie, although she can probably find it easy enough. I'll call the desk and let them know when it would be OK for you to stop up to the house to see the old man."

Don nods and the two leave Junior's office. They stop and give Millie not only the Motel number, which she says she has, but each of their cell phone numbers as well, then say goodbye.

Outside Tom says to Don, "Wow. That was easier than I expected. You didn't even have to do any kind of a dance to get him to agree."

"Now, we just have to figure out the best way to go about getting him to talk about himself. Maybe we can use the medium of fishing to get him to mention Antoine. You're the fisherman between us," Don says. "You'll be up for that when we get to talk with him."

"Now, I'm going to be useful. At last," Tom laughs.

Returning to the motel room, Tom continues writing things down on little post-it notes and then uses different colored string to connect the information from one note to another note; soon has the wall looking like a maniacal version of someone's "Cats in the Cradle."

Don and Tom spend a good deal of the afternoon trying to make sense of what they see. They look for patterns, they look for contradictions, they look for similarities. By 4 PM they are dizzy from all the things they have discovered and discussed. They decide to put everything aside for a while and just relax. They can come back to everything after dinner when they have to start putting together the questions they want to ask Emerson when they get to see him.

18

After dinner at the marina's restaurant, they return to the motel and stop at the desk to see if there is a message from Junior. There is. They should stop up to the house the next day around 3 PM, Emerson will meet with them then.

"OK. We've been chasing the car for almost a week now," Don says, "and now we seem to have caught it. Now, what?"

"Now, we create our scenario for his interview. Now it's my part of the game, I get to do what I do best.," Tom says.

"So what is our game plan? Where do we start? How do we edge into the conversation about Antoine? And what if he doesn't want to talk about it? What if, once he hears the name Antoine, he shuts down and tell us to get the hell out of his house and leave him alone."

"Well, if he does that, we will just regroup and come at it from a different direction. Let's not admit defeat before we even get there, though. I think we can get this done You'll just need to follow my lead tomorrow."

Don picks up the list of information he created earlier in the day and looks at the factoids he placed there. "We should probably add more points about his life that we already know, things we can ask him, to make him feel comfortable with us, and to let him know we are interested in him."

"Exactly, little brother. Now you're getting the idea. Let's create some cards with information about him and follow up questions we can ask. I think we can also have him comment on the success of Junior, and how well the company is doing. We should also mention how much the town admires the family and the company. We can mention his accidents and how terrible it must have been to lose his wife in that first accident.

"We'll move quickly off that subject, though since we know he doesn't have a memory of that and I don't want to stress him on things he doesn't remember.

"We can question him a little about how it felt after the second accident and how hard it must have been to come back from that.

"Then, I think, we should move on to whether he misses being involved with the company, and how does he influence the business now. At that point, we can jump into what his leisure activities are now. Hopefully, he will bring up the boat, but if he doesn't, we can. We can mention that we saw this beautiful boat in the marina and the dock boy said it belonged to his family. He should probably admit it is his because I'm sure he's proud of that boat.

"Once we establish that he likes to fish and has that nice boat, I'll tell a few fishing stories, and try to get him to tell me a few. I'll casually bring up some fishing stories I've had with friends, and how much fun it is to fish with friends, then mention that he must have a fishing partner that he enjoys going out with on the boat.

"If he doesn't mention Antoine, I'll say we were up in Canada the other day and stopped at a few of the marinas to look at the boats – I'll go into some long story about how I have an interest in boats – and say we met some people that know a guy named Antoine who fishes from a big boat that they thought comes from down this way.

"That should kick off a conversation about Antoine. From there I'll begin to ease him into discussing Antoine more candidly. At that point, you'll jump in with your questions. If he starts to get skittish, I'll come back into the conversation and regain control.

"If he gets too flighty, we'll ease out of the Antoine conversation altogether, and get him back into his comfort zone. Once he's secure again, we can thank him for his time, ask if we can come back to see him again, and try to exit gracefully."

"Had it all thought out already, didn't you," Don asks.

"It's what I did for more than fifteen years. This is the same thing, only I'm not trying to make a murderer or a thief confess, just trying to get some old guy with a boat and an invisible friend to tell us more than he seems to tell anyone else for the last 20 years or so.

"Now – write down everything I just said on some of those index cards you have, so we can review the game plan and adjust things that need adjusting. Then, let's get all the notes in order, add specific questions we want to ask and get a good night's rest before we see Emerson tomorrow."

It seems Saturday mornings at the Chicken and Cow there is a different waitress, and there was no Billy Shavers either. Since Billy works the night shift, his week starts on Sunday night until Thursday night, so he won't be there for breakfast today.

Don knows that Billy would love to know they are going to talk with Emerson this afternoon, but Billy will just have to wait until Monday morning to hear about the meeting. Don wonders if they should see if Gertrude is in her office and tell her they are going to meet with Emerson that afternoon, but decides against it.

After breakfast, Don and Tom walk over to the marina to take another look at the boat. As they walk down the dock they see the dock boy hosing down Emerson's boat. The kid sees them and stops working as they approach.

"I see he finally told you to clean up the boat, huh?" Tom says to him.

"Yeah. I guess he wants to take it out this week and told me to scrub it all down nice and clean. It's gonna take me almost all day today and a little bit of tomorrow to get it done since it hasn't been cleaned in a while. The fish scales are baked onto this deck in some places. And he must have fried fish inside cause it stinks in there."

Tom sees that all the operable portholes and hatches are open, and a fan is running inside the cabin.

"You might try opening some boxes of baking soda to absorb some of the odors inside," Tom suggests.

"Way ahead of you. I have ten boxes of the stuff set around the cabin. That'll take a couple of days to work, though, so I also have some candles burning. Hope I don't catch the boat on fire," he laughs.

"Just keep the engine compartment well ventilated and you should have no problem," Tom says.

"What can I do for you fellas today? More questions?"

"No, but I would love to see what the inside of this thing looks like. It is such a pretty boat. Mind if I come aboard." Tom asks.

The kid looks around, and not seeing anyone else looking his way motions for them to climb aboard.

"I know the old man wouldn't like it, so don't say anything to anyone, OK?"

"You got our word," Tom says as he pulls a twenty out of his pocket, folds it, and hands it to the kid.

"Gee! Thanks mister.," the kid says.

"Let's just keep this our little secret, ok?"

The kid nods, as he offers a hand to Tom as he climbs over the transom. The kid does the same for Don.

"Watch where I just mopped; it might be slippery," the kid says to Tom. "And wipe your feet on the mat before you start walking around inside. No sense in making more of a mess in there than there already is."

Both Tom and Don nod in reply.

Once inside they see a full galley to port and a dining area to starboard. A doorway starboard leads aft to a stairway to the engine compartment and the head. Forward on the portside is a stairway up to the bridge, and in the center of the cabin two steps lead down to an expansive open living area with a full-screen TV, a couch, and a couple of lounge chairs. At the forward bulkhead, a short passageway leads past one door off to starboard that houses a small guest cabin for two, and a door leading forward into a full sized bedroom.

"You could easily live in this thing," Don says to Tom.

"Easily, but not cheaply. Look at all the wood on this thing. I think it must cost even more than I thought it did. Grain processing must be very, very profitable."

They climb up the steps to the bridge where Tom is even more impressed. The boat has everything. Radar, a sonar scope, a million dials for the engine, electrical gauges, and other things even Tom doesn't recognize. This boat even has a solar panel, Tom notices. You could stay on this boat anchored somewhere for weeks with no need for shore power. This is more boat than could ever be needed for a lake this size. Maybe Champlain or one of the Great Lakes, but this lake?

"The man knows boats, that's for sure. This thing is more

suited for the ocean than for this lake and it must have cost a bloody fortune to have it shipped here and then moved to the lake, even though the rail line is less than a half mile from here."

They look around the boat for a while, hoping to see if there is anything that might give them a clue about Antoine, but find nothing. If the man uses this boat, Don thinks, he doesn't keep anything personal on it. There are clothes in the closets, but it appears they were all the same size. Same with the shoes and sneakers on the shelves.

As they leave the boat, they thank the kid again, and he nods.

"That's some boat. Why would anyone buy a boat like that for this lake?" Tom says to Don, as he looks back at the boat again. "It sure stands out, doesn't it. It's at least six feet bigger than Junior's boat but looks even bigger. It must draw four or five feet below the water line. It is definitely seaworthy, that's for sure."

Finding a bench at the top of the dock ramp they sit for a while looking out over the lake and talk about the boat. Neither can figure out why anyone would spend more than a quarter of a million dollars for a boat like Emerson's, only to fish on this lake. It made no sense.

"Let's take a ride past Emerson's place and see what else is nearby. It's a nice day and we have until this afternoon before we have to see him." Don get's up off the bench and begins walking to the car. Tom follows, looking back at the boat every few steps. That boat deserves to be on the ocean, he whispers to himself.

They drive south past the cement plant and Ben's house, and further south past Emerson's house. You cannot see Emerson's place from the road. Only a small sign that reads *Prescott* on a mailbox indicates that the well-maintained asphalt driveway leads to his house.

They drive for another ten miles or so and come upon a small but beautiful lake, completely surrounded by mountains. A winding road leads around the lake which has a beach for swimming at one end, and a small anchorage for about twenty boats, at the other. The lake is only about five miles long and less than a mile wide, but in some ways, it is a more beautiful than the lake at Dexter, and much less used. It is mid-day Saturday, well into the 80s, and still, the beach is less than half full and there are only one or two sailboats on the water.

"I like this lake better than the one at Dexter," Tom says as he pulls over to the side of the road to park near the marina. "You could definitely get away from everything living here."

"According to the map," Don says, "Half the lake is on State Park property, so there must not be a lot of development allowed on the lake. From what we can see from the road, most of the houses are really little more than one or two room cabins, and none look winterized. But, yeah, it sure is pretty.

"So, Tom, have you got everything you want to ask Emerson in that head of yours?"

"Yeah. A piece of cake. I'll have him eating out of my hand in a half hour," Tom laughs. "I wonder what the man is like, though. Do you think he will welcome us and be willing to talk, or do you think he is only doing this to please his son?"

"Maybe a little of both. I know we have to really flatter him and his family big time before we go after any information on Antoine. So, butter him up as much as possible before you start hitting him with questions about Antoine. I bet he'll love to talk about that boat. I know I would if I owned."

"Me, too," Tom says. He looks at his watch. "It is almost 2:30; we should probably start back. We sure don't want to be late and have him all kinds of mad at us for that."

Don agrees. Tom turns the car around and heads back toward Dexter and Emerson's house. I hope we get some info on Antoine this afternoon, Don says to himself.

They arrive at Emerson's driveway at 2:55 and turn onto the asphalt paved drive leading up to his house, which is set about 1000 feet off the highway. The driveway is lined every few hundred feet with oak and maple trees, which Tom remarks must be absolutely beautiful in the autumn.

They arrive in front of the house, and stop in the circular driveway, pulling to one side to allow any other cars that might arrive room to pass them.

The house is beautiful. Like most farm houses in Vermont, it is painted white and has a large porch that runs the width of the house and around one side. Seven or eight white ladder back rocking chairs line the porch looking like soldiers at attention, waiting for orders.

A gray set of stairs leads up to the porch. A large oak double door with stain glass in their upper half, welcomes visitors. A large, nearly one-hundred-year-old Oak tree towers over the driveway in front of the house, providing shade for the entrance way.

Tom and Don climb the stairs and ring the bell. The sound of footsteps are heard coming toward the door and finally it opens, revealing a tall, thin but not frail white-haired man, wearing a light tan polo shirt, tan khaki Dockers, and leather moccasins.

He stands there silently waiting for Don or Tom to speak first.

"Mr. Emerson Prescott? I am Don Winston, and this is my brother, Tom. I believe your son said we could come up here and talk with you this afternoon." Don extends his hand.

"Yes, yes," Emerson answers as he takes Don's hand. "Please, Please, come in." He backs away from the door slightly to give Don and Tom room to get by him. Once inside, Emerson closes the door.

Don looks around. The house is immaculate. It is airy and filled with natural light. A 25 foot long East Indian print runner runs down the hallway and a beautiful chestnut stairway rises to the left of the hall. To the right is what once was called a parlor, and to the left is a living room. Don can see the kitchen at the end of the hallway and assumes the dining room is to the left under the stairs.

"Please come in," Emerson says as he waves his hand toward the parlor on the right. As they walk into the room Emerson asks them if they would like something to drink; he suggests some ice tea he just made.

"Yes. That would be wonderful," Don replies.

"Please, have a seat. I'll be right back." Emerson leaves to get the tea.

Tom smirks at Don and mouths silently, *nice*. Don nods in agreement.

The room has an oak mantle and fireplace face, wood crown molding with wood baseboards, and a beautiful Persian rug covering oak floors. If this was a farmer's house at one time, it must have been one hell of a rich farmer.

Emerson returns with the drinks and motions for Don and Tom to sit down on the couch in front of the window at the front of the house. Once they are seated he hands them each an ice tea.

"So, gentlemen, Junior told me he spoke with you at the plant and that you were interested in the company and in me." Emerson chuckles. "He knows way more about that plant now than I do, and god knows I am not all that interesting these days.

"I assume you are aware that I had a couple of accidents years ago and lost most of my memory from before then. That limits my knowledge of the company, and sad to say, most of my own life and certainly most of everything I may have ever known about this town. Most of what I remember these days from before the accidents are things people have told me, of the town and the company, and even of myself. From what I have heard, I guess I was a pretty likable guy once." Emerson laughs as he tells Don and Tom this information.

"I'll be happy to talk with you fellows, though, so go ahead and ask me anything you'd like to know, I'll do the best I can to answer you. Junior said you are history buffs, and that you not only like to learn about the towns you visit but the people as well. I'd say that's as good a way to get to know a town as any, I guess. After all, a town really is her people, right?"

"You're absolutely right, Emerson…may I call you Emerson?"

"Certainly. That Mr. Prescott stuff is for formal occasions, and this sure doesn't feel like one of them."

Don starts the conversation by asking about the farm , how many acres, do they grow things anymore, is it profitable? Really small talk to get things going.

Don mentions Benjamin and how Emerson had bought land from him. Emerson's face turns a little sour at the mention of Ben, and Don only asks the one question and leaves that subject alone.

Tom mentions Emerson's boat and for the next twenty minutes or so he and Emerson talk about boats. Tom tells Emerson that he looked at Emerson's boat and admired his taste, which causes Emerson to tell Tom all about how and why he bought that particular boat.

Well into the conversation about the boat, Tom mentions how he has a really close friend of his that he loves going out fishing with and asks if Emerson has someone like that in his life, maybe Junior, who he likes to fish with him?

"No – Junior has his own boat which he uses more for pleasure, and he and I don't seem to be fishing partners anymore. We were once, from what he tells me, but not since my accidents.

"I go out fishing alone mostly, these days."

"I heard that you do go out with one person quite a lot. I think his name was Antoine?"

"Where'd you hear that?"

"Oh – Don and I took a little trip up to the other end of the lake and had a few drinks and dinner at one of the bars up there. We were talking with one of the bartenders about some of the boats we saw at the marina, and we asked him who had the biggest boat on the lake. He mentioned a few names and yours was one of them. He said you brought your boat up to that end of the lake quite often for fishing, and that almost all the time, Antoine was with you."

Don thought he saw a little twitch in Emerson's face at the

mention of Antoine, and Emerson also took a couple of extra seconds with his reply to Tom's questions, something that up to that point Emerson had not done when answering them.

"Well, yes. Antione and I do fish quite a lot together, come to think of it. I even let him use my boat without me."

"Wow." Tom laughs. " He must be some friend for you to lend him that beautiful boat of yours. I wish I was your friend.

"You must know him for a long time to trust him with that boat."

"Well, I do now. We must know each other close to twenty years now, I guess. Met him fishing one day and we just hit it off."

"Does he live around here," Tom was beginning the interrogation.

"No. He lives over in New Hampshire. Only see him during the summer. I think he travels a lot during the winter."

Tom steers the conversation off Antoine for a while and begins to talk about fishing, and friends, and good times. He and Emerson begin to swap fish stories and Tom eases into describing things he did on boats as a kid.

"Yeah, we sailed across the whole Great South Bay from Long Island to Groton Connecticut, in a 20-foot rowboat with a 25 horsepower motor and two six gallon gas cans. We just made it across – only had a half gallon of gas left. We didn't know we shouldn't have done that. When you are a kid you do those things."

"Yeah, kids are crazy that way."

"When I was a teenager I wanted to run away up to New England and work on one of those lobster boats off the coast," Tom says. "That always seemed like really exciting work. Go out in the early morning fog, lift those pots all day, and come back at night and sit around and get drunk with the other lobstermen. I always heard it was hard work but you made a lot of money doing it."

"It's hard work alright. I did that for a couple of years when I was a kid. The money is good but the work is rough and dangerous. And you have to go out in freezing cold weather and in weather that is so hot you can hardly wear your clothes, and when it is foggy you never knew what might run into you." Emerson was smiling as he told his story.

Both Tom and Don had to keep from smiling as Emerson repeated this story that Pete had said he could never have done. Tom wanted to keep him talking.

"So where was that when you did your lobstering?"

"It was up in Maine, in Damariscotta. Spent a couple of summers there senior year of high school…" Just then, he realizes what he has been telling them. "Aww, but you don't want to hear about that. Hell, I am not even sure if that is something I did then or something I think I did. My memory gets all joggled up sometimes. That damned amnesia really runs a trick on me at times."

"Well," Tom says, "it sure sounds like you know what you're talking about. You could sure fool me." Tom gives a soft laugh.

"You get to be this age and you start to believe everything you say must be true…especially when no one is around to remind you that it can't be." Emerson thinks he better stop talking so freely to Don and Tom.

"Listen, boys, it's been fun, but I am getting a little tired so we better cut this short for now." Emerson stands and extends his hand toward Tom. "I hope you had fun and found me as interesting as you had hoped. Heaven knows, I don't think I am that interesting."

Tom and Don stand as Tom shakes Emerson's hand. "We want to thank you so much, and could we stop by again sometime and talk with you some more? I know I found you very interesting and informative."

"I guess. Just check in with Junior to make sure I am up to it, OK?"

Don takes Emerson's hand and shakes it. "We will. And again, thank you so much for your time." Don smiles at Emerson and hopes they haven't pushed their luck with him. They turn and leave the room they have been in for more than an hour. When they reach the front door, they turn one more time and thank Emerson for his time, telling him they hope to see him again soon.

As they drive around the driveway, they pass a gravel drive that goes off behind and to the left of Emerson's house. At the end of the gravel drive they see an old barn, and behind that, what appears to be a more modern home. "Must be Junior's place," Tom says. "He lives up here, too."

As they leave the Emerson farm, Tom says "Did you catch that about lobstering in Maine. Exactly what Pete said Emerson told him. And just like Emerson did with Pete, Emerson tried to cover it up."

"Yeah – I caught that, and I caught that he said he was there during his last couple of years in high school. I guess we're going to take a trip to Damariscotta, Maine. We'll drive up there tomorrow and stay overnight. I am about due for some lobster anyway."

20

The next day they check out of the motel, telling the owners they will probably be back in a couple of days. The owner tells them he expects they'll have room but to call when they know they'll be returning, just to make sure.

They take the route through Harmony Corners, New Hampshire, home to the mysterious Antoine, and Lewiston, Maine, then on through to Wiscasset and into Damariscotta.

It is almost 3 PM when they stop for the night at the Lobsterman's Inn, a little ten unit motel on the outskirts of town. After settling in their room, they take a short ride around town, looking for the high school that Emerson said he attended for one or two years.

"What are the chances that Emerson really did go to this high school," Tom asks Don.

"Little to none, but we have to check it out."

"I guess leaving any stone untouched would be less than a good investigation." Tom slows the car and points, "Look. That looks like a high school. At least it has a track and a ball field."

Tom turns into the parking lot of a two-story red brick building. Over the front door embedded in the façade are the words Damariscotta High School, and under that, 1934.

"OK. We found the school," Tom says. "Tomorrow when it opens I guess we just walk in and ask if Emerson Prescott ever went to school here, and that will be that, right?"

Don laughs at him. "It should be so easy.

"I think we can walk in and ask if they have yearbooks for the years we think Emerson could have gone to school here. We'll tell them we're doing research on one of there alumnus and want some background on what went on at the school while they were here. That will get us to the books, I'm sure."

"That doesn't sound too hard. We'll do that first thing

tomorrow morning, as soon as they're open," Tom says.

"Good. Now that that's settled, let's go get some lobster. Let's drive further on down the river until we hit the ocean, and eat there."

Twenty minutes later they sit at Capt. Jack's Lobster Pound, plastic bibs tied around their necks, two large baskets of opened clams in front of them, waiting for their order of lobsters and corn to be delivered to their table. A cool ocean breeze blows across the deck of the lobster pound as they sit in the late afternoon sun enjoying the view of the Atlantic Ocean and the Pemaquid Point Lighthouse at the tip of land a mile away.

The next morning, after they eat their breakfast of blueberry pancakes and sausage at Misty's Riverside Restaurant, they drive over to the high school. High school is not in session so there is no problem parking. They enter the school doors, and Tom remarks they look smaller than he remembered them being when he went to high school.

Once inside, they find the Administration office where two women sit having their morning coffee while they catch up on the weekend. Don walks over to the chest high counter just inside the office and says good morning to the two women, who both smile at him.

"What can we do for you today," asks one of the women as she stands and walks towards Don.

"I'm doing a little background research on someone that went to your school about 50 years ago. My hope is that you might have some yearbooks from the year he graduated that we could look at, just to get a sense of what life was like for him then."

"Fifty years ago, huh? Gee. That's even before my time. He must be some pretty important person. You'd think I'd know if someone important came out of this school.

"What did you say his name was?"

"Well, I didn't but his name is Emerson Prescott. Ring a bell?"

"Can't say that it does. What year did he go here?"

"I'm not sure. One of these three years: 1961, 1962, or 1963."

"I graduated from here in 1972 and never heard that name, Then again that would have been almost tens years before I got here, so that doesn't really surprise me.

"Wait here a second." She walks back to her desk and picks up a phone. "Angie... this is Barbara down in Admin, hey you're in today, good...yes, hello to you too...yes, it is a beautiful day. Listen, I have two fellows here that would like to look at some of our yearbooks for a story they're doing about the school... yeah, think of that, about us, ain't that something? Yeah... the years? I think it was 1961, 1962, and 1963...can you get to them?... You can?... Great. Ok, then, I'll send them up to you. They're on their way. Thanks, Angie."

"Well, you're in luck. The librarian is in today for half a day. During the summer she pretty much comes in when she has to, but summer school is over now so there is little need for her to be here, but the gods must have known you were coming, cause she just happens to be here today.

"Now, you go out this door, turn right, take the stairs to your left to the second floor, and then turn right; it's the first door on your right after that. Do I need to write it down for you?"

"No – I think I have it. And I want to thank you so much for your help. I'll stop in to let you know when we leave. Thanks again." Don and Tom leave the admin office and follow the instructions up to the library.

They enter the library and see an attractive woman in shorts and a tee shirt looking through a closet behind the main desk. She turns as she hears them enter.

"Hi. I'm looking for those books for you. We have yearbooks up here that go back almost 80 years. They keep promising to shoot them for digital records, but you know how that is. That takes time and money, and most people don't think it's important enough to save these archived records so....ah, here they are." She pulls out three very old looking books and carries them to her desk.

"All I ask is that you be very careful when turning the pages and please, do not fold any of them. I'm sure if you fold a page it will simply crack, and we wouldn't want that, would we?"

Don laughs at the teacher phrasing the librarian uses...the collective *WE*. "No...we wouldn't want that," he smiles at her. "Can we use that tall counter over there?"

"Sure. Let me put these over there for you." She carries them over to the counter as Don and Tom follow her. "One more reminder. Please be careful. These are the only copies we have."

"We will be very careful. Thank you."

She walks back to her desk and continues doing what she was doing before Don and Tom interrupted her.

"You take '61, and I'll take '62," Don says to Tom.

They each reach for the appropriate yearbook and begin looking through it. The first pages have the normal things: the history of the school, a list of former principals by year, pictures of the school exterior and interior throughout the years. The next few pages are devoted to present day administrators and teachers. Then a few pages of events that occurred during the last school year. Finally, the pictures of that year's graduating class begins.

Most of the boys have crew cuts and the girls have either page boy haircuts or beehive hairdos. All the boys wear ties and a cardigan, a sports coat or if they are on an athletic team, a sweater with the letter D sewn onto it. Everyone faces to their left for their portrait, and the background is a drape with the school colors.

Tom begins to laugh as he pages through the pictures.

"Look at these kids, Don. Every single one of them has acne. You forget how hard it was back then to get rid of that stuff. Kids today have so many choices of medications to use to keep their skin clear."

"You don't have to remind me, Tom. I thought that stuff would never clear up." Don shakes his head from side to side, remembering those days in high school. Those weren't the best of times for him, and he was glad when he graduated and went on to college.

After another twenty minutes, Tom finishes leafing through his book. "Nothing there about Prescott. I'll grab the last book here while you finish looking at yours." Tom pushes 1961 away and opens up 1963.

He passes quickly through the school's history pages, and through the admin, teacher, and events sections. Tired of looking at all the pictures of acne scarred kids he has looked at in the first book, he decides to go straight to the section of the student body where the last names begin with the letter P.

- Paulson, Adam

- Pawal, Mary Lou

- Peterson, Jeremy

- Pentangelo, Elizabeth

- Pinto, Grace

- Porter, Robert

- Stephenson, Ronald

Tom sighs. "No, Prescott here."

Don, having finished looking at his book, sees that Tom has is only looking at the P section of the book. "Did you check every page? They sometimes place the names of kids who were late to the photo shoot at the end. Might as well look there, too, just to make sure.

"Yeah, you're right." Tom keeps turning the last three pages. When he gets to the last page he stops and points to a picture on the page. "You're not going to believe this, Don. Look here."

Don looks down to where Tom points his finger. There is a picture of a boy with long sideburns, greased-backed hair, with a little squiggle of hair pulled down over the center of his forehead. He was one of the few students who had not smiled for his yearbook picture. Matter of fact, he looked to be scowling at the photographer. No tie, no jacket, no sweater. He looked as if he was even uncomfortable about having to wear the open collar shirt he had on.

Don whistles softly, although the librarian hears it and turns. "Find what you were looking for gentlemen?"

"Maybe," Don answers. The tip of Tom's finger is right underneath the name of the boy in the picture: Beechen, Antoine.

"Antoine Beechen went to this school? I thought he was from New Hampshire. What was he doing in high school, in Damariscotta, Maine?"

"Ok – now this is getting officially weird," Tom says. "We come here looking for Prescott, but no Prescott graduates from here the year he should have graduated. Instead, we find Beechen, who lives in New Hampshire and somehow ends up graduating high school in Maine."

"Maybe we need to look at 1964, too," Don says. "Maybe he's there." He walks back to the librarian's desk and asks her for the 1964 book. "I think we may have been a year off," he smiles at her.

"Sure. Just give me a minute." She walks over to the bookcase that holds the yearbooks and retrieves the 1964 book for Don. "Hope he's in here," she says as she hands him the book.

"Me, too," Don replies. Inside his head, he repeats that: me, too!

He places the book on the counter in front of Tom and goes straight to the P section of students. No Prescott. Next, he turns to the end of the student picture section. No Prescott there, either.

"He had to have graduated in one of these years. There is a listing of all graduating students following the picture section. Let's check there as well." Don looks first at the list in the 1964 book. No Prescott there. He grabs 1961 and turns to the end of the student picture section, reads through the names, and shakes his head. "No Prescott in either of these books. How about yours?"

Tom finds nothing the 1962 book and is just finishing reading the list in the 1963 book. Shaking his head Tom says, "Nothing here, either."

"This makes no sense to me," Don says. "This seems to be all backward from what we know about everything."

"Let's see if they have a copier, so we can make a copy of Beechen's picture. At least we can get an idea of what Beechen looks like, anyway."

Don carries the 1964 yearbook with the picture of Beechen back towards the librarian's desk, while Tom gathers up the other three books.

"Do you have a copier we might be able to use to copy a page out of this yearbook," Don asks, as Tom sets the other yearbooks down on her desk.

"Yes, I do." Don swings the book around to face her and points to the face on the page. "Could you make a copy of this students face, and could you do it in as high a resolution as possible. Also," Don reaches for his key fob upon which he has a small thumb drive attached. Detaching it, he hands it to the librarian. "Could you save it to file for me and put it on here, please? I would really appreciate it if you could do those two things for me."

"Sure," she says. "I'll make the file first and then print the hard copy for you from the file." She takes the thumb drive and places it into her computer on her desk, then points to the picture I the yearbook and says, "This student, right?"

Don nods affirmatively, and she takes the book over to the scanner, placing it under the scanner's cover. She sits down in front of her computer and presses a few keys. The scanner comes to life and Don can see the light bar track across the book. The librarian hits a few more keys and the light bars travels under the book more slowly this time as the scanner completes scanning the page.

The librarian presses a few more keys and the printer begins printing a copy of the file. She walks over to the printer and removes the print of the yearbooks page. She turns and places it in front of Don. "Is this good enough," she asks him.

"Perfect," he replies and hands it to Tom. "You even enlarged it for me. Thank you for that."

"Well, you can hardly see anything at the original size. It's only, what, one by one and a half inches in the book. You should see what the photos look like from my graduating class. All the boys had hair as long as the girls and you could hardly tell the difference between them."

She sat and finished saving the photo file to Don's thumb drive, then retrieved the drive from the computer, and stood to hand it to him. "I hope this was a productive morning for you," she said.

"I think it was. Interesting, too. You have been so helpful. Thank you so much"

"It was a change of pace for me, so it made this morning go a little faster. I am almost finished here for today. Time to go home and get ready to join my friends at the beach and have a gin and tonic. In a little over three weeks school will be back in session. The summer is not nearly long enough for us that work in a school."

"I guess, not. Thanks again." Don smiles at her as both he and Tom leave the library.

On the way out of the building, Don sticks his head in the admin office to let the workers know he is leaving and thanks them again for their assistance.

Neither Don nor Tom says anything to the other until they are sitting in the car, then Don says, "Why do we keep finding new pieces to a puzzle we think is almost complete?"

"We do keep getting deeper into a mystery that we didn't even know we had." Tom starts the car. "Where to now, bro?"

"I don't know, Tom." Don looks out the window of the car as Tom pulls out of the high school parking lot. "I just don't know."

Emerson Prescott drives down to the Dexter marina a little after noon on Sunday. When he called earlier in the day to find out if the boat has been cleaned, the dock kid told him his boat was ready. He decides then to get away from everything for a couple of days. He has been a little upset about the meeting with the two brothers, Don and Tom.

It isn't that they have been intrusive or rude, but he has let his guard down and talked more than he wants to about his life. Since the accident where he hurt his head on the fender of his car, he never engages in deep conversation with anyone from around town. People try to talk to him about things that he has no knowledge of, and if he gets too comfortable talking with them, he starts saying things he doesn't want them to know.

He parks his car in the marina parking lot and walks over to the dock boy sitting in his shack.

"What do I owe you for cleaning the boat?"

"Mr. Prescott," the kid jumps up off his chair. "I didn't see you pull into the parking lot. How are you?"

"Fine. Fine. How much do I owe you for cleaning the boat?"

"Well, sir, it took me a long time, ya know. It was pretty dirty and we never cleaned it after your last fishing trip. There was a lot of baked on fish scum and the interior smelled pretty bad, too.

"I took me about 13 hours to clean it all up, so, uh, give me a minute to add that up," The kids says as he reaches for a pad and pencil.

"That's 195 dollars. Let's call it 200." Emerson pulls a money clip out of his pocket and peels off two one hundred dollar bills. "Keep the change," Emerson says.

"Do you need a receipt, Mr. Prescott?"

"No. And, of course, you don't need to tell the owner of this place about it either. He gets enough of my money renting me this slip."

"OK, Mr. Prescott. Let me help you get under way."

As they walk down to Emerson's boat, the kid tells him he provisioned the boat with a bottle of scotch, some bottled water, a nice steak and some fresh vegetables. He charged it all to Emerson's accounts around town, just as he always does. And as soon as Emerson is on board, he'll run back up to the shack and get him some bait.

When they reach the boat, he helps Emerson over the transom and then rushes back up to the shack. He opens the bait cooler and removes one container of worms and another container of cut bait. He places both in a plastic bag and returns to the boat.

He hands Emerson the bait bag and proceeds to untie two of the four lines holding the boat to the dock. Emerson has warmed up the engine and nods to the kid to let go the other two lines. The kid removes the forward line from the cleat on the dock and tosses it onto the forward deck. He walks to the aft line and removes that from the cleat, coiling it up and handing it to Emerson who places it on a cleat on his boat.

He nods at the kid, then says, "If anyone comes looking for me, just tell them I'm fishing for a day or two, and you really don't know when I'll be back."

"Yes, sir, Mr. Prescott. You have our number here at the dock if you need anything. Good fishing."

Emerson eases the boat out of the slip and into the lake. Emerson never guns the boat until he is well out on the lake. The lake isn't that big anyway, and there is rarely a need to get to where he is going faster than at a leisurely pace.

He opens his shirt to let the sun hit his chest and puts on his favorite blue cap, and sunglasses. It has been a while since Emerson has been up to the other end of the lake and he looks forward to having Antoine aboard again. Antoine knows how to have fun. He always has, and he always will.

Emerson turns on the radio and sits down in the vinyl captain's chair on the bridge. Now, he can relax. Now, he can be just a fisherman going fishing, with no one asking questions, no one demanding anything from him. He wonders what he's going to do once he is too old to go out on the boat alone. Antoine may not come around anymore when that happens. He'll miss Antoine. But you can't have everything I guess, he says aloud. Sometimes you have to choose between yourself and your friends.

Hasn't it always been the way?

The trip is an easy one. No chop on the water, although there is a slight northerly breeze, just enough to keep the heat of the day pleasant.

About two hours later Emerson decides to drop anchor and do a little fishing. Once the anchor is set, he baits up his hook and lowers it into the water. He sets his rod in the holder and goes inside to pour himself a scotch and water. Back out on the deck, he sits in the chair at the aft end of the boat and looks at the shoreline less than a half a mile away.

Another hour or so he'll up anchor and pull into one of his favorite marinas. Antoine should be there by then. I'll pour a drink for him and we'll see what happens. He'll probably want to go ashore after dinner and leave Emerson behind on the boat as he always does, but that's fine with Emerson. The less these folks up here know about him, the happier he is.

Too bad he can't share Antoine's friendship with Junior. Junior would probably like Antoine. There's always a space between Emerson and Junior now. Junior wants his pre-accident dad back and that will just never happen. Those days are other people's memories now, not Emerson's. Emerson only has the present and the last fifteen or twenty years, anything further back in his life is an unknown to him.

He bets that Junior was a great kid, and he wishes that he had those memories, but he doesn't. Emerson has looked at countless numbers of pictures of the family before the second accident, and that family looked like it was always having fun.

Now, the only family he has is the one he has had since the second accident, and of course, the memories that accidently pop up every once in a while. The ones everyone that has known Emerson for a long time find preposterous and unbelievable. The ones he keeps to himself rather than cause strange looks and reactions when he mentions them.

For some reason, he thought he saw one of those looks from one of those two boys that visited him the other day. When they were talking about boating and his time on the lobster boat. He saw a little light go on inside one of them. It wasn't recognition of a shared experience, it was more of something clicking in his head. As if he knew more than he let on he knew.

He'd make sure that didn't happen again if he spoke with them again. There really are some memories that are better not shared, and many of the memories Antoine and Emerson share will never be told to anyone.

Emerson pulls into the Saint Bernard Yacht club around 5:30 PM. After tying up the boat for the night, he goes below and cooks the steak the kid bought him. He boils some rice and also makes a salad. Once everything is ready, he sits down at the table in the cabin and has dinner. He turns on his radio and listens to the rock station out of Sherbrooke, Quebec.

After dinner, he cleans up the kitchen and climbs up to the flying bridge to watch the sun go down on the western side of the lake. By 9 o'clock, the sun is down behind the mountain on the other side of the lake and Emerson goes below and turns on a light in his stateroom for the evening.

Around 10 PM, Antoine strolls into the bar at the Saint Bernard Yacht club and walks over to Frank, the bartender, who greets him with a surprised look on his face.

"Well, where have you been this summer, stranger? It's been quite a few weeks since I saw you up here." Franks extends his hand to Antoine, who reaches out to shake it. "Did you come up with your friend or are you here alone?"

"Emerson is already here," Antoine says. "He's tied up at the marina. I stopped down there before I came up here to the bar, and I think he may be asleep already because there is only a night light on in the cabin."

"You just can't get him off that boat can you?"

"He likes his privacy, that's for sure."

"Why does he come up here and then stay on board when he ties up?"

"I think he likes the quiet. Also, if he knows I am going to be in the area, he comes up to see me."

"You and he must be real good friends."

"We go way back, that's for sure."

"So what have you been up to this summer?"

"I've been doing a little traveling, mostly just driving around, nowhere special. Went up through Maine for a couple of weeks, and down to the Jersey shore for a week when we had that stretch of hot weather up here the beginning of July.

"Have you been busy this summer?"

Frank pours Antoine a single malt scotch and places it on the bar in front of Antoine.

"Nice to know I haven't been forgotten," Antoine says. "Thank you."

Frank and Antoine talk about the summer and how busy the marina has been this year. Frank mentions that the owner may be expanding the restaurant during the coming winter and may even add a few more berths for boats.

After an hour of catching up, Frank starts talking about how just about a week ago there was some guy asking about his friend.

"He seems to know a little about your friend on the boat, and was surprised to learn that you knew him."

"Really? What was his name," asks Antoine.

"He didn't give me his name, but he stayed overnight at the Country Suite Motel down the road. I bet if you called them, they might remember the guy's name."

"What did the guy look like?"

"Tall, maybe 5-11 or 6 feet tall. Dark hair, maybe, mid-forties. He wasn't from around here, that's for sure. He had a slight New York accent I think. He was a pleasant guy. Just saw him that one night. He didn't come back again."

"I can't think for the life of me who that might have been. I'll have to mention it to Emerson tomorrow morning."

"So, how long are you going to be up here this time, Antoine," Franks asks.

"Maybe just a day or so. Depends on how long Emerson wants to stay. We'll do some fishing and then when he's done fishing, he'll want to go home and I'll get on my way, too."

Antoine stays at the bar until just after midnight, then pays his bill in cash as he usually does, says goodnight to Frank and walks down to the boat.

He sits in the chair on the boat's deck thinking about what Frank has told him: someone is looking for information on Emerson, and Frank has given him information on Antoine. He knows Emerson doesn't know this fellow, and he certainly knows he doesn't. Who the hell is this guy and why is he asking questions about Emerson and him?

The next morning, Antoine walks up to the bar and leaves a message for Frank asking if the guy who has been looking for him and Emerson comes around again, can Frank please get a phone number, so Antoine can contact him. He also says he's leaving early today, but he might be back by the end of the week.

Around noon, Emerson decides to leave the marina. He starts the boat engines, unties his boat, and heads back to Dexter. He is a little concerned that someone is using his name as a friend, to try to get people to talk about him and Antoine. No one knows he stays at this marina, except for Junior, and the people at the marina.

There certainly are a lot of people interested in me this summer, Emerson thinks. First those two fellows in Dexter, and now some guy in Quebec. For someone that stays out of the limelight, I seem to have created a lot of interest. I wonder why?

The trip south back to Dexter is a quiet one. This was supposed to be a few quiet, relaxing days away from everything, but now he is wondering what's going on.

By four o'clock, the boat is back in Dexter and tied up at his slip. He leaves the boat and walks right by the deck boy who asks him if he should wash down the boat. Emerson doesn't reply. He's busy trying to figure out who's asking questions and why. Most of all, though, he wants it to stop.

Emerson does something he normally doesn't do, he walks over to the processing plant and into Junior's office.

"Dad? What are you doing here," Junior says when he see his dad. "This must be the first time you've been here this summer. What's up? Are you alright?"

"Yeah, yeah, I'm OK." Emerson sits down in the chair

opposite the desk. "I have a couple of questions to ask you."

"Sure. Fire away."

"How well do you know those two fellows you told me to talk with the other day?"

"I just met them last week. They came in to ask me about the plant, and you, and the town. Billy Shavers brought them in to meet me. Why?"

"They told me they wanted to talk with me to get a better idea of the town, and me and the family, and to see why the town likes us so much, etc., etc. What did they tell you?"

"Pretty much the same thing. They were very impressed by how you grew the company into what it is today. Then after they heard about your story, they said they wanted to meet you."

"They say anything about going up north to the lake and asking around about me?" Emerson stares at his son.

"Not a thing," Junior replies. "Did they do that?"

"I don't know, but someone was up there asking about me and my friends. It just seems odd that there would be more than those two asking about me at the same time, don't you think?"

"Well, so what if they were asking about you up there? Maybe it was just interest on their part. They seem like really nice guys. What could they…." Emerson cuts him off.

"You know, I hate it when people have questions about me," Emerson says in a loud voice. "I should have never agreed to talk with them, and I don't want you talking with them anymore either. Understand?

"Our business is our business; no one else's. God knows who else they been talking with around here. I don't want them in our business, do you understand, Junior?"

"Yeah, dad. I got it. Don't get upset."

"OK. Just so you know, no more interviews with those two."

"Ok, dad. No more interviews with them."

"I'm going home." Emerson stands, "If you want to stop by for a drink after work, I'd like that." He turns and walks out of

Junior's office, passing Millie without saying a word.

Emerson walks back to his car mumbling to himself about people asking too many damned questions. Even as he pulls into the circle in front of his house, he continues to mumble about that.

I'm going to find out what they want to know and why they want to know it. I can push back pretty hard if I want to, and they'll find that out if they push me too hard.

He slams the car door and just misses catching his pants leg in the door as the lock clicks closed.

Don and Tom pull into the motel at almost the same time that Emerson pulls into his driveway. They stop at the motel desk to register for a room and ask if there have been any calls for them?

The desk clerk says no, no one called or stopped by while they were gone. The clerk gives Don the same room. Key in hand, Don walks over to the room as Tom parks the car in front of their room.

Once inside Don pulls out the thumb drive containing the picture file of Antoine and inserts it into his laptop. He opens the lid and turns it on. The screen comes alive. He selects the thumb drive directory and clicks on Antoine's picture file.

Tom walks over and sits down next to his brother as the picture displays on the screen. "Can you enlarge that so we get a bigger picture?"

Don pushes a key and the picture enlarges, "A little bigger, please," Tom requests. Don hits the key again as the picture enlarges to take up more than half the screen.

"It's a little grainy, but not too bad. Man, that kid had one hell of a greaser hairdo," Tom laughs.

Don stares at the picture, squinting his eyes a little and turning his head to the side, then squinting his eyes again. "There's something about those eyes that look familiar," he says. "Do you see it?"

Tom looks hard at the photo on the screen. "Yeah, I think so. I just can't match it up to anyone I can think of."

"Me, neither," Don says. "Well, if they look familiar to both of us, it must be someone we both know."

"Makes sense to me. Thing is if we both think we recognize those eyes, then we should both know whose eyes those are like. But even if we could identify who we are thinking of, what would that mean as far as Antoine is concerned? Just that he reminds us of someone we know?"

Don keeps staring at the picture. "I think I know whose eyes they remind me of...Junior Prescott."

Tom takes another look at the picture. "Yeah, I can see that. I wonder if that is kind of a regional trait up here in New England. Sort of like when you use to go into parts of Brooklyn when we were kids, everyone looked Italian in certain areas. Everyone had dark hair, and heavy beards – always looked like they needed a shave, even at 10 in the morning."

"I guess that could be it. Antoine would have been around 18 in this picture, and Junior is what, 45 or 50 now? I guess some of his features would have either mellowed or gotten stronger, which might cause his eyes to look like this kids eyes. Maybe I am just seeing things."

"Tomorrow we should drive up to Emerson's place and talk with him some more," Tom says. "Maybe show him this picture and see if he recognizes Antoine at that age. That might explain why Emerson talks about lobstering as a kid. Maybe he's swapped stories with Antoine, and now has the stories mixed up in his head as being his own."

" Ya know, I think I'd like to stop and see Ben first. Show him this picture and see if he's seen this guy around town at all."

"That may be the way to go. Get a little more information before we go back up to talk with Emerson. Always good to have more information than to be in the dark."

"I know there's a big story here somewhere, but I don't know if it's just something I'm pushing to be more than it is, or if it is something that should be investigated more. I already have enough to formulate an idea for the book, and I wonder if there is that much more to discover that would benefit me in any way.

"What do you think, Tom?"

"I think we need to ride this pony a little further to see where it wants to roam. Maybe after we talk with Ben tomorrow you'll have a better idea of what you want to do."

"OK. Sounds fair," Don says. "I could go for dinner pretty soon, how about you?"

"Let's go now. We never did eat lunch today. Want to drive

up to the other end of the lake for dinner? You haven't been up there yet."

"Yeah, let's do that. How long does it take to get there?"

"Maybe forty minutes, maybe a little longer if I drive slow," Tom says.

An hour later they sit on the deck at the Saint Bernard Yacht Club, overlooking the lake and the marina, where just earlier in the day Emerson had his boat tied up. They sit about twenty feet from where Antoine had been talking with Frank about Tom, although neither Antoine nor Frank knew it was Tom they were talking about.

The waitress comes over to take their drink orders and to recite the specials for the evening. When Tom looks over at the bar to see what kind of liquor they have, he sees that Frank is tending bar.

They both order drinks and dinner, and as the waitress walks away, Tom says, "The bartender I spoke with the other day is on duty. After dinner let's talk to him a little. It'll give us something to do for a while." Tom snickers a little as Don nods his head.

After eating their steaks, which were perfectly cooked to a medium rare temperature, they get their check from the waitress, pay her and leave her a good tip. They walk over to the bar and sit down. Frank is at the other end of the bar talking with a customer, but when he sees Don and Tom, he walks over to them.

"Well, I see you're back sooner than you expected to be. And you brought a friend with you, too." Frank looks at Don "My name is Frank, and you are..." Frank says, extending his hand.

"Don. I am Tom's brother," Don says as he shakes Frank's hand. "Good to meet you."

"So what can I get you guys to drink?"

"I'll have a Clan McAllister, water on the side," Don says.

"A stiff gin and tonic for me," Tom says.

Frank nods and returns with both of their drinks. After placing them in front of Don and Tom, Frank rests one elbow on the bar and says, "You know that guy we were talking about the other day, Antoine? Well, he was up here yesterday, and that friend of his was with him. When I mentioned that you were asking about them, Antoine said he didn't know you, and he was pretty sure his friend wouldn't know you either. You sure you were asking about the right people?"

"Were they both in here together," Tom asks.

"No," Frank answers. "Matter of fact, only Antoine was here. The other guy stayed down on his boat. And come to think of it…" Frank turns and walks back toward the cash register, then retrieves a piece of paper. "Antoine wants me to get your phone number should you come in again. Is there a number he can contact you at?"

"Yeah, sure," Don says and gives his cell phone number to Frank. "He can call anytime he wants. Let him know that.

"Do you plan on seeing him soon?"

"He said he may be back up this way toward the end of the week, so if he does come up, I'll make sure he gets your number."

"Thanks a lot, Frank," Tom says.

Tom and Don continue talking with Frank about the lake, Sherbrooke, and Magog. Don is more fascinated by the stories that Frank tells than is Tom. The more Frank talks, the more Tom wants to leave and finally suggests to Don they do just that.

They bid a good night to Frank, telling him to make sure that Antoine gets their phone number. Frank says he will and watches them leave before turning his attention to his other friends that line the bar.

On the drive back to Dexter, Don goes over almost everything they have learned and asks Tom what he thinks about everything.

"Well, it certainly is very interesting, that's for sure," Tom replies. "We have a lot of information but it's hard to tie it together enough to produce a good ,clear, picture for us.

"I think it's funny we just missed Antoine and Emerson by a day. We could have put this all to bed had we been here."

"Yeah, it would have been easy to tie it all up in a bow if we had just been here earlier.

"I think it is time to confront Emerson with this Antoine guy, and see what he has to say for himself. I think I'll be satisfied if Emerson can explain to us what his relationship is to Antoine. If we can just find that out, I will be happy to put a period at the end of the sentence, and go home."

"OK, then," Tom says. "But didn't you want to talk with Ben first?"

"Yeah – we should still do that. Then we can ride over to Emerson's house and ask him about Antoine."

Tom nods in agreement, and the two of them ride silently back to their motel for the rest of the night.

24

The next morning they see Billy at the Chicken and Cow. He is excited in anticipation of what they might tell him.

"So what have you been up to? I missed seeing you yesterday. Did you find out anything more?" Billy is full of questions.

"Yeah, we found out things we didn't expect to discover," Don tells Billy. He brings Billy up to date on the picture they have of Antoine, and how Antoine has asked the bartender up north to get their phone number. He also tells Billy that they have already spoken with Emerson on Saturday and that Tom and he are going to see Ben again this morning, and then go see Emerson once more.

Billy's eyes are wide with fascination. "Oh, god, I'd love to go with you guys. Is that possible?"

"That probably isn't wise. Probably not a big problem with Ben, but with Emerson, he'd probably clam up tight if there was anyone there except us," Don replies.

"We'll fill you in on everything tomorrow morning. We won't leave you out on any of this."

"Good, because I was so upset when I didn't see you yesterday at breakfast, I almost started to drive around town trying to find you," Billy laughs. " You have me hooked on this, ya know?"

"Well, maybe in a day or so I'll even have more news for you about something else that will make you smile," Don says, referring to why he has been so interested in all this in the first place. He never told Billy he is a writer searching for material for a new book, and Don knows he will create a character based on Billy for an important part in the book.

"Oh, no! More mystery from you. You are just loaded with that crap," Billy laughs.

If only Billy knew, Don thinks.

Once the three of them finish breakfast and leave the Chicken and Cow, Billy heads home, and Don and Tom head out to talk with Ben. Don has his laptop with him, as well as the printout of Antoine. It's a long shot, Don thinks to himself, but maybe Ben knows Antoine.

Soon their car stops in front of Ben's house and they stand in front of the door on Ben's porch. Don reaches out to knock on the door, but as his hand hits the door it magically opens, and Ben stands there looking at them strangely.

"What are you two doing here so early in the morning?"

"May we come in? I have something I'd like to discuss with you, and I have a picture I'd like to show you," Don replies.

"Sounds important. Yes, yes, come on in. I have some coffee cooking. Follow me to the kitchen." Ben turns and shuffles through the entrance way into the hallway and finally into the kitchen, with both Ton and Don at his heels.

"Don't forget to shut that door," Ben says loudly. Tom closes the door behind him as he clears the doorway.

Inside Ben's kitchen is an old wood burning stove and oven as well as a newer gas fired stove. The kitchen looks as if it has never been upgraded, except for the stove and refrigerator, but it is neatly painted and the oak floor is in excellent condition. The cabinets are painted white and it is apparent they are hand crafted and not store bought. There are three windows: one over the sink, and one at each end of the kitchen facing the side of the house. That make the kitchen very bright, and with everything painted white, the kitchen has a very cheery feeling.

There is a round pedestal oak table in one corner of the room, with a red and white checkered cotton tablecloth covering it. A sugar bowl, salt and pepper shakers, and a candle sit on top of the table cloth.

He motions for the two men to sit down at the table then faces the upper cabinet next to the sink and reaching in, pulls out two coffee mugs. He sets one in front of each brother and goes to the stove to retrieve the coffee pot.

He turns and fills each cup with coffee, then asks, "Either of you want cream or milk? I have both, but I always prefer cream." He returns the pot to the stove.

"Cream would be great," says Don.

"Same here," echoes, Tom.

"Sorry, I don't have breakfast pastry for you." Ben walks to the refrigerator, opens the door and grabs a small bottle of cream. "I wasn't expecting company this morning. I usually have better manners." He closes the door and sets the cream on the table.

"Not a problem, Ben," Tom says. "Besides, we already ate, thank you."

Ben grabs his coffee cup and joins the two brothers. "Hope the coffee is OK," he says. The men nod.

"So, what's so important that couldn't wait until the sun was overhead? I've only seen you boys here in the afternoon. I thought maybe you didn't get up until noon." He chuckled and smiles at them.

"Ben, we've been doing a little investigating about Emerson," Don begins. "It seems you aren't the only one he has cut out of his life since the second accident. Of course, he's cut Gertrude out, and you, and Billy's father in law, Pete.

"There are others here in town no longer friendly with him as well. But there seems to be someone he has become good friends with since his second accident, that no one around here knows; his name is Antoine Beechen. Ever heard of him?"

"Beechen? Nope. Never heard that name before. Antoine sounds French. Maybe he's from Canada or maybe somewhere in Maine. Lots of French Canadian Acadians up there."

"I have a picture of him. Would you mind looking at it to see if you recognize him?"

"Sure. Why not?" He reaches into his shirt pocket and pulls out a pair of wire-rimmed glasses and puts them on. "Only need these to read," he smiles, "or to be able to see what's in a picture."

Don opens up the laptop he has carried in with him and turns it on. The screen flashes and he locates the icon on the screen that links to the picture of Antoine. He clicks on the icon which opens the file.

He turns the laptop towards Ben and says, "Do you recognize

him?"

Ben squeezes his eyes tightly to focus on the picture appearing on the screen. Then his face shows a look of amusement. "You're kidding, right?"

Don looks at Tom, and then back at Ben. "What do you mean, Ben? Do you recognize the man in the picture? That's Antoine Beechen when he was around 18 years old."

Ben's head pulls straight back and his smile vanishes into a frowning smirk. "If you say so, but I'd bet everything in my bank account, that was Emerson Prescott.

"Are you sure that's a picture of this Antoine guy?"

"Are you telling me this man looks like Emerson Prescott?"

"No. I'm telling you that is Emerson Prescott. I think I know what Emerson looked like when he was that young. I've known him his whole life. The man in that picture is Emerson Prescott or its one heck of a doppelganger. I'd know those eyes anywhere. Even Junior has those eyes. So did Ernie. I think those eyes are the most distinguishing feature of that family. Even Junior's son has those eyes."

"Ben, we got that photo from a high school yearbook in Damariscotta, Maine, from 1963. Did Emerson live in Maine then?"

"Not to my knowledge. And I bet if you look in the yearbook from the town's high school here in Dexter, you'll see I'm right. Emerson was a popular guy in high school. I bet there are plenty of pictures of him in the yearbook."

Don and Tom look at each other. Don turns the laptop back to face him and takes a good long hard look at the photo on the screen. Yes, the eyes are the same. He even said that to Tom, that they looked familiar. He also looks at the cut of the jaw. It seems to be the same as that of Emerson's. Of course, the hair is way different now. It isn't jet black like in the picture, and the skin is now more weathered; but yes, it could look like what Emerson might have looked like when he was a teenager.

"How could that be, Ben? How could Emerson be in two places at the same time?"

"I don't know, Don. Are you sure about where the picture

came from?"

Don turns the laptop around to face Ben. "Look at the caption under the photo, Ben."

Ben looks at the photo a second time and reads aloud the words under the picture; *Antoine Beechen, Class of 1963, Nickname – Curly.* "Yeah, it says this guy is Antoine Beechen alright, but I'd bet what remains of my farm that is Emerson Prescott. You go look at the high school year book for Dexter. The hair is combed different, Emerson used to have close-cropped hair back then. Ernie hated that greaser look and never let him wear his hair that way. But otherwise, that's Prescott."

"Ben, you are a treasure of information, thank you. I think Tom and I have to take a trip over to the high school to see if we can find that yearbook." Don shuts the laptop off and closes the cover.

"How'd you come across that picture anyway," Ben asks.

"We drove over to Damariscotta yesterday and went to the high school there to look through the yearbook trying to find a picture of this guy Antoine."

"What did you want to find a picture of him for?"

"Well, we heard Emerson and Antoine are good friends. We wanted to ask him about Emerson. We had a hard time locating him and I figured having a picture of him might help us find him."

"So, have you found him yet?"

Don looked at Tom with a perplexed look on his face, then looking at Ben says, "I don't know."

25

Dexter high school sits six miles northwest of the center of Dexter. It looks like a much newer structure than the high school in Damariscotta. It is a flat roofed, two-story building that looks more like a factory building than a school. Don thought it must have been built in the late 1960s or early 1970s by its design. The parking lot sits off to the left side of the building, and on the right side, a road winds its way back toward what looks to be an administration office building, and the athletic fields. Tom points the car in the direction of the administration building.

"I bet there is a lot of Prescott money in this school," Don says to Tom. " I bet Prescott paid for these athletic fields. They look well maintained, and that takes more money, I bet, than this town can afford through taxes."

"Certainly nicer looking that the one in Maine, isn't it?" Tom pulls the car into the space in front of the doorway to the building.

"I can't just use the same story here that I used in Maine. I'll just say that I was curious about what Emerson looked like as a kid and see if that gets us anywhere."

They walk into the building and find the administration office directly to the left of the entrance. They hear a couple of voices talking inside the office and it stops when Don enters the room.

"Hello there," one of the voices yell from across the counter. "Are you looking for someone?"

" Actually, we were wondering if we could look at a couple of your yearbooks. We're kinda like history buffs, as well as rural America buffs, and have been spending the last week getting to know your lovely town and some of its people.

"Some of the folks who we've gotten to know are Gertrude Revere, Ben Harper, Billy Shavers, and Junior Prescott and his dad, Emerson. We were wondering if we might be able to find some pictures of Emerson when he was younger, maybe from when he went to school here. I always find it so interesting to see what people looked like when they were young. Don't you find that interesting, too?"

The woman who had shouted out the greeting to them walks toward Don. "Why yes, I do. It's fun to see where someone comes from and compare that to where they are now. Sometimes you can't believe the trip they took," she laughs. "I think the biggest changes in people are the ones that came of age in the 1960s. All the boys had such long hair and beards, and of course, the girls all dressed so freely in hip hugger jeans and loose flowery blouses. Now, they're all mothers and fathers, some even grandmothers and grandfather, and they all dress so conservatively. It's so funny to see how they have changed.

"I have nothing pressing right now, so I could walk you over to the library where the yearbooks are. We have a few copies of every year since the mid-1950s so we keep one copy of each year out and available to the kids so they can look at what their parents use to look like way back when. They get a kick out of seeing them.

"Marge, I am going to take these gentlemen over to the library; I should be back in a half hour or so.

"If you follow me, I'll show you where the books are and you can take a peek at what Emerson looked like back then."

"Thank you so much. By the way, my name is Don and this is my brother Tom."

"Nice to meet you, Don, and Tom. I am Dorothy. How do you like our little town?"

The three of them begin walking toward the back of the school building to a door near some picnic tables. "It's so peaceful here and the lake is beautiful," Don says. "We've only been up here for a week, but I can tell you, I will probably return up here one day for another vacation. Everyone is so friendly and helpful."

A minute later Dorothy takes her key ring out of her pocket and unlocks the door. They walk into the cool air in the dimmed light of the building.

"The library is just up these stairs," Dorothy says as she turns and enters the stairwell. "Be careful. Most of the lights are shut off since not too many people are in the school right now."

"We'll be careful," Don says.

They exit the stairwell on the second floor and turn right. Three doors down Dorothy turns right into the library. She continues walking toward the back of the library where a trophy case holds all the regional and statewide trophies the school has won over the years. To one side is a bookcase with forty or fifty books, each with a year printed on its spine. She turns to Don and asks, "Nineteen sixty-three, correct?"

"Yes, mam."

Dorothy reaches for that yearbook and pulls it off the shelf. "Please be careful. Even though we have extra copies, they won't last forever. We're having our Information Technology students scan all of these into a database, but that takes time. We've got about half of them done, but there's a lot to scan in each book and they are particular about how well they scan the material to get the best possible results. So until then, this is how we access the goods," she laughs.

"Here you go. Feel free to sit anywhere. I'll be back in about ten minutes. Sorry about no light on here. Probably best to sit by one of the windows, where there will be more sunlight."

"Thanks so much, Dorothy. We should be done by the time you get back."

"OK...take your time." Dorothy walks out of the library as Don and Tom sit at a table near a window where the light from the sun shines the brightest.

Don opens the book and goes through the book which looks amazingly similar to the yearbook in Maine. First the school history, then the administration section, then the teacher section, then some photos of some school activities, and then the pictures of the kids.

Don turns the pages to get to the section where Emerson's picture is. On the second line down, third from the left, there is a picture of Emerson Prescott. Tom and Don's eye almost pop out of their heads. With the exception of the hair style, the picture they see looks like a duplicate of the one of Antoine.

"How is that possible," Don says to Tom. "Could two people look more alike?"

"It's pretty amazing." Tom takes out his phone. "I'll take a few pictures of this. When we get back to your laptop, we can download the pictures, and maybe we can overlay them on top of one another to see if the head shapes are the same too. Do you have a photo program on your laptop?"

"Yes. It's not very powerful, but it can do layering so we should be able to do what you just said." Don laughs as he looks at the picture. "Look. They are even turned the same way. Must be a thing about high school portraits."

Tom begins taking several shots of Emerson's yearbook picture to make sure he has one that is good. When he is satisfied, he puts his phone away.

Don continues leafing through the book, stopping every now and then when he finds a picture of Emerson. There is one of him playing basketball, another one of him on a debating team. Still another one of him and others in his class, picking up trash at the elementary school. Every picture looks as if it could be Antoine. Finally, there is one of the whole graduating class – all fifty-two of them.

"Wow! Fifty-two graduating seniors. My homeroom class in high school had almost as many as that, and we had five graduating classes," Tom says.

"I guess that is one of the benefits of living in a small town. You sure do get to know each other," Don says.

Don closes the book just as Dorothy comes back into the library. Don stands, then walks over to the bookshelf and replaces the book in the space where it been.

"Did you find what you were looking for in the book?" Dorothy walks towards them.

"Yes, we did. He sure looks different now than he did in the book," Don laughs. "I guess 50 years does that to a person. I'm sure I'll look strange in my yearbook to how I'll look when I'm his age."

"Won't we all," says Dorothy. "Ready to go?"

The three of them walk out of the library, down the stairs, and back to the administration building. Don and Tom thank her for her help as they reach their car, and Dorothy continues her walk up the steps into the building.

"Let's go somewhere and download the pictures you took," Don says to Tom.

A few minutes later they sit in a park near the marina and download the files from Tom's phone into the laptop.

First, Don opens both files of Antoine and Emerson to do a side by side comparison. Don and Tom stare at the photos that appear side by side on the screen. "Almost looks like a reflection doesn't it," says Tom.

"Except for the haircut. Let me load them into the photo program and layer them." He presses a few keys and the program opens. Soon he has layered the two photos and placed one over the other. He adjusts them so each photo's eyes are almost in the same identical place. The closer he gets them centered, the more the two photos look the same.

"It's the same person, isn't it," Don asks Tom.

"It sure looks like it. But how is that possible?"

"We know they are two separate people, I have the birth certificates to prove it. There's only one reasonable explanation: they have to be twins."

" Ya think," Tom says.

"Look…we know they were born at the same hospital, only about twenty minutes apart, and one doctor delivered both of them. They are the spitting image of each other. What else could explain it?"

"What about the mother's names? They're different, right? How could that be if they are twins? Surrogate motherhood was not an option at that time, it was the mid-40s, and having an egg split and placed in separate mothers was impossible then. I don't even know if they can do that now."

Don keeps staring at the composite picture. "So what's the explanation? Twin brothers, born to different mothers, brought up in different states, separated for who knows how many years, and the family of one of the twins doesn't know anything about it, and neither do any of his friends?

"Is that possible?"

"Well, there is one person who knows what the answer is, and we need to talk to him." Tom stands up. "Close that thing up, and let's go talk to him. Now."

While Don and Tom are looking at Dexter's high school yearbooks, Antoine calls Frank to see if anyone came around asking about him. Frank tells him, yes, two men were there and they left their phone number, which he gives to Antoine.

Antoine asks Frank when they had been there and Frank tells him late yesterday afternoon. He tells Antoine they asked a few more questions about his friend and about Antoine, but nothing out of the ordinary. Antoine thanks him and hangs up.

He needs to call whoever these guys are and find out what they want. He wonders if they are going to try to contact Emerson. That could be a problem and there would only be one way to correct that, but that way would change his life forever and he wasn't really ready for that yet.

Emerson stands at the front window of his house, looking out at the lawn. Another beautiful day in Dexter, if only he didn't have this sinking feeling something is going wrong.

Then he sees the car turn into his driveway. Who the hell is this, he wonders. Then he sees the two figures in the car. It is those two brothers. What do they want?

He moves away from the window so as not to be seen. He contemplates going upstairs and not answering the door when they knock, but figures they will just keep coming back until they corner him. He walks over to the front door and before they begin to climb the steps, he opens the door.

"Gentlemen," he says. "What can I do for you?" He steps through the doorway and stands there, effectively blocking the entrance making it clear the brothers will not be invited in this time.

Don and Tom stand at the foot of the stairs, looking up at Emerson.

"Good morning, Emerson," Don says. "Have you got a few minutes?"

"Actually, I don't and it would be nice of you to not bother me again. Please leave." He turns and steps back into the doorway.

"Emerson," Don says, taking a chance. "It's about Antoine."

Emerson freezes. He knew something was wrong, and now his worst fears are confirmed. He turns around to face them.

"Who?"

"Antoine Beechen. I think you know him."

"And why would I know him?"

"Well, for one thing, you've been friends with him for almost twenty years, at least. For another......I think he's your twin brother."

Emerson feels his face flush in anger. How dare these two

come into his world and try to disrupt it like this.

"My what? Are you crazy? And even if he was, what difference does that make to you? Why is it your concern?"

"Well, all the secrecy about your relationship with him piqued my interest. Care to talk to us about that?"

"Talk to you about what? A ridiculous theory you have about me? A theory that I have a twin brother? Don't you think I would know if I had a twin brother? And to think that this imaginary twin brother is, what's his name? Antoine Beechen?

"You want to talk to me about all this and wonder if I am interested in doing that? Well, not in the least. Now get the hell off my property and stay out of my life and out of my affairs."

"Emerson, we have pictures of each of you from high school and they look exactly the same. How do you explain that?"

"I don't have to explain anything to you two. So what if two kids in a picture from almost fifty years ago look the same. How does that prove they are related, let alone twins?"

"Well, I have birth records showing you were born only twenty minutes apart, too, and..."

"Listen, I don't care what you have. You're nuts. There must hundreds, maybe even thousands of people born within twenty minutes of when I was born. Does that make them all related to me?

"Now go away! Leave me alone! And leave this ridiculous story alone as well.

"And trust me, you don't want to fuck with me, young man. I have a lot of friends in this county, in this state; I could make it uncomfortable for you.

"Now go! Go away!" He gestures with his hands, then turns and walks into his house, slamming the door behind him.

Don smiles. "Let's go, Tom, he's not going to talk to us anymore."

"So what are we going to do with this information, Don? Hell, is there even anything we have to do with this information?"

"No. I guess not. I have all the information I need to start formulating that book. Let's return to the city tomorrow."

He turns toward the car shaking his head. It would have been nice to tie up the loose end about Emerson and Antoine, but he has enough to begin writing the book. That is what he came up here to do, and it is now time to start doing it.

The drive back to the motel is a quiet one.

After Emerson slams the door, he stands just inside the house, shaking. It is starting to unravel. These bastards know more than he thought anyone would ever learn about him. How they figured it out is beyond him. Now his concern is how can he extract himself from this? How far will they take it? Must he plot a way out or let things ride for a while to see where they end up?

If things explode, there's only one way to get out and it will have to happen soon. Emerson goes into his study and begins to list the things he needs do to facilitate his exit from Dexter if that becomes necessary, although he thinks it is time to do this even if it isn't necessary. He spent way too many years living this way. It's time to move on.

- need to transfer money into Antoine's account for temporary cash availability

- move the balance of cash from savings into offshore secure account or cashier checks

- cause his own disappearance, leave no trace of his existence

- check on that barrel in the barn that he placed there more than 20 years ago

He'll start everything this afternoon. First, transfer the money. Not much; a few thousand will tie Antoine over for a couple of months. Then draw a few hundred thousand dollars in cashier's checks. It's risky, but he'll have to leave the payee name blank until he finds out who will be receiving the checks.

He'll have to go down to the bank to do those things in person. In case they ask, he'll explain he needs the money in cashier's checks to complete a deal he is pursuing. Most likely he will conduct his business with the bank manager, an old friend, who he will instruct not to divulge this information to anyone, not even his son, Junior. It's not strange for a businessman to draw a large sum of money in cashier checks for a business deal. Once the checks are created, he can deposit them at a future date in an overseas account, maybe down in the Cayman Islands somewhere. Open an account there, and no one will know about it. Emerson knows an attorney in Boston that can help him do that. He'll have to remember to contact him later today or tomorrow morning at the latest.

The big thing he must figure out, though, is how is he going to disappear without a trace? Maybe some kind of an accident, something where a body might not necessarily be found. Having an accident right after withdrawing a large amount of cash might indicate someone was out to rob him and that might add to the mystery of his disappearance.

He thought about a boating accident; it could blow up somewhere on the lake and sink. He could be lost in the lake. People drown in that lake every once in a while and are not found for years.

Getting back to shore after the boat is in position to blow up, well, that could be difficult, but if he could jump off the boat close to shore and swim in, that would work. Making sure the boat sailed toward the center of the lake would be the hard part. He couldn't use the auto pilot because investigators would wonder why it was in use in the middle of the night. How could he guarantee the boat would steer true toward the middle of the lake once he was off the boat?

Well, maybe leaning a seat cushion against the wheel might be enough to do that. He'd have to take the boat out tomorrow and try it out. He doesn't think he has much to worry about from the wind or current in the lake detouring the boat from where he aims it. Most nights the wind is calm, so it won't affect the drift of the boat, and the lake has no discernible current to affect its course either.

The explosion could be set to occur out in the middle of the lake, long after he is already on his way out of town. Do it at night, and while it will wake people, it will still take a while for anyone to get to the boat. He'd be long gone by then. They'd be looking for him in the lake, not on the highway.

A fuel leak or a propane leak could cause the explosion. He can't use a timer, they might be lucky enough to find that. Whatever he uses as a fuse will have to disappear, though. No candles, they leave a wax deposit. No gasoline leading to the spot where the fire starts; that can be detected by the arson squad. He has to do a little research on this point. Maybe a spark from a cell phone. Yes, that might work. He'd have to get two of those cheap cell phones, "burner" phones Emerson thinks they are called. He'll leave one on the boat to ignite the explosion, and carry one with him just long enough to call the first one, and then destroy that one too.

Once everything is done, though, he'll be out of Dexter and he can live his own life again. He knew one day he might have to do this, but with each passing year, there seemed less and less of a need to plan for it. Now, that has all changed.

He leaves the house and drives into town to the bank. An hour or so later he has transferred the money, and the cashier's checks are in his pocket. All that is left is for him to have Antoine buy a car, and for him to figure out how to cause enough of an explosion to sink his boat.

Don and Tom stop at the marina on the way back to the motel to have a drink at the restaurant. Don still feels unsettled about the way this is ending.

"We should really try to find Antoine to talk to him. I'd love to know how they were separated and how they found their way to each other."

"Me, too," Tom says. "They must have gotten really close, but why didn't Emerson tell his son about his brother?"

"You know, we're still missing a big piece of this puzzle. What about the birth certificates. Why are there two different mothers listed? That makes no sense. And if they are twins, and I am now sure they are, why were they separated and why all the mystery about it. Why wouldn't Emerson tell his kid that either Emerson was adopted or Antoine was adopted, or maybe….maybe, even, they were both adopted.

"Tom, I changed my mind. We're not going home tomorrow. There's more to this story. A lot more. We're going to Manchester tonight. I have to find out why those hospital records show two different mothers. One of them has to be the birth mother and one has to be the adoption mother. We need to figure out which one is which."

"Oh, boy. And here I thought we were going home tomorrow," Tom laughs. "You're something else, buddy boy."

"Come on, let's get going. Maybe we can get there before the hospital administration office closes. It's not even two yet and Manchester is only a couple of hours away, especially the way I know you can drive when you want to."

Don stands and pounds his brother on the back. "Come on bro, let go!"

They arrive in Manchester at 4:05 PM, thanks to Tom's driving. New Hampshire General Hospital is located just three blocks off I-93 and they locate the administration offices with no trouble.

Once inside the hospital, they go straight to the main office and speak with an administration secretary. After Tom explains what he wants to find out and after he shows her his retired police shield, the secretary calls the hospital's administration attorney, who agrees to see them. They go up to the sixth-floor office and he sees them right away.

"What can I do for you, gentleman. The secretary said this was police business."

"Mr. Jamison," Tom says after seeing his nameplate on the desktop. "Is that correct?"

"Yes, William Jamison. And you are?"

"I'm Tom Winston," Tom displays his shield to the attorney, "and this is my brother Don, who just drove up here with me to keep me company."

"This is police business, isn't it?"

"Well, I'm really here for procedural information about an investigation I am conducting. I need information on hospital procedures," Tom says. "I have no idea how that information will affect my investigation, and finding out will help me answer some questions I have. This will have nothing to do with any litigation or breaking of laws, and in no way will it be used for a criminal case against you or this hospital in any way. It is strictly to help me understand hospital procedure."

"OK. Ask away."

"I understand that you cannot divulge information of a personal nature on any patient in this hospital, or that was ever serviced by you or this hospital. That's all protected by HIPAA."

"That's correct."

"Ok, here's what I need to know.

"When a mother is admitted to a hospital to have a baby, and let's say that baby is to be adopted immediately, with arrangements made before the mother ever comes to the hospital, adoption papers already signed and everything, legalized, when the baby is born, whose name goes on the birth record? The birth mother or the adoption mother?"

"Normally, the birth mother's name would go on the birth record, and then the birth certificate would reflect the adoption mother's name."

"You just said normally. When might that not be the case?"

"Well, if the mother is a surrogate, then the biological mother would be listed on the birth record rather than the birth mother or surrogate mother."

"Now, let's say the surrogate mother gives birth to a baby, but the biological mother is not around to accept the child, but it has been put up for adoption; how does that work?"

"Well, in that case, the adopted mother's name might be used since she will be the mother of record if the adoption mother so requests it.

"There is one more option that might occur, though. The birth record may indicate a Jane Doe name as the biological mother for record purposes only, and of course, the birth certificate would indicate the adopted mother's name."

"OK. I only have a few more questions. Would there ever be a case where a birth mother would come in to have a baby, thinking she would only be having one baby, and that baby is going to be adopted, and then by chance there turns out to be a second baby born as well, could the first baby have the adopted mother's name listed for the first baby, and the biological mother's name listed for the second baby?"

"I don't think that would change the procedure for the first baby. If they knew the biological mother's name for the first baby, then that name should be listed as such."

"What if I showed you two birth records from this hospital where it appears that did not happen. What would you say then?"

"I'd say that was impossible."

"Don, can you bring that up on your laptop and show it to Bill?"

Don fires up the laptop and brings up the records of Antoine and Emerson. He walks around the desk and places the laptop on the attorney's desk, so he can read the records.

The attorney reads both records, taking the time to make sure they say what Tom has described. After a couple of minutes, the attorney leans back in his chair and nods.

"It certainly looks like what you described is the case here. Where did you get these records? They look like our records, but before I admit to anything, I need to know how you got these records."

"They were provided to me by a reliable source. That's all I can say. Please remember, nothing you tell me will leave this room or be used for any criminal case. If you want me to sign something to that effect, I will do it."

"Well, yes, I would like you to sign something. Please give me a few minutes to write it up." Bill stands and walks into an adjoining room. Tom and Don hear him talking with someone and then he returns.

"Can I get you something to drink? Some coffee or a soda? Water?"

"No thanks, we're fine."

"May I ask why you need this information?"

"It is very complicated, but I will try to make it short and sweet. Someone we know, just discovered they might be adopted, and at the same time, they discovered they might have a twin brother. When looking over the birth records and the birth certificates it wasn't clear that this was the case, although now it looks like it may be.

"One of the brothers knew he was adopted, but never knew he had a brother until 20 years ago. The other brother never knew he was adopted, his parents never told him, and was surprised and cautious when contacted by the first brother. Both of them are in their 70s now, and just want to clear things up for their families."

"Wow! That must have been a shock to them when they found out."

"Yes, it was. And the funny thing is they only lived about 100 miles from each for their whole lives."

A woman walks into the office and addresses the attorney. "Excuse me, sir, here are the papers you wanted." She walks across the room and places the papers on the attorney's desk.

"Thank you, Susan," he says.

"Anything else, sir?"

"Actually, yes. You're a Notary, right?"

"Yes, Sir."

"Would you bring your stamp in and certify this for us, please."

"Yes, sir."

"Thank you," Bill says. He turns to Tom and hands him the papers. "Would you both read this, and then when Susan returns, sign them for her?"

Tom reads the papers. It is a straight forward confidentiality agreement, coupled with a general release from harm for the attorney and the hospital. Tom hands the paper to Don, who reads it and hands it back to Tom.

Susan returns and walks over to Bill's desk.

"Tom, would the two of you sign those in Susan's presence, please."

Tom signs his name and passes the paper to Don, who does the same. Tom hands the papers to Susan, who then affixes her stamp to the papers and signs them.

"Please file them, Susan. And thank you."

"Yes, sir," she says and leaves the room with the papers in her hand.

"So," Tom says, "are we all set now? Can we continue this conversation?"

"Yes," says Bill.

"I think we can assume these records are from this hospital, and that they are real. I am sure you noted the dates of the births, so I would be quite certain that if there were any criminal laws broken that by now the statute of limitations has run out. Would you agree?"

"Most likely."

"OK, then. Let's talk freely. How could something like this happen?"

"Tom, I am almost 65 years old, and I have been with this hospital for more than forty years. I started back around 1974, so I wasn't here when these records were created. Matter of fact, I would venture a guess there is no one here today working for this hospital that was working here then.

"There were a lot of older attorneys, as well as older doctors, working here when I started. Many of them had worked for this hospital during the war, some even from before the war. They used to tell stories about how during the war they didn't have enough supplies to do the things they needed to do. How there wasn't enough staff for the demand. How they were always working overtime, extra shifts, sometimes without pay because they knew the hospital could not afford it.

"Remember, people didn't always have enough money for medical care back then. Private practice doctors could let patients owe them money, but hospitals weren't allowed that luxury, so sometimes corners were cut, doctors did work in hospitals at night, sometimes things that weren't completely by the book.

"A lot of women got pregnant by men that weren't their husband, and then the men never came back from the war. Sometimes, the father died before the child was born and women were forced to consider abortions, and abortions were illegal then.

"Doctors sometimes aided those women. They could have

lost their licenses, but they did what they thought was moral considering the circumstances. Other times, when a woman didn't want an abortion and felt they could give their child to a loving couple who maybe couldn't have kids, well, the doctors went ahead and facilitated that.

"As I said, this usually happened outside of normal hospital hours. It was war time. It was hard enough to make enough to feed yourself, let alone try to take care of an infant and work at the same time. From what I understand, doctors sometimes altered the birth records to indicate a birth mother different than the real mother. This eliminated the cost of going through an adoption process, which was expensive then, just as it is now, and relieved the pressure on the birth mother of having to give up her baby to someone she didn't know, or worse yet, to an orphanage.

"If you ask for my opinion, looking at these records, I would say the birth mother had arranged an adoption for one child, and surprise of all surprises, she had twins. It wasn't always easy to tell if someone was about to have twins back then.

"Since she didn't have a second adoption set up, she kept the second child. I see that the second child was also adopted, and it was probably done later, rather than at the moment of birth."

Don stands and walks over to his laptop. He clicks on the two birth certificate files.

"Bill, first look at the hospital records. See where the number of live births is blacked out and then corrected? Now look at the birth certificates. Each one only indicates one live birth.

"I think from what you have told us, perhaps the correction was made on the birth record because originally it was recorded as two live births, but to cover things up it was later changed to one live birth for each birth mother name.

"I think that supports your explanation."

"Do you have the State birth certificates of these men," asks Bill. "I'd like to look at them as well."

Don opens up both birth certificates.

Bill studies them, going back and forth between the birth records and the birth certificates.

"Did you guys notice that on the Beechen baby, there are different parents listed on the certificate and the record?

"On the hospital record the parents are listed as Emily Holden and François Beechen, but on the birth certificate, the parents are listed as Louise and Pierre Beechen. From this, it indicates that the Beechen baby stayed in the Beechen family and was legally adopted, while the Prescott baby was the one originally set up for the unrecorded adoption.

"My guess is that the amended birth certificate for the Beechen baby was amended because he was adopted and because the hospital birth record for the number of live births was corrected. The reason for Prescott's baby's amended birth certificate was probably due to the hospital birth record being changed for the number of live births. It probably wasn't noticed until the next day after the copies were filed with the health department."

"I never caught that," Don says.

"So Don does this make more sense now," Tom asks Don. "Do we need anything more from Bill?"

"No. I think this answers a lot of the questions we had." He turns to the attorney. "I want to thank you, Bill, for trusting us, and for giving us such valuable information. We could never have guessed any of what you told us." Don clears the screen of his laptop and shuts if down.

"Listen, guys, this conversation never happened, and the only reason anything came of this discussion was because of that badge you have there. I would never have talked to you about any of this if not for that."

"Understood, Bill," Tom says. "It all stays here and you never spoke with us."

Bill stands up and holds out his hand. "Now, get out of here."

Tom and Don each shake his hand and thank him again.

Once outside, they look at each other in amazement. Don speaks first.

"Who knew things like that happened during WWII. When you think of it, though, it all makes sense. Doctors helping mothers whose lovers had died. Hard decisions made during hard times."

Tom nods as he unlocks the car door. "Let's get back to Dexter and look at all this again. Maybe we're taking too hard a look at Emerson. Maybe this is nothing more than a doctor trying to make things work out for a mother who couldn't care for her child, and two sets of people who wanted to have kids and couldn't."

"You may be right. It sure got complicated, though, but it all makes sense now. Let's go home."

The first thing Emerson does when he returns home is to go into the barn behind the house and crawl up to the second-floor loft where the family had been storing things for more than fifty years. There are so many things up there that to get to the back of the loft, Emerson has to climb over boxes, wooden crates, bed frames, old kitchen tables, broken lamps and chairs, rusted rolls of wire fencing, boxes of fishing tackle and a few old fishing rods, and some rusting steel 55-gallon oil barrels filled with stuff people just can't throw out.

He shares the barn with Junior, although Junior rarely if ever put anything in it, and even more rarely ever takes anything out.

Finally, Emerson gets to the back of the loft and sees the large folded blue plastic tarp that lays on top of a sealed barrel. On top of the tarp is even more junk, thrown there for no other reason than that is the only place left in the loft for it to sit.

He pulls the junk off the tarp, then pulls the tarp itself aside. There sits a black barrel, its lid sealed with a steel ring securing it to the barrel. Emerson sits looking at the barrel, remembering the last time he saw the contents. The barrel still looks intact. There is no sign of any deterioration of the steel. He sighs heavily, wishing there was no need for all this secrecy, but this secret the brother's share is part of their reality. It happened, and now it is time for Emerson to move on.

He replaces the tarp over the barrel and throws everything he removed back on the tarp. He moves more broken and discarded things in front of the barrel, then picks his way over and around the rest of the junk in the loft, back to the ladder that leads down to the floor of the barn. Just before he reaches the ladder, an old lamp crashes off the loft onto the dirt floor of the barn. Damn it, he says. He climbs down and pushes the broken lamp off to the side.

Walking to the house, he decides there are a few things he needs to pick up to get his plan in motion, but he can't get them in Dexter. Maybe it's time to take a trip to Burlington, someplace far from Dexter where he can purchase some of the things he needs. Someplace where no one recognizes him.

Instead of going into the house, he returns to his car and begins his drive to Burlington. A little more than an hour and a half later, Emerson stops at a Big Box Builders Supply store and buys an inexpensive prepaid burner phone. Next, he drives to an America Drugs Store and he purchases a second phone. So as to not leave any paper records of his purchases, he pays for everything in cash.

He locates a library a half mile away and enters just before closing time, hoping he will have time to find a book on how to use a cell phone ring to create a spark to set off an explosion. They do it all the time on TV and in movies; how hard can it be, he wonders.

Walking through the library to the home improvement section to find a book on electricity, he spots a bank of computers. It dawns on him he can do an electronic search for this information. He chooses a computer at the end of the row and sits down at the keyboard.

He types into the search field:

how do you create a spark from a cell phone ring

He watches as the computer performs the search. The search returns a stream of sites with that information. He clicks on one that has a video attached. He goes straight to the video and clicks on it. A message comes on the screen stating the video has been removed in violation of the site's safety rules.

Damn it, Emerson says to himself. Of course, they aren't going to let everyone know how to build a detonator using a cell phone, not in these times anyway. He returns to the search page to see if there is anything else on the subject. He comes across a site that explains how to use the cell phone to remotely ignite fireworks. He clicks on the link and a video opens that shows how to wire a cell phone to ignite fireworks. Emerson laughs. They restrict videos showing how to use the cell phone as a detonator but allow videos that instruct you on how to use a cell phone to ignite fireworks. Typical useless restrictions, like most things.

He watches the video a couple of times, noting what else he will need to buy to make this work. It is going to be a little trickier than he first thought, but not out of range of his knowledge of electricity. He needs some wire, a small circuit board, tape, solder, an ignition source, and a way to ensure this will all disappear into the lake after the explosion, leaving no trace of the phone or the cell phone. He watches the video a few more times and sketches out how to put it all together, then deletes his search, wipes the keyboard of any fingerprints he may have left on the keys, then stands and leaves the library, just as the librarian begins to clear everyone out.

He is back in his house by 8 PM. He goes straight to his study and to his liquor cabinet. He places a glass on the small bar in front of the cabinet and retrieves a bottle of Jack Daniels from the shelf. He pours some into the glass and leaving the bottle on the bar, walks over to his favorite chair. Emerson knows tomorrow is going to be a very busy day. He has to make sure the boat can be kept on course with a seat cushion, he has to also construct the cell phone detonator and test it. Then he has to ensure that Antoine buys and insures a car.

And he has to hope that those two nosy guys don't get in his way anymore. He is sure he can get everything else done tomorrow, but the wild card is those two guys. If they go around stirring up more trouble for him, he will be forced to accelerate his projects and that could cause him to make a mistake somewhere, and he can't afford that.

He's in the home stretch now, and all he has to do is execute his plan; then he'll be home free.

Coincidences keep occurring between Emerson and the Winston brothers. They both return to Dexter at almost the same time. Emerson from Burlington, and the brothers from Magog. Matter of fact, if Emerson had needed to drive through Dexter to reach his house that evening, he might have passed Don and Tom driving to the marina restaurant for dinner. It has been a long day for the two brothers and they just want to relax for the evening.

During dinner, they just can't stop talking about everything they discovered today. They have talked everything through so many times they start to get confused about what they think they know and what they now believe to be true. A couple of after dinner drinks allow them to calm down enough to stop discussing the day's events, and they finally return to their hotel room.

As soon as they enter the room, though, Don picks everything up again.

"I think we need to look at everything again tomorrow

morning with new eyes. I also think we need to put Antoine back in the picture again. We need to talk with him, especially since Emerson won't talk with us anymore."

"Yeah, you're probably right, Don," Tom replies. "But can we just watch some TV tonight and vegetate a little?"

Don laughs, grabs the remote off the nightstand and presses a few buttons. Soon they are watching some inane sitcom, but neither is completely able to rid their brain of thinking about Emerson Prescott and Antoine Beechen.

At 9 AM, Thursday morning, Antoine arrives at Uncle Mike's Pre-owned Auto Emporium, Woodsville, NH, about an hour south of Dexter. He has 7,000 dollars cash in his pocket and hopes to find a non-descript car which he can purchase for Emerson, who will use it to drive to the Boston or Hartford airport, where he will board a plane out of the country. Antoine will purchase the vehicle and the tickets for Emerson, as well as have a change of dry clothes waiting in the car for him.

Once the vehicle is purchased, insured, and licensed Antoine will have it delivered to a small picnic area near the lake, where no one will notice it parked, at least not for a few days. Those few days will give Emerson all the time he needs to put his escape plan into action. Having a car available for transport away from Dexter that is not registered in his name, but in Antoine's name, won't steer authorities to suspect that Emerson might have survived the accident. There would be no reason for the authorities to look for a vehicle registered to Antoine.

He roams the lot until a middle-aged man in a bad sports coat approaches him to see if he needs help. Antoine tells him he is looking for a fairly inexpensive, but reliable automobile. Antoine tells him he just wants something that will get him back and forth into town, a distance of five or so miles. He tells Fred he lives in Harmony Corners, 40 or so miles north of Woodville, and has been borrowing his friend's car for a few weeks while he searches for a new one.

The salesman, who tells Antoine his name is Fred, Mike's right-hand man, nods his head in understanding. Fred asks him what amenities he needs in the car, to which Antoine tells him just the basics, then steers him toward a gray 2008 Chevrolet Malibu (Classic) LS Sedan with 121,489 miles on the speedometer.

"We just had this checked out last week and everything is in top running order. I wouldn't show this car to someone that was going to do a lot of highway driving, it can do it but you would be pushing it. Other than that, it is a great car, especially for what you are looking to do with it." Fred says. "Are you trading anything in? Sounds like you're not, though, am I right?"

"No," says Antoine. "'My last car died."

"Do you need financing?"

"No. I am paying cash."

"My favorite type of customer," laughs Fred. "Want to take it for a test ride?"

"Absolutely," says Antoine.

Fred opens the door. "Go ahead and sit in it while I get the keys and a plate. I'll be right back."

Antoine sits down in the driver's seat and looks at the interior of the car. No tears in the upholstery, not much wear on the floor mats, and no dings on the dashboard. Not a bad looking car, he thinks.

Fred returns with the keys and hands them to Antoine. He walks around to the back of the and places the magnetic dealer plates on the license rack on the trunk. He returns to the passenger side of the car and gets in.

"Feel free to start it up and take it out for a ride," Fred says. He closes the door and fastens his seat belt.

Antoine puts the key in the ignition and turns the motor over. It spurts to life with no hesitation. Antoine closes his door, and drives the car out of the lot.

"Drive down to the interstate and take her for a ride to the first exit. I think you'll be impressed by the power she still has."

Antoine enters the highway a few block down and rides it up to the next exit, exits the highway, and reenters the highway in the return direction towards Mike's Emporium. He pulls into the lot and up to the front door.

"Well, what do you think," Fred asks.

"What's the price?"

"Sixty-four hundred, and it will have a full tank of gas."

"Get it down to fifty-eight hundred, and we have a deal"

"I'll have to check with my sales manager, on that, so come on in, and we'll see what we can do." Fred opens his door and gets out.

Antoine opens his door and but doesn't get out. "I am not going to waste our time by going through the normal dance unless you agree to the fifty-eight hundred. That's the best I can do. I need insurance and plates and I have enough for that and the car at fifty-eight hundred. So, do that, and I'll follow you in to sign the papers."

Fred looks at him, trying to size him up. "You're a tough man…but OK! Fifty-eight hundred."

"And I need insurance and plates."

"I can do the registration and plates for you, and there is someone in town that will do the insurance for you as well."

"Great. And one more thing. I need the car delivered to a town near Dexter, VT, about 50 miles away, not to my house in Harmony Corners. I'll have someone drive your delivery guy back down here.

"I'm doing a little business up there and it will be hard to coordinate picking it up here or even getting it at my place. The guy I borrowed the car from lives up that way and it'll make everything easier to just drop his car off and have you deliver mine there at the same time.

"How much would that cost?"

"Dexter is about fifty miles, right? We can do that for one hundred dollars if you return our driver. How does that sound?"

"Let's go sign the papers, and while you process everything, I can give the insurance guy a call and get that started."

"Let's go then," Fred says as he turns and waves to Antoine to follow him inside.

An hour later, Antoine picks up his insurance papers and then returns to the dealership. Fred tells him he can have the car the following day if he wants it. Antoine tells him he will get in touch with him tomorrow to let him know where and when he would like the car delivered. He gives Fred the fifty-eight hundred plus tax for the car, and the one hundred dollars for the delivery charge.

Antoine thanks Fred for working with him, then gets in his car and drives away. Everything will have to be timed perfectly if Emerson is to disappear the way he planned, and Antoine knows it all depends on how he sets things up. He'll have to get the plane tickets ordered after it is decided when Emerson wants to get away.

In Dexter, Emerson sits at his workbench in the workshop of his garage. It is a little after 1 PM, and he is getting a later start than he wants to on modifying one of the phones to act as a detonator. After reviewing more videos on the internet, he determines he needs to use a couple of AA batteries to provide the spark for ignition, and finds a couple in the workshop. Following the guidelines from the videos, he now makes the adjustments and modifications to the phone that will create and allow a spark to ignite the fuel of his choice.

All he has to do is test the apparatus he is creating. Everything is in place on the phone, so he picks up the other phone and dials the first one. He hears the phone ring, first, in the one he uses to call out from, and then he hears the ring on the detonator phone. The next thing he sees is the glow of the low voltage wire he uses at the sparking point connected to the phone. It glows white hot then breaks. He hangs up his phone. It works.

Now, he has to decide exactly what the explosive will be for the accident. He decides that propane may be the easiest and quickest way to ignite a fire. Hook up the phone detonator wire inside a closed container, maybe even a balloon filled with propane would work. Place the balloon near a leak in the gas line coming from the fuel tank, he could crack the fuel line and let a little gasoline flow out and pool below deck. Then ignite the detonator, spark the balloon and propane, and that in turn would ignite the gasoline, and boom…no more Emerson.

He sets everything up except for the balloon. Where the hell is he going to get a balloon, he says to himself. He spends fifteen minutes looking around the workshop for a balloon before he realizes he is making this way to complicated. All he has to do is catch a rag on fire and have it fall into the space where the gasoline leak is and the rag will ignite the gasoline fumes.

He stands by his work bench picturing in his head where the phone has to be in relation to where the rag will be. He needs the phone to drop freely into the water as soon as the explosion occurs, preferably before that, maybe even as early as when the rag catches on fire.

OK, he says to himself. The phone will hang just over the side of the boat tied to the rag with string. When the phone rings, a spark is created at the rag, causing the rag to catch fire. The fire burns toward the string, catches it on fire, and when the string breaks, that causes the phone to drop into the water, and with no pressure pulling at the rag, it falls into the engine compartment where the fuels has leaked, catching the leaking fuel on fire and ultimately the gas in the fuel tank, causing an explosion. It will look like the rag fell on the hot engine causing the rag to catch fire and then the rag caused the fuel tank to ignite.

There is probably a much more professional way to do this, Emerson reasons, but I don't have time to become a professional. He locates an old oily rag, frays the edge where the wires will touch, and soaks it and the string in gasoline. He ties the phone to the rag with the string. He sets the low voltage wires on the rag where he has frayed the rag and places the phones and batteries over the edge of the chair to simulate the edge of the boat.

He steps back a safe distance, then dials the phone. He hears the rings from both phones, then sees the wire begins to glow. The heat from the wires ignite the frayed edge of the cloth and then the cloth catches fire which ignites the string. In less the two minutes, the string burns through and the phone falls to the dirt floor. Within three minutes the rag is completely in flames and Emerson stamps it out with his foot. It works.

Now, he has to figure out the rest of the logistics, which won't be hard. The last thing he has to do is figure out how much gasoline he will have to let flow into the engine compartment to cause a fire by the fuel line, but that will only be trial and error. He'll have that done before the end of the day.

By 4 PM, Emerson has tested everything and his plan solidified. The only thing left is to determine what day is best to do this. It is already Thursday, and he doesn't want to do this on a weekend, which means Monday morning is the earliest opportunity. It should be around 2 AM after everyone is asleep and well before the morning fishermen rise to go fishing. The lake is normally dead calm with no one motoring around at the time. There will be no one awake to see what happens, especially where he will be on the lake.

He wants Antoine to call Mike's Emporium tomorrow and have the car delivered late Saturday afternoon. That way the car will only have to remain at the picnic spot on Saturday night and during the day on Sunday. No one will think it strange to see a car there for the whole day Sunday; they'd assume it is somebody out on a boat.

Things are falling into place and Emerson feels good about everything working as planned. To be sure, though, he will retest everything Sunday prior to taking the boat out. He just hopes those two brothers don't interfere with his plans. He doesn't need them poking around anymore. Not now. Now when everything is so close to being over.

29

Friday morning, Billy Shavers waits for Don and Tom at a table in the Chicken and Cow. He hasn't seen them since Wednesday morning and to say he is excited to have an update from them is an understatement. He sees them walk in and waves them over to his table.

"Good gosh, where were you yesterday? I am half out of my skin waiting to hear what's going on." Billy is smiling but his eyes look frantic. "What have you found out since I last saw you?"

Don and Tom fill him in on everything. When he hears about the picture of Antoine from high school almost matching the one of Emerson in high school, his eyes get even bigger.

"How is that possible," he asks.

"That's what we asked, too," Don answers. "The only things we can think of is that they are brothers, probably twins. But we can't prove it."

"We even went to the hospital where they were born and spoke with the administrative attorney who told us about some odd procedures they performed there during World War Two that might explain how the brothers were separated, but we can't prove anything. That information, though, is off the record, so we can't quote anything with authority."

"But, we're 99% sure they're brothers and twins."

"Wow," Billy says softly, elongating the "ow" part of his statement. "Have you confronted either Emerson or Antoine about this yet?"

"We asked Emerson, but he told us we were crazy, that we had no idea what we were talking about, and basically threw us off his property. He told us not to come back."

"Oh, he's hiding something alright," Billy says. "No one does that unless they're hiding something."

Both Tom and Don laugh at the seriousness with which Billy

is taking this. Both Tom and Don are sure that if it was up to Billy, he would march right up to Emerson's place and demand he tell everyone the truth immediately.

"Easy, Billy. We'll put this all together. We just need a few more pieces of information to link everything. Maybe we can find Antoine and see what he has to say about all this. Matter of fact, we need to call the marina at the north end of the lake and talk with our contact, Frank, to see if he gave Antoine our number yet.

"Maybe Antoine will even call us this morning, who knows."

"Hey, I want to ask you guys a favor," Billy says. "I've been helpful to you guys, haven't I?"

"Absolutely," Tom says.

"Then let me shadow you for the next couple of days. I think I deserve that." Billy folds his arms across his chest and stares at Don. "I'll stay out of your way, but I can't wait until Monday morning to see what you find out. I'll go crazy waiting."

Tom shrugs his shoulders at Don, and with a little smile says, "What do you think, Don? Sounds OK to me."

Don laughs a little and says, "Sure. But you need to know, we follow the clues where they take us, even if it is to Maine for an hour or to New Hampshire for an overnight.

"Are you OK with that?"

Billy smiles approval at Don. "You bet. No problem. If I miss work Sunday night cause we are somewhere where we can't get back, I won't hold anything against you for that."

"OK, then, Billy. Let's have breakfast and then get started. We'll fill you in after breakfast."

Billy nods in agreement. "Oh boy, I can't wait to see what you have up your sleeve now."

Don and Tom both laugh out loud at Billy's statement. They aren't even exactly sure what they have up their sleeve.

Having finished breakfast, they walk to the brother's car. Once inside Don turns to Billy in the back seat. "I am going to call the bartender up in Magog to see if he's heard from Antoine yet. We'll see what he says, and then make plans." Don dials the marina's restaurant. A kid answers.

"Is Frank there?"

"No, not yet. Frank doesn't come in till around one or two. Want to leave a message?"

"No. I'll drive up there later and see him. Thanks."

"OK," says the kid and hangs up.

"Here's the plan," Dons says. "We have no plan."

"Tom, should we have another talk with Ben this morning? Think we have anything to gain there?"

"Who knows, but it's worth a try."

A few minutes later they pull into Ben's driveway and knock on his door.

"Oh, my god," says Ben, when he opens the door. "They're multiplying. There's three of you now."

Everyone laughs. "Come on in. I am going to have to start keeping morning pastries around if this is going to continue."

They all walk back to the kitchen and settle in. "Coffee," Ben asks them. They all shake their head.

"Ben, we are kind of at a dead end here," Don says. "Emerson won't talk to us anymore, we can't get in touch with Antoine. We know that Antoine and Emerson must be twins but won't admit that to anyone else, and we can't figure out why.

"Do you have any idea why Emerson would keep all that a secret from everyone? After all, since his accident, he hasn't remembered much about his life and you would think if a long lost family member came back into it, especially one he seems to like, he would embrace that, right?"

"Yeah. I know I would, and maybe you would, but we ain't Emerson, are we?"

"No, and I guess everyone is different, right?"

"Yep. It's always hard to figure out what someone else is going to do in any given situation. Thing I don't understand is, what do you expect to find rummaging through all his old history? Do you think the two of them did something they're trying to hide?"

"All my years of being a detective tells me there is something hinky about those two. Their behavior is consistent with people who feel the need to keep information from others," Tom says. "I just can't put my finger on what it is they could be hiding."

"Me, too," Don says. "I know we have gone over this more times than we want to admit, but in order to find out what is missing from the big picture, let's do it again. It's possible you or Billy may remember something you failed to mention before. Is that alright with you two?"

Billy nods yes, and so does Ben.

"In talking with people here in town, I started seeing little pieces of information missing about Emerson's second accident and subsequent non-recovery from the amnesia. Especially, things that should have obviously happened.

"He had two accidents a few years apart and has amnesia. Tom and I checked on how that's possible and are satisfied it can occur as described. One of the really puzzling things about the second accident is why Emerson didn't want to at least go to the hospital for a check up? He was adamant about only letting the doctor check him out at his house. By all descriptions, the bump to his head was bad enough to cause the amnesia to occur again, but not bad enough to have a doctor give him a total physical? I'd think his doctor would've insisted the next day at the latest, to say nothing of worrying about a concussion.

"And here's an interesting question…when was it decided that Emerson had lost his memory again, and how? Ben, I remember you telling me Emerson knew who Junior was when Junior found him, but a few minutes later Junior had to tell him who he was. If so, when did the amnesia start again? Was the amnesia as total as the first time. Was there a period where Emerson knew some people, like Junior, but not other people? Was his history wiped totally clean again?

"If he had amnesia, how come he knew he fell and hit his head. No one finds that strange? Should he have been able to recall that?"

"Then, Emerson begins to alienate so many of his long time

friends, even terminating many of those friendships. Why? Because those people called him on some things he mentioned about his childhood; things he said he did that he couldn't have done?

"A few years later, as Tom discovered, the mysterious Antoine, a friend no one has ever seen in Dexter, appears. He is sort of an invisible friend, although he's not made up, he's real. Emerson then trusts Antoine so much, he allows Antoine the use of his expensive boat. In trying to locate Antoine we discover he lives in New Hampshire, where none of his neighbors have seen him for a long time. We do a little more research on Antoine and discover he lived in Maine while in high school.

"We go to his high school in Maine and locate a picture of Antoine that when Ben sees it, swears it is a picture of Emerson. We find out Emerson and Antoine are born in the same hospital, delivered only twenty minutes apart by the same doctor. We contact the hospital only to find Emerson and Antoine are both adopted, independently of each other, and may well be twins separated at birth, never knowing who the other is or where they might be.

"So, not only is Antoine real, but possibly he is Emerson's twin brother that no one knows he has. We locate Emerson's high school picture at the same age as Antoine's high school picture, and in a side by side comparison, the two pictures could be the same person.

"Over the years, Emerson slips a few times in telling a story about his time in Maine when he worked on a lobster boat. He even slips up on that story when he talks with Tom the other day. Thing is, by all accounts, Emerson never lived in Maine and could have never worked on a lobster boat; but Antoine did both.

"Oh, one more thing I haven't mentioned. Antoine doesn't receive mail at his home address in Harmony Corners, New Hampshire. It is forwarded to a mail drop in Burlington, Vermont. Also, guess who pays Antoine's credit card bills each month?

"Emerson Prescott. All of Antoine's mail, even those credit card bills, seem to be sent to that mail drop. I couldn't find out who owns or pays for the mail drop, but no doubt it must be Emerson."

"So, you think Antoine is Emerson's twin brother, and Antoine, what, just happened to contact him after Emerson's second accident, and now Emerson pays all of Antoine's bills?" Ben whistles. "Whew! That's putting a lot of ducks in a row, isn't it?"

"Yeah, but how else can it all fit together," Don asks. "I'm open to suggestions."

"You know, you mentioned how at times Emerson didn't seem to know his friends," Ben says. "Also, that thing about telling people he did things that people knew damn well he couldn't have done? Well, what if that wasn't Emerson? What if people had run into Antoine those times and not Emerson, ya know, maybe he was just walking through town or something. Meeting him on the street no one would have guessed it wasn't Emerson. The two of them look so much alike in those pictures you showed me, I bet he would've even fooled me."

"I never thought of that," Don says.

"As for Emerson paying for his brother's bills," Ben says, "so what? Nothing strange about a more successful brother paying for the least successful brother's bills."

Tom snickers at that, as he looks at Don. "Did you hear that, my more successful brother?"

"I agree," Don says, "but why not just have the mail forwarded directly to Emerson, and why is all of Antoine's mail sent there? That's why I'm stumped. I know something is out of place here, but I can't put my finger on it.

"I guess I want to know what you two think the next step might be. Should I pursue this further? Is there even something there to pursue? Do we just let it drop and assume it's just Emerson taking care of his brother whom he didn't know he had until after his second accident?"

"I'll agree, there's a mystery here," Ben says. "But is it a mystery that needs solving? Maybe it is just a family thing, and we need to let it go as that. What else could we do anyway? No laws are being broken, and nobody seems to be getting hurt."

When even Billy agrees with Ben, Don and Tom are forced to admit they might be right. Maybe they need to drop it and chalk it up to an interesting town story, and leave it at that.

Don, Tom, and Billy get up together and leave Ben's house after thanking him for all his help and for his input on Emerson. During the trip back to Dexter, Don invites Billy and his wife to dinner that night, and Billy accepts. Don suggests they drive up to the marina and restaurant in Magog at the north end of the lake, and asks if he and his wife have ID's that will get them across the border, to which Billy answers yes.

They agree to meet at 7 at the motel, and Don suggests they all go up there in his car. Tom drives back to the Chicken and Cow where Billy's car is parked, and drops him off. Don and Tom take a quiet ride back to the motel.

When they get in the room Tom is the first to speak.

"I really hate to leave this story unfinished, but Ben's right, how much more to the story could there be?

"Yeah – I agree," replies Don. "After all, I came up here to get the start on a book, and I have that, and I should be satisfied, right? I'm a writer, so I'll start the book using Emerson's story as inspiration, and do what I do best…make up an ending."

"There you go, bro. Now, let's enjoy our last night here with a new friend and his wife, and tomorrow we'll take a nice leisurely drive through Vermont and New York back down to the city.

"You know, we haven't even gone swimming in that beautiful lake out there yet. Or maybe we could ride up to that other lake we passed the other day. Either way, it's warm enough to have an enjoyable afternoon swimming, maybe consume a couple of beers on the beach, and certainly we deserve some time relaxing in that lovely sun that's out today.

"Get your suit and let's go. It's a little after noon and we can get a whole afternoon of getting some sun."

As Don and Tom leave the motel to enjoy the rest of their Friday afternoon swimming at the lake, Antoine is on the phone with Fred at Uncle Mike's Pre-owned Auto Emporium, in Woodsville,

NH, scheduling the delivery of the car Saturday afternoon.

"Yes, Mr. Beechen, the car is all ready to go. We received the insurance papers this morning, and the car was registered at the motor vehicle bureau as well. Matter of fact, Emmet just returned a little while ago with the papers, plates, and stickers. The car is inspected, and the gas tank is full."

"Great," says Antoine. "I would like the car delivered tomorrow as late in the day as possible. What time do you close?"

"Well, on Saturdays we try to get out of here no later than five, sometimes even a little earlier if there's no traffic here on the lot."

"So, can your guy leave then? I could meet him and drive him right back so he would probably be back there by 7 PM, give or take a few minutes."

"How about I let him leave here at 3 PM, that way he could get back here by 5 when he normally gets off?"

"No. I can't do that. It has to be around the time I mentioned. If it's a big problem I can throw him a few more bucks to do this for me."

"No, I think it will be alright with him. I mentioned to him today he might have to work a little overtime, and he was fine with that.

"It would be nice of you to give him a little extra tip, though."

"No problem. Then we're set to go for tomorrow afternoon. Great."

Antoine proceeds to give Fred instructions as to where to meet him and then hangs up.

Everything is set in place with the car. After the driver meets him, Antoine will return the driver to Woodsville, then return and park the car deep into the picnic area near the last picnic bench near the water. He'll place a dry set of clothes in the back seat, and place the keys for Emerson, under a leg of the table. That point is where Emerson will swim back to shore after the boating accident and ultimately drive out of Dexter forever.

Again the coincidences that occur between Antoine, Emerson and the Winston's are amazing. At 7:15 PM. Don, Tom, Billy, and Billy's wife, Diane, drive up the east road to the marina in Magog. The same road the picnic area is located on. The same picnic area where Antoine will meet Emmett and the Chevy the next evening, before driving Emmett back to Woodsville.

Had this been Saturday night, none of them would have seen a car parked in the picnic area behind some bushes covering the license plate from view. That car would be replaced later that evening by the Chevy Antoine will place there Saturday night.

Don and company arrive at the marina on the north shore of the lake around 7:45 PM. After having a couple of drinks on the deck while watching the sunset over the mountains, they order dinner.

Conversation, for the most part, is light, and only occasionally do any of the men mention anything about Emerson or Antoine. Billy tells Don and Tom that he has kept Diane up to date on what has transpired regarding Emerson and Antoine. Don asks that Diane and Billy keep that information to themselves, explaining he has a reason which he can't divulge. He also tells them that he will let them know when it is OK to talk about everything. Both Diane and Billy promise to honor Don's request.

"Tom and I discussed something this afternoon," Don says, "and we decided that we are going to see Emerson one more time before we leave tomorrow morning. We are going to lay everything out in front of him and see if that shakes him up enough to fill in the blanks for us. If he says anything, we'll let you know, but our guess is he will remain tight-lipped and tell us to get lost again.

"So, that's enough talk tonight about Emerson and Antoine. I want to hear more about everything you guys have done up here in this beautiful part of Vermont."

The night passes with much laughter, and much information shared about lifestyles and occupations, except, of course, Don still doesn't reveal to Billy or Diane he is a writer; he'll reveal that information once the book is done.

They decide to return to Dexter a little before midnight, again passing the picnic area where on Saturday night the gray 2008 Chevrolet Malibu (Classic) LS Sedan, (which by then will have the now increased mileage of 121,698 miles on it) will be parked where Antoine leaves it for Emerson. It will remain there until Monday morning when Emerson swims into shore, gets the dry clothes out of the back seat, changes into them, and then drives away.

Back at the motel, Billy and Diane get in their car as Don and Tom say goodbye to them. They exchange phone numbers and email addresses so they can keep in touch, and Don invites Billy and Diane to visit him in New York if they ever get the notion.

As the Shavers' leave the parking lot, Don says to Tom, "I'm going to miss him. He's a really nice guy. At least we can keep updated on Emerson since I know Billy won't be able to help himself from writing to me if anything happens." Don laughs.

"Let's get to bed, Don," Tom says. "We have a long drive tomorrow."

Within ten minutes the lights are out in the motel room and they are both fast asleep, tired from their swim earlier in the day and from all the drinking and eating they did that evening. They hear nothing except the low sound of air being blown in through the air conditioner sitting under the window by the door to their room.

Emerson is also in bed; he's been there since almost 10 PM. While there is little noise outside his window save for the occasional cricket chirping, he lies awake going over plans for the next two days. Finally, around 2 AM, his mind exhausted, he falls asleep.

Tom and Don sleep in until almost 8 AM. They rise, shower, pack their clothes, and check out of the motel. They drive over to the Chicken and Cow for one last breakfast, and when they are done drive over to Emerson's house for one last conversation with him.

When they pull into his driveway a little after 9:45, they see Junior's car parked in the driveway. They park the car next to Junior's and walk up the steps to the front door. They knock, and instead of Emerson answering the door, Junior greets them.

"Listen, fellows. I am not sure what you did or said to dad the other day, but he doesn't want to talk with you anymore. I apologize if he was rude, but he's my dad, and since I have no idea what you may or may not have said to him to make him angry, I have to ask you to leave and not bother him anymore."

"OK, Junior. But you might want to ask him a couple of questions, questions we were going to ask him today. Maybe he will give you the answers he has been denying us this week.

"Ask him who Antoine Beechen is. Ask him about Emily Holden, and François Beechen. Ask him who Louise and Pierre Beechen are. And ask him who Dr. Raymond Foster is.

"I think these are all things you might want to know. I'll leave it at that. If he wants to tell you, he will.

"Thanks for the time you gave us last week, it was genuinely appreciated." Tom and Don turn to walk away.

"Wait, a minute," Junior says. "What are you talking about"

Don turns to him. "That's for your dad to tell. We only have the questions, he has the answers."

"Answers? Wait, wait just a second, please," Junior turns and walks down the hall to the kitchen. Don can hear him calling, "Dad. Come here for a minute, please"

"I don't want to talk to then, I told you that," Emerson can be heard saying. "they're sticking their noses in where they don't have any business being. Get rid of them."

"No dad, you have to explain this to me. Come on."

"Nope. Not gonna talk to them."

Junior walks back to the front door, signaling them to come in and follow him to the kitchen.

Don and Tom enter and walk down the hallway to the kitchen, where they find Emerson sitting at a table having coffee.

Looking up at Don and Tom as they walk in, he shouts to Junior, "Get them out of my house, right now."

Junior turns to Don and says, "Go ahead and ask him those questions."

"Good morning Emerson. We've tried to have you answer these questions not only for our own inquisitiveness but because some other folks in town are interested as well.

"Emerson, who is Antoine Beechen and what relation are you to him? You must know who Emily Holden and François Beechen are, as well as Louise and Pierre Beechen, Antoine's adoptive parents. We know you know who Dr. Raymond Foster is, and how he fits in with all of this.

"So, Emerson, why not tie up all the loose ends and explain to us and your son, who all these people are and how they relate to you, and to Junior."

Emerson just stares at Don, then he stands up and turns to face him. "Get...out...of...my...house," he says slowly and deliberately. "Get...out...of...my...house...now! I swear I'll get my rifle and blow your fucking brains out! Both of you! GET OUT!"

Emerson begins to move towards them.

"Maybe you'd better leave," Junior says to Don and Tom. He stands between Don and his father and turning to Emerson says, "Sit down dad. They're going right now."

"Emerson, talk to your son. Tell him," Don says. "He deserves to know. He's your son for god's sake."

Don and Tom turn, walking back down the hallway to the front door, and down the steps to their car.

Just as they are about to get into the car, Junior appears at the door. "What the hell is that all about? What is it I need to know?"

"Ask your father. If he doesn't want you to know, well, he won't tell you. Goodbye, Junior. Good luck with him."

They get in the car and pull out of the driveway, back to the main road and turn southeast toward New York.

After a few minutes Don says to Tom, "Well, if that doesn't get the gears turning, nothing will. Did you see how mad Emerson was? Whew! Glad we got out of there before he went for the shotgun.

"He really doesn't want his son to know anything about all that. I bet they are having one hell of a discussion right now."

"Well, it's all over for us now. You have what you came up here to get, and you started a little trouble as an extra added bonus," Ton adds sarcastically.

"Let's let it all sit for the rest of the trip home. Let's drive through New York and down the Taconic Parkway. That's always such a pretty ride."

"OK, big brother," Don says. "You win. We'll drop it for today. Nothing more we can do anyway."

They spend the next eight hours driving through small towns in Vermont and New York, stopping every so often to look at an interesting shop or to look at a scenic turnout. They arrive back in NYC around 7 PM and after parking the car, retire up to Don's apartment.

After Don and Tom left, Junior confronts his father, asking him to answer the questions they asked him. Emerson refuses, finally telling Junior to get the hell out of his house and to leave him alone.

Once Junior is gone, Emerson sits in his kitchen, surer than ever that he has to go ahead with his plan. He is right, he thinks; it is all blowing up in his face and it is time to go. Once he calms down, he goes out to the workshop in the barn and begins rigging everything up for the last test he wants to perform on the detonator before going out on the boat Sunday night.

After an hour, he completes the final test and feels secure it will perform as designed. Now, all he needs to do is take the boat out and test his theory that the boat will steer a straight course with a cushion leaning against the steering wheel. He can do that around dinner time when traffic on the lake crawls to a halt for the night. Then all he has to do is wait until Sunday night to execute everything.

He knows that once he is gone, Junior will one day clean out the barn, find the barrel, open it, and discover the secrets hidden inside. By then, though, he will be long gone and his new life be established somewhere warm, maybe on some Caribbean island, or even on an island in the Mediterranean in Europe. No one will be looking for him except at the bottom of the lake, so he will have disappeared, never to be found. Everyone in town will believe he died in the boat accident, and that's that. As anxious as he is about the coming event on Sunday morning, he reflects on the last twenty something years. It has been a good life, and he knows he will miss much of it, and miss Junior, yet it is time to let it all go.

Emerson cleans up his work area – no need to leave a bunch of clues around for investigators to find – then climbs the ladder to the loft. He can't see the barrel from his perch on the ladder. Good, he thinks. No one casually looking up here will see it.

Remembering back to the day he moved the contents up to this barrel, and the subsequent months following that action, he wonders where he got the strength to do that.

It was hard enough getting the contents of the barrel up to the loft that day. Then he needed to weigh down the barrel to ensure it never accidentally tipped over. He found a couple of bags of Kwikcrete, a ready mix cement, and emptied their contents into the bottom of the barrel, saving some to place around what he would put inside. He needed something to absorb any moisture that might condense inside the barrel once it was closed.

Sometimes, over time, things have a way of emitting an odor and he didn't want anyone investigating a strange smell in his barn. But this was a farm, and there were strange smells everywhere. Still, not much trouble to put something in the barrel to mask any odors coming from the barrel. He didn't have to look around the barn very long before he located a couple of bags of fertilizer, which he carried to the loft and poured into the barrel. To fill the remaining space in the barrel, he carried some dirt from the pens in the barn up to the loft and topped off the barrel.

He put the top on the barrel and placed the ring around the rim, closing but not tightening the clasp. Air needed to escape for a few weeks. When it was safe, he would reseal the lid. For now, he just piled some things that were in the loft around and over the barrel. He would come back in a few weeks, when he had more time, and seal the barrel for good. He would also get some kind of a cover up there to better hide that old barrel, but right then he had to get down from the loft and back out to the car before someone came along.

No one would understand why he decided to store the contents inside this barrel. He felt then, that was his only option. Now, after more than twenty years, he feels he might do things differently. He would be free today to do anything he wants to do without having to give into subterfuge. His relationship with Junior would have been different, and he wouldn't have had to protect himself from the people of this town as he has done. He could have had real friends, maybe even a romantic partner.

All that is lost to the past, though, and in two days he will be able to begin to live again as he wants, free from scrutiny and free from suspicion.

He climbs down the ladder and looks up to see if he can see the barrel. He can't see it because of the objects in front of it. He is satisfied it will remain hidden until Junior gets around to cleaning out the barn, and that could take months, maybe even years.

He places the materials he needs for the explosion in a brown grocery bag and walks to his car, where he puts the bag in the trunk. He gets into his car and drives into town and to the marina.

At the marina, he sees the dock boy sitting on the end of the pier near his boat. Emerson walks to his craft, boards, and places the bag inside the cabin, out of sight. He returns above deck and walks forward, calling out the boys name. He waves him to the boat and asks him to untie him. He starts his engines and in five minutes he is a few hundred yards out into the lake.

One last tour of this, he thinks. It sure is pretty out here in the autumn. He'll miss that, and he'll miss the fishing. There will be time for fishing wherever he decides to go, and there will be new vistas to admire. Transition. That's what life is for him now.

An hour later Emerson is almost out in the middle of the lake. He takes one of the cushions off the seat near the pilot's chair on the flying bridge, then slows the boat to the minimum required to keep headway on the boat. He sets the rudder amidships and holds it steady to determine exactly where the rudder needs to be to steer a straight course. When he locates that point, he places the cushion against the wheel, lodges it between the interior wall of the cockpit, and lets the boat steer itself.

As the boat moves forward at its minimum speed, Emerson adjusts the cushion until the boat steers true. He then looks at his watch to determine the time it will take to cover the distance he deems necessary to have it get to the center of the lake, the spot where he will activate the detonator phone.

He stops the boats and shuts off the engines. He goes down to the main deck cockpit area and opens the engine access lids in the cockpit deck. He locates the fuel lines from the gas tanks and sees the crossover valve located in the middle of the boat. He bends down to feel around the area below the valve and discovers a slight depression in the hull below the valve. Perfect, he thinks. The gas will catch there and the fumes will congregate in that area. He can set the rag just above the opening and once on fire, it will drop directly into the engine compartment and next to the crossover valve. All he'll have to do is loosen the valve nuts to the fuel diverter and enough fuel will drip down into the engine compartment to cause a backup of fumes.

He measures the distance between where the rag will be placed and the edge of the boat where the wires will run over the gunwale and connect to the phone. He notes this in a small notebook and sketches how it should be placed. He also adds into the notebook the speed needed to maintain headway, and the heading he will have to have the boat moving.

He goes back up to the flying bridge and very lightly makes a small pencils mark to indicate where the wheel should be. He places the cushion in the spot needed to keep the wheel secure, then pushes it a few time to determine how much force will be needed to knock it free from the wheel. He note in the book where he needs to lodge the cushion and replaces the cushion back on its seat.

Once he verifies everything checks out, he starts back to the marina. He leaves the engine compartment lids up. He plans to tell the dock boy to remind him to have the mechanic check the engine for overheating issues on the following Monday. Emerson figures this is a good alibi as to why the engine compartment lids are open when they inspect the boat after the accident: he needed them open to allow the engine to remain cool.

The dock boy is at the dock to assist him in securing the boat when he returns. Emerson tells him to contact the mechanic on Monday to check out an engine overheating problem and asks him to close the lids in an hour, once the engine has cooled down.

Emerson leaves the marina and drives home to wait for Sunday to come. In a little more than 36 hours, Emerson Prescott will disappear and his new life will begin.

Soon after Emerson returns home, Antoine books a flight to the Cayman Islands from Boston's Logan airport.

He selects a 7:15 AM flight with one stopover in Atlanta, scheduled to arrive at Owen Roberts airport in Grand Cayman, Cayman Islands, at 12:31 PM. He tries booking a flight from the there to Rio de Janeiro, Brazil, for the next morning, but the only flights to Brazil go through Miami and once out of the states, there is no returning. He finds a local inter-island flight from Owen Roberts airport to Montego Bay, Jamaica, at 11:26 AM, Tuesday morning, and from there he books a flight through to Sao Paulo, Brazil, leaving at 6:43 PM Tuesday night.

He selects business class for the long flight to Brazil. He pays for the flights directly from his own account, making sure to not leave a charge card trail back to Emerson.

Satisfied he has all the travel arrangements completed, Antoine calls it a day, and turns on the TV. Sunday night will be here soon enough, and once everything is in play, Emerson will be gone and Antoine's life will be easier.

32

Emerson wakes early on Sunday morning after a restless sleep. During the night he woke almost every hour with thoughts of Monday morning. When he sees the sun begin to peek into his bedroom, he decides to give up the illusion of sleep and dresses in a pair of old jeans and a polo shirt. This is the last morning he will wake up in this bedroom. The last morning he'll see the sunrise through this window after all these years of living in this beautiful house. This has really, truly been more than a house to him. It has been home.

He goes downstairs to the kitchen and makes his morning coffee. He sits at the table looking out at his backyard and into the fields that fill out his sight lines. Where did the time go? Why did those two guys from away have to invade his space and his life? They even spoiled the last few hours he might have spent with Junior. He vows to reconcile that with Junior before he leaves tonight. He has to make sure that Junior knows he has always cared about him.

Finishing his coffee, Emerson walks to his study and over to his desk. He opens up the lower draw and fishes around for his passport. He places it on the desk. He opens the middle drawer of the desk and takes out a manila envelope containing twelve cashiers checks, each with a value of 30,000 dollars, for a total of 360,000 dollars. There is another, smaller legal sized envelope in the drawer, and he withdraws that as well. It contains 9,000 dollars cash. Between the money on his desk and the almost 10,000 dollars transferred into Antoine's account, Emerson has withdrawn almost 375,000 dollars from his personal account. There is still more than 100,000 dollars left in the account. No need making anyone suspicious, wondering why he cleaned out the account. Lastly, he removes the phone he will use to send the signal to the detonator phone

He carries all this back into the kitchen where he gets a plastic zip bag from one of the drawers, into which he places all of these items except the phone, then seals the zipper closed. He will later place this into a leather bound note folder and along with another change of clothes, he will place everything into a carry-on bag for the trip to the Cayman's, and ultimately, Brazil. This money will have to last him the rest of his life and he knows that once he is settled he'll have to invest most of it, but he's not going to worry about that now. Soon, he'll have plenty of time to figure out the best place to invest it.

He places the bag under his arm and walks out to his car. He drives out of his driveway and turns towards the picnic area where Antoine has parked the car. It is still so early that there are no other cars on the road; not even the folks that will go to church this beautiful Sunday morning are up and about yet.

In a few minutes, he pulls off the road at the picnic area where Antoine parked the Chevy. He walks over to the picnic table by the car, and lifts up one corner, revealing the car keys. He takes them and sets the table back down. He walks to the trunk of the Chevy, opens it and throws in the plastic bag. He closes the trunk, walks back to the picnic table, lifts one corner of it off the ground, and places the keys back where he found them. He lowers the table and returns to his car. Ten minutes later he is at the marina to make sure the boat is all ready to go for the night.

The dock boy is there and Emerson tells him he wants to take on some fuel. The kid goes over to the fueling dock and waits for Emerson to warm up the engines. When the engine reaches operating temperature, he motors over to the dock where the kid leans against the pump. The kid grabs the line from Emerson and ties him off, first at the bow, then at the stern.

"How much you need Mr. Prescott?"

"I think about 30 gallons will do it," Emerson says to the kid. "I'm going to do a little night fishing tonight and may troll a little, so I don't even want to have to think about running out of fuel."

"I don't know if you could ever run out of fuel on this baby, Mr. Prescott. I think she holds almost 100 gallons. You'd have to troll her for two days before she ran out."

"Maybe so, son, but better to be safe than sorry, right?"

The kid nods as he places the nozzle of the gas hose into the gas filler port. He begins pumping the fuel, looking back over his shoulder at the fuel gauge on the pump. "30 gallons, right?"

"Yep," replies Emerson.

The kid pumps the 30 gallons in less than four minutes, then replaces the cap to the tank and puts the hose nozzle back on the pump.

"I'll put it on your bill, sir, as always. You ready to cast off?"

Emerson starts the engines again, the kid unties the stern line first and then the bow, throwing the line on the deck after each line is untied.

"See you at your slip," he says.

Emerson pulls the boat into his slip as the kid catches first the bow line, then the stern line that Emerson throws him. He shuts down the engine and disembarks the boat.

"Don't forget about contacting that mechanic tomorrow and have him check out the engine. I'm taking her out tonight, but I won't push her hard, and if she starts having a problem, I'll just drop the hook and you can come out in the morning and get me, OK?"

"Sure thing, Mr. Prescott," the kids says. "You want me to clean her up today for your trip?"

"No, no, don't bother. You can clean her tomorrow." Emerson opens the door to the stern and exits the boat. "See ya later."

"Yes, sir, Mr. Prescott."

Emerson drives back to his house and spends the rest of the day watching TV, puttering around the attic, looking at all the relics from the past that are stored up there, just trying to stay busy to make the day pass quicker.

Around 4 PM Junior stops in and asks him if he has calmed down from their argument. Emerson puts a hand on Junior's shoulder, and tells him yes, everything is OK between them. Emerson offers Junior a drink in the study, and they sit and talk for a while. Emerson does as he planned earlier, and tells Junior how proud he is of him in the way he has run the company for all these years and that he cares for him deeply.

Around 5:30, Junior says he's going home. Emerson tells him he's going fishing on the boat for the night, so he'll see him tomorrow. They hug and Emerson looks at Junior as he walks away, knowing neither of them will ever see the other one again.

Emerson goes up to his room and chooses his lightest pair of shorts to wear for the night. The less clothing he has on when he swims to shore later, the easier it will be for him. He puts on his boat sneakers, but wears no socks, and changes into a light cotton dark colored polo shirt.

He goes downstairs and makes himself a light dinner which he eats slowly, not finishing everything on his plate. He is too anxious about the evening and knows he will have plenty of time to eat after everything is done.

He makes sure he has everything he needs and goes over the plan a few times, trying to make sure he has all his bases covered. He knows he only has one shot at this, and if he fails he is going to have a lot of explaining to do.

At 7:15 PM, he takes one last look around the house, and unceremoniously walks out through the front door for the last time.

By 8 PM, Emerson is on the water, headed out to the middle of the lake to do a little fishing. It is still light enough for people to see him, and he has his navigation lights on as well to make his boat more visible. He sets out a couple of lines for trolling and settles into his captain's chair. For the next few hours, he trolls the middle of the lake in full view of anyone that might be looking, stopping every now and then to adjust his lines, or to just sit there fishing.

He opens the engine compartment lids and keeps them open so if anyone sees him, they will attest that he might have been having engine problems.

He waits until around 12:50 AM to anchor off the point where the picnic area is located. He begins to set everything up. He first loosens the diverter fitting to allow a little fuel to leak. He then takes an awl from his tool chest and punctures a small hole in the fuel line, causing more fuel to drip into the engine compartment. He soaks the rag in the fuel accumulating in the bottom of the engine compartment and places the rag in the right position directly over the diverter and fuel line. Then he sets the phone on the gunnel as he ties it off with the line running across the top of the rag, so it will ignite when the cell phone charge ignites the rag. He goes up to the flying bridge and engages the engine, setting it to the rpm he had noted Saturday. He turns the wheel to the preselected position and makes sure the boat tracks true before placing the cushion where it will hold the wheel until the explosion.

He hurries down to the main deck and lowers the phone over the side. Lastly, he climbs over the aft transom and quietly slips off the stern into the water. He treads water while watching the boat ever so slowly pull away from him. Satisfied all is well, he turns and begins swimming the 100 yards into the point where the car is waiting for him. It takes him about ten minutes to get to shore and he is near exhaustion as he steps on the rocks near the shore. He should have taken a life preserver with him, he says to himself.

He looks out at his boat and it looks to be steering true, straight out to the center of the lake. As he surmised, there is no wind and he hears no one else on the lake. No parties seem to be happening on the shore anywhere, and the moon is partially obscured by clouds. Perfect evening, he thinks.

He hurries to the picnic bench to retrieve the keys from under the leg of the bench, then opens the trunk. He takes out the plastic bag and removes the sender phone. He unlocks the driver side door and throws the bag into the front seat. He then walks to the lake edge and sees the boat is almost at the point where he wants to initiate the detonation.

He decides it is time and dials the number of the detonator phone. He hears the ring in his phone. It rings once. Nothing happens. It rings a second time, and still nothing. Finally, he hears it ring a third time and he sees a small spark on his boat. The spark begins to glow brighter, then it disappears. Oh shit, he thinks, the damned rag didn't catch fire. Oh, damn.

He has no need to worry. Fifteen seconds later there is an enormous explosion on his boat, and the lake begins to light up like a meteor has broken through the atmosphere and landed nearby. He hurries back to the car, gets in, and starts the engine. He almost puts the car in gear but remembers he needs to pull the SIM card out of his phone and destroy it. If they ever find the detonator phone, they can use the record of the received call to locate where the call came from. It won't be bad if they determine the location of the phone call was in Dexter, but if he travels with the phone they might be able to tell from GPS tracking where the phone has gone after the phone call. That might lead them south, and then that might lead them to Boston, and if that happens, it might make them think to check the airport, and he didn't need them doing that. Better to destroy the card right away, and then ditch the phone at another location.

After doing that, he slowly and carefully pulls out of the parking area and onto the road. He drives away at just below the speed limit so as not to draw attention to himself if someone actually happens to see the car. He crosses a bridge and opens the window, then wipes the sim card clean of his prints with his shirt, and tosses the broken sim card into the water under the bridge. Now all he has to do it get rid of the phone and his wet clothes. He'll do that at the rest stops along the road before he gets to Boston.

He is wet, he is terribly nervous, and he knows that Emerson Prescott is now dead. He turns on the heater; he is cold from the swim into shore and he has not taken any time to change his clothes. He can do that later. Within ten minutes he is out of Dexter, heading south to Interchange #27 on I-91, and on his way to Boston, less than four hours away.

In 45 minutes he turns onto I-93, and a few minutes after that, he sees a rest area and stops. He hurries into the Men's room with his dry clothes and his phone. He changes into his dry clothes and dumps the wet shirt into the refuse container.

In another 38 miles, he sees another rest area and gets rid of the wet shorts, dumping them into another refuse container.

Driving across a bridge near Concord, New Hampshire, he slows down a little, opens the passenger side window, and throws the phone as hard as he can over the guard rail into the Merrimack river. He closes the window and relaxes a little. It's only another hour or so to the airport, and that makes him feel a little better because once he is in the terminal, he knows he is home free.

He arrives at Logan airport and finds the long term parking lot. Checking with the attendant at the security and rental office he prepays for a month long stay. The clerk shows him a map and circles a spot where he is to park his car. When Emerson is ready to go to the airport, he is told to call the office from the phone at the pickup station, and a shuttle bus will be dispatched to pick him up.

Emerson pays in cash, returns to his car, and drives into the lot in search of his spot. Once he parks the car, he removes all traces of Emerson Prescott from the car. He has his checks, cash, and passport in a manila envelope, which he will place inside a travel bag he plans to purchase once inside the terminal. He made good time getting to the airport and has more than an hour and a half until his flight leaves, so he doesn't feel rushed doing things. He wants to make sure everything is perfect before he leaves the car.

Sooner or later they will notice no one has picked up the car and they will try to locate the owner. Since the car is registered in Antoine's name, the won't link it to Emerson. The car will be towed to an impound lot, a notice sent to Antoine Beechen in Harmony Corners, New Hampshire, that he owes towing and storage fees, and after three attempts in six weeks to contact Antoine, they will sell the car at auction to cover all costs. So what if they trace the car to Antoine. Antoine will be gone.

After making sure everything is as it should be, Emerson walks to the pick-up station and places a call to the office. In five minutes a small transport bus arrives and takes Emerson to the terminal where his plane is leaving in a little more than an hour.

He enters the terminal, walks over to a kiosk, types in Antoine's name, enters Antoine's verification number, slides Antoine's credit card into a slot in the kiosk, and a second later his ticket prints. He is now verified for boarding the flight, and he still has time to shop for the travel bag and a change of clothes.

Logan Airport has everything anyone might need to purchase at the last minute. It is almost like a department store. He finds a travel store and gets a leather bound legal sized portfolio binder, a small carry-on travel bag, and a neck rest for the flight. Then he finds a store that sells clothing and picks out a pair of slacks, a shirt, and some socks. Lastly, he stops at a breakfast fast food store and gets some coffee and a Danish. Normally, he pays for things by credit card, but not wanting to leave a trail, he now pays for everything by cash.

He finds the entrance to his airline and goes through the security line with no problem. No one questions his resemblance to his identification documents since he and Antoine share the same face. From this point on, Emerson will be Antoine, and no one will ever see or hear about Emerson Prescott again.

Forty-five minutes later, Antoine boards the flight to Owen Roberts airport just outside of George Town, Grand Cayman Island.

A few minutes after that, the plane lifts off and Antoine is on his way.

A plan well executed, and no one is even going to know.

Billy Shavers is working at his station when one of his co-workers comes into the building yelling that there has been a big explosion out on the lake. He's not sure what caused it, but it looks like it might be a boating accident.

Since almost everyone in the plant lives in town, everyone is concerned it may be someone they know. They all leave the plant and run over to the marina just down the block and look out over the lake.

The fire on the lake can just about be seen between the two points of land between the marina and the accident. Sirens are going off on both sides of the lake as well as in Canada and at the border station situated on the east side of the lake. There are no fire or police rescue boats headed out to the fire yet, but a few small pleasure crafts can be seen heading to the fire.

The small boats circle the fire, but don't dare getting close enough to even try to perform any rescue operations, even if there is anyone on board to be rescued. It is more than ten minutes before the police and fire rescue vessels arrive at the boat and can begin to spray fire suppressant foam onto the vessel. It takes a full five minutes for the flames to be arrested, and then they have to wait another ten or fifteen minutes before the smoke clears enough to get close enough to see if there is anyone on board. It is another fifteen minutes before they feel it is safe to board the half-sunken vessel to perform a search for any survivors.

All the small boats shine lights into and on the water looking for anyone that might have been blown overboard by the explosion, or that may have jumped into the water to escape the fire. The search is soon joined by official vessels and a couple of salvage workboats, and it continues until day break. No one is found swimming or floating and even though the search continues for the rest of the day, nothing is found to indicate anyone survived the blast.

Within minutes of the first boats arriving on the scene, a report comes by telephone into one of the workers at the marina. The boat is Emerson Prescott's boat, and it looks like a fire started in the engine compartment causing a gas tank explosion. The aft section of the boat is heavily damaged and sits low in the water with only the foam flotation material keeping the boat from sinking.

It is also reported that there is no sign of Emerson on board or in the water around the boat. Some of the onlookers say he may have been able to swim to shore, but Emerson is a man in his 70s and most question if he could have been forced off the boat and made it to shore safely, a distance of more than two miles in any direction. Others disagree saying he could easily have made it if he been able to get a hold of a life jacket.

As Billy watches the scene out on the lake, he wants to go back to his locker, and get on his phone to Don to tell him what has happened. It is incredible, Billy thinks, that with all the work Don and Tom have done over the last couple of weeks trying to solve the mystery of Emerson Prescott, it has come to this less than forty-eight hours after they gave up and went home.

As soon as the boat is identified as Emerson's boat, two state troopers notify Junior at his house and drive him to the border marine control station on the east side of the lake where the search is being coordinated.

At the marina, the plant supervisor selects a few workers to shut down plant operations, suggesting everyone go back to the plant and retrieve their belongings, and either go home or stay down by the marina in case the rescuers need any assistance.

Billy goes back inside and gets his lunch and his phone. He goes out to his car and calls Diane to let her know what has happened. He tells her he is going to remain at the marina in case he is needed and that he will see her later. He looks at the time on his phone. It is already 3:30 AM. He'll wait until six before he calls Don with the news. By then there should be more information about what happened and he can share that with Don.

By 6:30 AM the sun is up, and one of the salvage vessels involved earlier in the search and rescue operation tows Emerson's boat back into the marina. The complete aft section of the boat is a charred mess. The fiberglass engine compartment covers are both burned and melted in what appears to be an upright position The rear bulkhead that serves as the entrance way from the swim platform suffered the same fate. The glass windows and portals are blown out on the first deck, and there is smoke damage everywhere including inside the main cabin below. The canvas covers over the flying bridge have caught on fire and are destroyed, as are most of the cushions up there.

The dock boy arrives just as the boat reaches Emerson's slip. He's allowed to go down to the dock and help secure the boat, then told to stay off the dock until further notice. He goes back up to the dock house and sits down. Once the boat is secured at Emerson's slip, authorities place crime scene tape at the foot of the dock, and station a trooper there to protect the boat from anyone tampering with it.

Billy walks over to the dock house. "What's it look like inside?" he asks the dock boy.

"The inside of the cabin has a lot of smoke damage, but it doesn't look like the fire made it in there," the kid says. "But the engine compartment is a different story. That looks like where the fire was.

"My guess is the engine overheated again and somehow the heat caused a fire. He told me the other day he wanted me to contact our mechanic this morning and have him check it out.

"The engine must have gotten hot on him. He said he was going to troll a lot last night and that prevents air and water from circulating in and around the engine. It looks like he had the engine compartment lids up like he did the other day to allow extra air to circulate in there, so that's my guess."

"Have you mentioned that to the police yet?"

"No," the kid says. "Do you think I should?"

"It sounds important to me," Billy says. "It might help in their investigation."

"Geeze...OK, then." The kid gets off his chair and walks over to the state trooper at the head of the dock and begins talking with him. Billy sees the trooper take out his notebook and start to record the kid's information down in his book.

Billy can see boats searching out in the middle of the lake as well as along the shoreline in hopes of finding a body or a survivor. Everyone is sure that Emerson must have been the one on the boat and they expect it will be Emerson that they find.

By 7 AM, Billy decides it is late enough to call Don, so he dials his number on his cell. A sleepy Don answers, obviously irritated that someone is calling at 7 AM. He doesn't even bother to check the number to see who it is calling him so early.

"Yeah," he croaks into the phone. "What do you want," he demands.

"This is Billy Shavers up in Dexter."

Don doesn't say anything for a moment as he tries to process this information. Why would Billy be calling him at 7 AM on a Monday morning?

"What is it, Billy? It better be good because I was having a hell of a dream when you called."

"It's about Emerson."

"What about Emerson?"

"It seems like he might have been involved in a boating accident around 2 AM this morning, and they can't find him or a body yet. There are a bunch of boats out on the lake searching, but nothing yet."

Don sits up in his bed. Emerson had a boating accident at 2 AM, and they can't find his body? What the hell is Billy talking about?

"Why do they think Emerson is missing?"

"It was his boat on the lake. There was an explosion and it burned half the boat. By the time they could get on the boat, Emerson wasn't there, and they haven't found him anywhere along the shore nor in the water. They assume he was blown overboard and was either unconscious when he went in and drowned, or drowned trying to swim to shore."

"This is Emerson Prescott, right? Not Junior, but Emerson."

"Yes. The police got Junior out of bed and brought him down to the border patrol station where the search is being coordinated. It's Emerson, alright."

"But they haven't found a body yet, right. So it is possible it was someone else, maybe even Antoine, who had the boat out."

"Nope. The dock boy said it was Emerson. Emerson told him he was going fishing last night, and even told him he was having problems with the engine overheating, and for the kid to contact the mechanic here today to look at it."

"OK – let me wake up and call Tom. Thanks for calling me. I'll be speaking with soon. Keep your eyes and ears open, and don't volunteer any information to the police or anyone else about Antoine or what we suspect."

"Got you," Billy says. "Are you coming back up?"

"I don't know yet. I want to talk with Tom first. I'll get back to you." Don disconnects the call. Ain't that a bitch, he said to himself. I was there two weeks and nothing big happens. I leave for forty-eight hours and look what happens. I haven't even started writing the damn book yet, and everything I was thinking to write may all change.

He dials Tom's number, and Tom answers with the same gruff voice Don had just used on Billy.

"Get ready for a road trip, bro. I think we're headed back up to Vermont today."

Don picks up Tom around 11 AM, and they drive up to Dexter. About an hour outside of Dexter, Don calls Billy to get directions to his house. By 5 PM, Don and Tom sit in Billy's living room as Billy updates them on what's happened since that morning.

"They started dragging the lake around noon after they were sure there was no one floating in the water or resting on shore. They won't be able to drag the lake exactly where the boat had the accident since it is almost 150 feet deep there. If there is a body out there, and it is underwater, it cold take weeks, maybe even months, to surface, and when bodies have disappeared like this, the bodies usually make it to the other end of the lake before they are recovered. We've had five or six disappear on us over the years, and that's what happens.

"Is there any chance we can see the boat and the damage," Tom asks. "I've covered a few boating accidents in my career, and I'd like to be able to see the evidence."

"They are not letting anyone on board the boat," Billy says.

"A trooper is stationed there to prevent any tampering with the evidence in case they determine it wasn't an accident."

"Do they suspect that?"

"Not that I have heard, but the trooper said the forensic people are coming down, and so are the insurance people. They don't want anything disturbed until they have a chance to inspect the boat."

"Yeah – that makes sense, I guess. Maybe if I flash my badge they'll let me at least get a look at the boat from the dock. We'll see what they do tomorrow."

"Listen," Billy says, "Have dinner with us tonight. We have a guest bedroom upstairs, and the sofa here pulls out to a bed. If you want you can go to the motel tomorrow, or stay here if you'd like.

"The plant is closed for a few days, which is why I am even awake right now. I am usually upstairs catching the last bits of sleep before leaving for work in a few hours."

Don shakes his head affirmatively and sees Tom agrees.

"Only if I get the bed upstairs," Tom says.

Don rolls his eyes and laugh. "OK, you big baby."

"Great. I think Diane has dinner ready, so let's go eat. You are going to love dinner; she's a great cook."

By noon, the Vermont State Police Arson Squad, the State Police Forensic Investigation Team, and the United States Border Patrol are all at the marina in Dexter. Working together, they begin compiling evidence. Hundreds of photographs are taken, surfaces on the boat are swabbed for trace elements, sections of the boat are cut off and bagged, and there is even a discussion about exactly where on the lake the accident occurred, since the first responders on the scene give varying descriptions of exactly where the boat was in relation to the US – Canadian border that divides the lake up into northern and southern sections.

The insurance company's people show up around noon, having driven in from Boston. They speak with the State Police representative and perform their own inspection of the damaged boat. Their longest conversation is with the Arson Squad which seems to think that there is a 90% chance this was an accident, but before signing off, have a few tests to conduct at their laboratory.

The consensus at the site, though not official, is that the fire started in the engine compartment caused by an oily rag falling on an overheated engine causing the rag to catch fire, igniting gasoline pooling in the after bilge. Once the gasoline caught fire it heated the fuel lines causing them to burst, pouring even more fuel onto the fire, and ultimately causing an initial burst of flames simulating an explosion. The gasoline pooled most likely from either a loose fitting in the fuel line or a small break in the fuel line. Since the engine compartment has been destroyed and there is so much debris in the engine compartment, the on-scene investigators have collected as much evidence as possible for a more thorough investigation and review of all the evidence back in their laboratories. They want to complete all lab work before saying for sure it was an accident. There doesn't seem to be any direct evidence pointing to arson at this time.

As for the recovery of whoever was on the boat at the time, there is still an ongoing recovery effort and that will continue for most of the day or until they find a body. It is believed that Emerson Prescott was the person on board and he is presumed deceased. That part of the case will remain open until a determination is made of his whereabouts at some later time.

At noon, Junior makes a decision to shut the plant until further notice. He instructs Millie to contact the workers to tell them they have the week off, with pay, and that they will be notified before the weekend as to when to return to work.

Around 4 PM, the state police investigators and the insurance folks have left the marina. The only police presence left are the two troopers stationed at the head of the dock to prevent anyone from tampering with the boat. There are still a couple of local police and fire rescue vessels out in the lake dragging for the body, and searchers continue checking every cove and island in the lake in hopes of finding Emerson lying on the shoreline somewhere, waiting for help.

Most everyone from the plant has gone home, though people from all over the area have been arriving off and on all afternoon to take a look at the boat and find out more about what happened last night on this beautiful lake. Even Gertrude Revere and Ben Harper go to the marina earlier in the day, meeting at the entrance, and commenting on how bad the boat looks. They both agree they hope Emerson will be found safe, perhaps somewhere on the edge of the lake, or better yet, that it wasn't him on the boat after all.

Ben wonders if it wasn't Antoine that took the boat out and that Emerson has just gone somewhere overnight, and will return soon. There's been a lot of things happening around Emerson Prescott the last few weeks, and Ben wonders if it isn't some kind of, what do they call it, Karma, coming back to bite Emerson in the ass. He refrains from mentioning this to Gertrude, who he can see is visibly upset at the thought that Emerson may be dead.

Both Ben and Gertrude stay around for a couple of hours, then each go back to their respective homes to await more news.

A little after noon, Antoine's plane lands at the Owen Roberts airport on Grand Cayman Island. He clears customs and finds a cab to take him to the Cayman Island International Bank, Ltd., just off Elgin Avenue a little more than a mile from the airport. He has an appointment at 2 PM with Hamilton Garvey, Director of New Accounts, to open an offshore account, where he will deposit his cashier checks.

Once seated in Mr. Garvey's office, the process of opening an account in the Cayman Islands begins. Antoine had to get a number of documents notarized before leaving the United States, and there are still more that need to be notarized here on the Island. After singing the cashier checks, he hands them to the banker who deposits cash into Antoine's account. He also requests a credit card to draw against his account until he sets up residency in Brazil. It takes until almost 4 PM to conclude the paperwork and have the credit card issued in Antoine's name before he receives his account number and instructions on how to access his money remotely.

He walks the less than half a mile to the coast where he finds a Hyatt hotel and checks in. He decides to shop for more appropriate clothes for a Caribbean Island and Brazil, and buys a larger suitcase. He drops them off in his room and decides to do a little sightseeing. Walking around the beach area for an hour or two he finds a restaurant just off the beach, and stops for dinner and a few drinks.

Sitting on the deck of the restaurant after dinner, Antoine watches the sun set over the Caribbean while he sips on a margarita and contemplates his new life in Brail. No more winters, no more having to play games about who he is. People will only know him as Antoine Beechen from now on. One man, one life.

He gets back to his hotel room by 10 PM, showers, and reviews his travel plans for the next day, then packs everything into the new suitcase leaving out only what he will wear the next day for his trip to Montego Bay, Jamaica, and then Sao Paulo, Brazil.

He doesn't bother setting his alarm since he doesn't have to be at the airport until a little after 11AM. The flight to Jamaica won't take long, and the flight to Brazil will leave a little before 7 PM. He'll be able to sleep on the plane, and when he wakes up he will be in Brazil.

As Antoine wakes the next morning, Don and Tom are already having breakfast with Billy and Diane. They discuss what they might do today, wondering if they should mention Antoine to the police. Don suggests that if Junior thought it was important, he would have already done that. He is not sure how much he wants to get involved in an investigation into the disappearance of someone who might be dead. That kind of thing can tie you up for a long time.

Tom says it is better for him to do the sleuthing this time since he can use his shield and police experience to mask his reasons for asking questions. Don agrees, and right after breakfast Tom takes the car and drives into Dexter, parking at the marina. He casually walks over to the trooper at the head of the dock and begins talking with him. The trooper is nice enough until Tom begins to ask questions about the accident, questions that go a little beyond "what happened".

"Is there a reason you're so interested in this, sir," the trooper asks.

"Well, yeah. I was here on vacation last week and met Mr. Prescott and his son Junior." He reaches into his pocket and withdraws his wallet where his shield resides. He opens it and shows the trooper. "I was on the job for more than twenty years and retired a couple of years back. You know, once a cop, always a cop." He looks at the trooper as the trooper looks down at his shield.

"Yeah, I guess it never really leaves you, does it?"

"Not really. You always want to be a part of a thing like this," Tom says. "You always have questions, and you can't always get answers once you are off the force. It can drive you nuts."

"I bet."

"So, are they pretty sure this was an accident? No foul play suggested?"

"Looks that way so far. The dock boy seems to think the guy went out by himself to do some night fishing, and the engine overheated. The investigators seem to back up that theory. They also found some evidence that a rag must have fallen on the hot engine, caught on fire, and then fell into some gasoline in the bilge or something, then that caught fire and then the boat blew up. That's about all I know. They're still doing lab tests on some of the evidence and reviewing all the photos and hard pieces back at the lab. Probably be weeks before anything is official, but you know how that goes. Depends on who is pushing for the result in how fast you get something back."

"My guess is, this guy is pretty well known in this section of Vermont, so they might have a hurried pace on this one."

"Do you think I could just walk down there and look at the boat? I won't disturb anything, I promise you."

"Yeah, I guess. I'll walk down with you, that way if anyone sees us, they'll just assume you are from the department and not think any more of it.

"Come on."

Tom and the trooper walk down to the boat. Tom walks back and forth along its port side, trying to get the best view into the engine compartment and into the main cabin. After ten minutes, he and the trooper return to the head of the dock.

"That must have been a very hot fire, and started very quickly," Tom says.

"I don't know much about how fires start or how they burn," says the trooper. "I know nothing at all about burn patterns, do you?"

"A little, but only what I learned from watching arson inspectors on the job."

"If you ask me, I think it was an accident, and I think this Prescott guy is floating down at the bottom of the lake and won't become a floater until late fall or even next spring. This lake freezes up pretty solid from what I hear, so once the ice sets, that's it until the spring thaw in March."

"Do a lot of people die on this lake?"

"I heard the mayor tell one of the inspectors that in 90 years there have been about eight drownings, mostly from boating accidents where two boats run into one another, and one of the people is injured, falls into the water unconscious, then drowns. A couple happened because some fools tried to swim across the lake, and didn't make it."

"How many were not initially recovered, do you know?"

"I think I heard three or four."

"Where do the floaters usually pop up?"

"At the north end of the lake, there is a small waterfall and a dam next to it. The dam was constructed to hold back water for the lake. I guess the falls were smaller before the dam was built from what I have heard. They built the dam as high as the shoreline on the north side of the river outlet up there, and now they can control how much water flows. Keeps the lake at useable levels."

"So they pop up near the dam then?"

"From what I heard today, yeah. They usually float over to the rocky side of the damn where the water pools before spilling over the ledge there. That's where they find them."

"Interesting. Hey, thanks for letting me look at the boat. Have a great day."

"You, too."

Tom walks back to his car convinced this was an accident, although there are a couple of telltale burn marks he isn't so sure of on the hatch covers. Something tells him the scorched burn marks on the separation between the hatch covers were much deeper than burn marks on the compartment covers themselves. A fire that started at the bottom of the compartment should have caused similar burn marks, but he isn't an arson expert, so this is all just a guess.

A few minutes later, Tom is back at Billy's house talking with Don about what he observed at the dock.

"So it seems to me it is probably an accident," Tom says. "I didn't see or hear anything that would lead me to believe otherwise. I don't know that we'll find out anything more until all the tests are completed. That may be a few weeks."

"I wonder if Antoine knows. He has to have heard about this by now. It must be all over the area, even up to Magog."

"Maybe," Tom says. "What do you want to do now. I don't think there is anything else to be discovered here."

"I think you're right. I think we'll go back to NY. I'll make sure Billy keeps us updated on everything, but there's nothing to keep us here."

Don finds Billy and tells him they are leaving. He asks Billy to email him if anything comes up, and especially if he hears of any police reports.

The two brothers thank Diane and Billy for their hospitality, and once again drive back to NYC.

Don doesn't hear from Billy for another four weeks and this time it is through email. The reports are completed and the fire is ruled accidental. No body has been found and the feeling is it won't be until the spring. It is probably caught on something on the bottom of the lake, and the lake won't give it up until the spring thaw forces winter runoff to flush the lake.

Billy says that Junior is sure his dad is dead but will have to wait until a body is found before holding any kind of a funeral. The plant reopened the week after Don and Tom left. Junior accepts his father's death and even started cleaning out things in the old barn.

Billy offers to help Junior with that task, and Junior accepts. So far, he and Junior have cleaned out old broken pieces of furniture, some lamps, and a bunch of really old broken tools. They plan on getting a start on the loft pretty soon.

Billy says some of the stuff in the barn looks to be 100 years old. He says it's fun seeing what's been hiding in the barn all these years. Even Junior says he's never seen some of the stuff his dad stored in there. Every once in a while, they come across something Junior remembers from his childhood, and he'll stop and tell Billy a story about it. Doing that seems to help Junior deal with his dad's disappearance, so he never stops him.

Billy promises to keep Don and Tom updated on what's going on in Dexter, and how Junior is coping with everything. No one has seen or heard anything about Antoine, and the Insurance company hauled the boat away for salvage. And oh, yeah, Ben says hello, and so does Gertrude. The last thing he writes is that Diane says hello and that the brothers are invited up for a visit anytime.

It is more than a month since he left the United States, and Antoine is settled into a small apartment on the Av. Antonio Rodrigues in Santos, Brazil, steps away from Gonzaga Beach on the Baia de Sao Vicente. All the amenities of home are available to him within walking distance. He has no need for a car since public transportation around town is excellent. The Sao Paulo International Airport is 60 miles away, about an hour and a half by car, but that is little bother to him; he has no travel plans. He takes Portuguese lessons, something he never thought he would have to do at this age, and it is difficult, but he is learning. Most businesses can understand his English, but he has problems understanding their answers to his questions. Still, he is assimilating well and does not miss the States at all.

The weather is warm the year round with high temperatures around 90 degrees F in the summer, and lows of 50 degrees F in the winter. For a month or so in January, humidity levels can be high, but generally, the weather is comfortable, and Antoine finds it to his liking. Supermarkets are reasonably priced for most food, and he is learning to eat local foods when available. Finding a new and interesting restaurant to eat at is never a problem, as every ethnic food is available.

Every morning he strolls along Gonzaga Beach, both a pleasant diversion and an excellent way to exercise for his health. He misses having a boat and plans to get one soon, though this time it will be a more modest boat, one that can sail open water. His 38 footer would have done well here.

There is a small contingent of expatriate Americans and he makes friends with them. He never mentions Emerson Prescott and the processing plant, or the town of Dexter, relying on Harmony Corners and Damariscotta as his hometowns. He does miss the people up at the marina in Magog. They always treated him well.

He plans on staying in Brazil for as long as he feels comfortable and doesn't rule out moving to another country in the future. He can now go anywhere he wants, and do anything he pleases, within the law. As long as he doesn't withdraw too much money at any given time, he will be fine for many years. His investments, suggested by the bank in the Caymans, are paying well and already his bank account is increased. He is happy and content.

Up in Dexter, Junior runs the plant just as he has for the last 30 years or so. He can't rule out that his father may be found alive, but after more than four weeks, he knows that will not happen. He decides to begin clearing out the house and barn. Billy helps him in the barn, but most nights Junior goes through things in the main house alone.

Dr. John Prescott arrives in Dexter the day after the accident, staying with Junior for a few days until he has to go back to the hospital where he works in Boston. Now, John and his family return to Dexter to discuss what they want to do with the house. Junior urges John to take it as a summer home rather than sell it off with a chunk of the farm. A decision is made to continue cleaning out as much junk as possible, then see what circumstances dictate later. The house cannot be deeded over to John until a determination of death is ruled for Emerson, and there is no rush for that to happen, nor can it happen until they find a body.

John and his family leave Dexter after a long weekend and Junior returns to his day-to-day schedule. Junior continues cleaning up the house during the week, and Billy helps him out in the barn on weekends.

This Saturday morning Billy shows up at 9 AM to help Junior empty out the loft. They begin removing easy things like old bags of clothes, a few flower planters, a couple of old oak end tables, and 25 pieces of 1" x 10" x12' pine boards that Junior didn't have a clue were stored up there. He comes across some small bales of hay that had to be more than 25 years old and throws them off the edge of the loft. Next, he finds an old oak pedestal kitchen table he remembers eating at when he was a kid. He and Billy set up a block and tackle from one of the barn beams and use it to lower the table gently to the floor.

Some oak ladder-back kitchen chairs follow (two of them have broken rungs), then Junior hands Billy some more lamps. Finally, there is little left in the loft except for a few steel containers. Two of them have no lid and Junior can see they have pieces of wood inside. He rolls them, one by one, to the edge of the loft and tells Billy to stay clear as he lets one loose over the loft's edge.

It hits the dirt floor with a thud, and some of the wood spills out. Billy rolls it off to the side as Junior takes the next barrel and does the same thing. Billy once again moves the barrel out of the way.

Junior rolls the third barrel, this one still has a lid on it, to the edge and suggests they lower this one using the block and tackle.

"This one may have liquid in it so I don't want to just drop it off the side. If it is liquid, I have no idea what kind of liquid it might be. Could be acid for all I know. Who knows what he stored up here," Junior says. "It's pretty heavy so once I secure the barrel to the ropes, I'll come down and we can both lower it down to the floor."

He loops the rope around the barrel and is satisfied it will not slip free when they move it. He rolls it close to the edge of the loft floor with almost half of it over the edge of the loft, then climbs down to help Billy lower it. Together, they take a strain on the rope and the barrel begins to lift off the floor. Suddenly, no longer resting on the floor, it just sort of jumps out, and off the loft. They hold on for dear life until it stops swinging, then lower it down to the floor of the barn. Junior unties the rope, then he and Billy roll it outside.

"I wonder what the hell is inside this," Junior says to Billy. "What kind of liquid would dad go through the trouble of storing up there on the loft rather than just leaving the barrel down here?" He can't find any latch on the rim. It seems to be sealed by tabs all around the outside rim, much like a big five-gallon can of paint or stain. It looks like it was opened once and then resealed. He finds a long sturdy screwdriver and begins flipping open the tabs, one by one until they are finally bent free of the barrel. Very carefully he starts knocking the top free from the barrel until he has freed it up completely. He removes the top and looks into the barrel.

"Oil," Junior laughs. "The old man kept used motor oil up there.

"What was he thinking? What was he going to use that for?"

"You know, farmers used to soak fence posts in oil before placing them in the ground. It helped preserve them and keeps termites and carpenter ants away, too. Maybe that's what he saved the oil for. If he was like my dad, who never threw ANYTHING out, he probably had a damned good reason for keeping it. Why he kept it on the second floor of the barn has me, though," Billy laughs. "Now that's a little weird."

"I'll have to have one of the guys from the plant come over here and take it away this week," Junior says as he replaces the lid and begins to knock the tabs down, resealing the top as best he can.

"He saved that damned oil for more than 35 years. Wow."

He looks back up at the loft. "Let's get that last barrel down and then we'll call it a day. The loft is almost completely empty now, except for a tarp and one more barrel. I don't think I ever saw it that empty in my life. There's a lot of room up there."

He climbs the ladder to the loft and grabs the tarp from on top of the last barrel. "Heads up," he yells as he throws the tarp over the edge.

Looking at the last barrel he sees the ring that secures the lid to the barrel is broken but the ring still holds the top to the barrel, although if there is liquid in this one, it most likely will spill over the edge when he rolls it. He leans against the barrel a little and tries to move it enough to tell if there is any liquid in it. He doesn't feel or hear anything sloshing around inside and decides there is no liquid in it. He rolls it over to the edge of the loft floor and once again ties the rope around the barrel until he feels it is secure enough to be lifted and lowered.

He climbs back down to the barn floor and again, he and Billy pull on the rope. The barrel comes free from the loft floor and swings over the edge a little. This barrel is not quite as heavy as the one with the liquid in it. They begin to lower it slowly to the floor. Once on the floor, Junior removes the locking ring and sets it aside, then he opens the lid.

Inside he can see what looks like sand or maybe commercial fertilizer. "Why the hell would he keep commercial fertilizer in a barrel up on the loft," he says to Billy.

"For the same reason he kept the oil up there," Billy laughs.

"I guess so. I guess he had his reasons, huh?"

"Let's roll this bad boy out to yard over near the compost

heap, and empty it out. Even if the fertilizer is no good anymore, it will mix well with the waste."

He places the lid back on the barrel and they take turns rolling it the 100 feet to the compost pile. Positioning it so the top of the barrel will spill into the center of the heap, Billy removes the lid, then the two of them push the barrel over. Old fertilizer pours out of the top of the barrel and when they turn over the barrel to empty it, not only fertilizer falls into the compost heap, but something that has been sitting in that barrel for more than 20 years falls out as well.

"What the hell is that," Junior says.

"I know what it looks like, but it can't be that," Billy Shavers says. "Can it?"

"It looks like a dried up body. But that can't be. What would a body be doing in a barrel in our loft?"

"I don't have any idea, but I think it's probably a good idea not to touch it, and for us to call the police." Billy already has his phone out and is dialing 911. The dispatcher answers quickly. "What is the nature of the emergency, sir?" Billy answers with "I think we just found a dead body. Can you send out the Sheriff?"

Within fifteen minutes, Darren Prichard pulls into Emerson Prescott's driveway and over to the barn where Junior and Billy are standing waiting for him. He gets out of the car and walks up to them. "What's this about a dead body," he asks.

"Over here, Darren." Junior motions for Darren to follow him. "We aren't sure it's a body, but don't know what else it could be." The three of them walk over to the compost heap.

"Whoa. Sure looks like a body, don't it," says Darren. "You find it dumped here?"

Junior looks first at Billy, then at the Sheriff. "Well, no. Darren. We dumped it here. We emptied that barrel over there and out it popped."

"You don't say. You don't see that often, do you?" Darren walks around the compost heap to get a good look at the body. "Sure looks like a body to me.

"This is out of my league. I gotta call in the state guys for this one. Follow me back to the car while I call it in."

A little more than 30 minutes later a state trooper drives into the driveway and over to the Sheriff's car. "Whatcha got Darren?"

"Not sure exactly. You're going to have to see this one for yourself. Come on."

All four walk over to the compost heap and Darren tells the trooper what Junior and Billy have told them.

"OK. Everyone stay away from there from now on. I'll get the forensics team, and maybe even the Coroner down here. It'll take a few hours for them to get here." He places the call to headquarters and they tell him to secure the site and wait for everyone.

"Show me where you got this barrel from," the trooper says to Junior. They walk over to the barn and Junior points up to the loft.

"It was sitting in the back corner, over there, under this old blue tarp on the floor here. We were cleaning out the loft and it was the last barrel we removed."

"OK – we need to get out of here, too. Let's go over to the porch and wait for everyone. They should be here in an hour or so.

"You've sure had you fill of troubles this year, Junior. Sorry to hear about your dad. I remember him from when I was a kid. Whenever our high school baseball team played yours, he always bought everyone soda and ice cream after the game. He was a good man. I can't believe they haven't found him yet."

"No, not yet. I know he's down in the weeds somewhere out in the lake, but I keep hoping I'm wrong and he'll show up one day."

36

The investigation of the contents of the barrel takes up most of the day. Once the forensic team and the coroner arrive on the scene, the state trooper requests that Billy and Junior accompany him to the state trooper station located a half mile from interchange 29 on I-91, east of Dexter.

They arrive in separate cars at 4:15 PM and park outside the trooper's station house. The trooper tells them he needs to go over some facts and then write up the report and have them sign it.

The small concrete block building has four businesses and the trooper station. There is a now defunct video store for rent, a Pizza restaurant, a Dollar store, a laundromat, and at the end, the State Police station. They enter the station, which is little more than a large room containing two desks, a radio dispatch table, some file cabinets, a few chairs and a table. The trooper indicates to Junior and Billy to sit at the table as he walks to his desk and gathers a few papers and a yellow tablet.

Joining them at the table, he places the tablet in front of him and begins to read from one of the papers he carried with him from the desk.

"We are going to have a conversation about the incident at Emerson Prescott's house on Abenaki Trail, where you called the Vermont State police to report a body you found on the property. I will ask you a few question relating to this incident and you have the right not to answer any question I ask.

"You are not under arrest, nor are you at this time suspected of any infringements of the law.

"The reason for this conversation is to verify the facts as we understand them to be at this time, and for you to add to these facts anything you have failed to disclose to the state police. Also, if you have any suspicions as to what may have caused this incident to take place, this is the time to inform the interviewer.

"Do you have any questions?"

Junior shakes his head no, but Billy asks, "Are we suspected of anything? We didn't do anything here except empty a barrel and report what we saw. Do we need a lawyer or anything like that? I don't understand all this."

"No, you are not suspected of doing anything wrong. This is just a conversation to review what you told me already, and for you to add anything you think you forgot to tell me before." The trooper turns the paper around to face Junior and Billy. "Would you both sign at the bottom of the page please, where indicated by an "x"."

Junior signs first, and reluctantly Billy also signs.

The trooper opens his notebook and begins to transcribe, point by point, what Junior and Billy have already told him. He asks if there is anything they can think of that they didn't tell him earlier, and they reply no.

"Do you have any idea how that body might have gotten into that barrel," the trooper asks.

"None at all. Matter of fact, there was a barrel of oil up in that loft as well, and I have no idea why or how that was there either," Junior answers.

"Who had access to the barn other than Emerson, your father?"

"I did. But as you saw, the barn is open to anyone that wants to just open the door and go in. We have no lock on it."

"So, anyone could have placed that barrel in the barn, hoisted it to the second-floor loft, moved it all the way to the back corner of the loft floor, and covered it with a tarp, and neither you nor your father would have known? Is that what you are saying?"

"Yes," answers Junior.

"And you, Billy, you have never been up in that loft before today, is that correct?"

"Yes," replies Billy. "I've been helping Junior move some stuff out of the barn for the last few days but today is the first time we removed anything from up there. Come to think of it, I never even went up to the loft at all, did I, Junior?"

"No, you didn't," replies Junior. "You were always below me

to move the stuff I threw over the edge. You were keeping the floor area under me clear."

"And neither of you have any idea at all who that person in the barrel might be," the trooper asks.

"I sure don't," answers Billy.

"Nor do I," says Junior.

"Please don't take this the wrong way, either of you, but Junior, your dad is still missing from that boating accident, is there any chance…"

"Whoa! Wait a minute. If you are trying to indicate that this body is my father's and that either I or Billy have anything to do with my father's disappearance, I'm done here." Junior begins to get up, but the trooper waves his hand and shakes his head negatively.

"I'm sorry, but I had to ask."

Junior sits back down. "I don't want any more questions like that one. I had nothing to do with my father's disappearance, and only wish that he could walk through that door right now. I loved my father, and would, and HAVE, done almost anything for him."

"OK. Gentlemen, that concludes the interview. Please sign at the bottom of each yellow sheet of paper and our interview will be concluded."

Junior and Billy each sign their name where the trooper indicates and stand to leave.

"It is going to be a few days before we get any information back from the coroner or the labs on who that body might be. Do not go back into the barn for any reason. Do not remove anything from the barn. Do not do anything at or near the compost pile. It is all off limits to you. We'll have the places cordoned off, so please respect these instructions. If we need to contact you for anything we have your work and home numbers, and of course, I know where you live. Matter of fact, you even know where I live. Who doesn't know where anyone lives here in Dexter…we're not that big a town."

"We're apparently big enough to have had a body in a barrel for who knows how many years without anyone knowing about it," Junior says. "Maybe the town is bigger than we think."

The trooper looks at him. "Well, almost no one, right? Someone knows how that body got there, we just don't know who."

Junior drives Billy back to his farm and stops next to Billy's truck.

"Been quite a day, huh, Billy?" Junior turns off his engine and gets out of his car.

"Excitement is one thing," says Billy "but this is something else. Who the hell could that be and how long has he, well I guess it could be a she, been in that barrel?"

"That body looked almost mummified, or at least parts of it did. My guess it's been in there a very long time," replies Junior. "I guess we'll know more in a few days when they get the reports back."

Billy shakes hands with Junior and walks to his truck.

"Thanks for helping me out these last few days," Junior shouts to Billy. "You've been a friend. Thanks."

Billy touches the bill of his cap and gets into his truck. He drives out of Emerson's driveway and turns for home. As soon as he is out of Junior's sight, he pulls over to the side of the road and gets out his cell phone.

Don is on speed dial, and Billy pushes the buttons to make the call. Don is going to want to know this.

Don's phone rings five times and then his message comes on. "This is Don Winston. I cannot answer your call at this time, so please leave your name, number, and a short message. I will call you back at my first convenience." Then a beep.

"Don – this is Billy. Ya gotta call me back immediately. Something interesting has happened up here that I know you are going to want to know." Billy hangs up.

He sits there at the side of the road trying to figure out who could possibly have been in that barrel. No one other than Emerson has gone missing from this town in more than twenty years. This is one hell of a mystery, he tells himself.

He puts the truck in gear and drives off to his house. By now, Diane has heard he has been taken to the trooper station, and she is probably worried about him. He'll be home in ten minutes, then he can tell her the whole story, or at least as much as he knows. He, like everyone else, will have to wait for the completed reports before anyone can say they know the whole story, and even then, there is probably more to the story than even the investigation can possibly reveal.

In New York, Don looks down at his cell phone when it buzzes. He is out for a light jog around Pelham Park, something he recently started doing again. He likes Pelham even more than Central Park for running. There are more hills and a much more varied landscape than Central Park. After dark, it is a little more dangerous but as long as you run during the day it is safe. There is always parking in the lots except Saturday and Sunday mornings when people play ball on the ball fields and families use the park for picnics.

He sees it is Billy calling. He laughs and rolls his eyes. What is he calling about this time? He decides to check the message after his run. It's getting near dusk and he wants to finish the run before dark.

Forty minutes later he sits in his car and searches his voice mail for Billy's call. He finds Billy's call and presses the play button.

"Don – this is Billy. Ya gotta call me back immediately. Something interesting has happened up here that I know you are going to want to know." That is the entire message. Man, he sounds a little crazed. Wonder what's so important, Don says to himself.

He accesses Billy's number from his directory and presses the call button. Billy answers. "Don?"

"Yeah, Billy. I got your call. It sounded urgent. What's up?"

Billy proceeds to tell him of the day's occurrences, including that he was questioned at the troopers office for over an hour.

Don asks if anyone has any idea who was in the barrel, and Billy says no one knows anything. Don thanks Billy for calling and tells him he'll be up in a few days, but to let him know if anything comes back from either the coroner's office or from the forensic labs. Billy says OK, and they hang up.

Don then pushes his speed dial number for Tom, who answers on the second ring. "What's up, bro?"

Don proceeds to relate everything Billy told him and asks

Tom if he wants to drive up to Vermont with him in a few days.

"Are you kidding? I wouldn't miss this for the world," Tom says. "I can see this will mess up that book you've been writing since we returned last month. Hope you haven't written the ending yet."

"No, not yet…and I bet I may even have to rewrite the beginning once I find out what's going on with that body up there."

"So, we leaving Friday night or Saturday morning?"

"Not sure yet. We should probably wait until they get the preliminary reports back. Won't be any new information before then."

""Probably not," says Tom. "Just let me know; I'll be ready when you are. I'll keep my dance card open."

After hanging up, Don tells himself that this is a story that just keeps on giving. Driving home, he goes over what Billy told him on the phone. This may end up being a bigger mystery than what happened to Emerson.

At 1:30 PM on Friday afternoon, detectives from the Vermont State Police enter Emerson Prescott, Jr.'s office at the processing plant. One of the detectives carries with him a yellow manila envelope containing three pictures of objects found amongst the contents of the barrel from the barn at Emerson's farm.

They stop at Millie's desk and present their credentials to her. She rises from her chair and walks into Junior's office to announce that the police are here to see him. He stands and waves his hand for her to show them in. She steps into the doorway and motions for the men to enter. As soon as both men are in the office, she leaves and closes the door behind her.

"I am Detective Sgt. Robert Goldstein," says the shorter of the two men, "and this is detective First Class Henry Marsh. We are with the Vermont State Police, Coroner's Office.

"I have a couple of photos I would like you to take a look at." He doesn't tell Junior that the pictures are of objects from the barrel. He opens the envelope and removes the three 8 x 10 pictures, laying them out on Junior's desk.

"Do any of these items look familiar, and if so, why would you recognize them?"

Junior walks around the desk to stand next to Detective Goldstein. He picks up one picture and looks at it.

"I recognize this ring," Junior says. "It's my father's pinky ring. I haven't seen that ring in at least twenty, maybe twenty-five years. Where did you get a picture of it?"

"Sir, please look at the other pictures first. Do you recognize those articles?" the detective takes the picture of the pinky ring from Junior.

Picking up the second photo, junior says, "This looks very much like a coin my dad used to carry around with him all the time. He called it his lucky charm.

"See that little nick on the rim, just under the last "T" in the words 'In God We Trust'. He told me he notched that to remind him that was the year he married my mother. He said that was the luckiest day of his life."

Detective Goldstein takes the second photo from Junior and hands him the last photo, asking "Do you recognize this item?"

It is a picture of a button. "I don't recognize that at all," Junior says to the detective. I mean, I know it is a button, but other than that, I have no idea what it's from."

"Our forensics team traced it to a windbreaker manufactured overseas and sold by Northwest Outfitters, in Seattle. Did your father ever wear clothes from that store?"

"I'm pretty sure he didn't. He ordered almost all his clothes from LL Bean up in Maine. He said they were the best, and if anything went wrong with their product, they always replaced them free. He always told me that they knew how to keep a customer and that we should always try to behave the same as them when it came to our customers."

"So you have no idea how this button or any of the other articles could have ended up in the barrel you found in your barn?"

"None at all. I have no idea how any of those items ended up in the barrel."

"I am sorry to tell you this, but the ring was around a finger bone of the corpse we found in the barrel. With that information and your identification of the half dollar as belonging to your father, it appears the body found in the barrel may well be your father."

"That's impossible. You know as well as I do, that decomposed body has to be a lot more than a month old, and dad was alive then. Hell. Half the county looked for him after his accident out on that lake last month. How could what you say be even a possibility?"

"We still have a few tests to complete at the lab, but you should prepare yourself if the results come back confirming our theory that those are his remains.

"To be sure, though, may I take a DNA swab for comparison? We only need to swab the inside of your mouth."

Detective Marsh removes a small sealed package from his

coat pocket and sets it on Juniors desk. Then he removes a package of latex gloves from the same pocket, opens the package and puts them on. Opening the swab kit, he removes a long cotton-tipped swab and a plastic tube. He walks over to Junior and says, "Open your mouth, sir."

Junior opens his mouth and the detective swabs the inside of Junior's cheek with the cotton swab. He opens the tube, places the swab into it, then replaces the rubber stopper. He removes a clear bag from his pocket, opens it and places the tube into it, pressing the seal closed. Laying the bag on the desk, he signs his name across the seal, then removes the gloves and places them in his coat pocket.

"Thank you, Mr. Prescott. We'll be in touch when we compare this sample with the sample from the body. We will probably have preliminary results by Thursday or Friday." Goldstein removes the last picture from the desk and replaces all three pictures back in the envelope. The two detectives turn, open the door, and leave the office.

Junior stands there watching them leave. How did they get those two items of his father? They couldn't have been in the barrel, could they? He tries to remember the last time he saw his father wearing the pinky ring or saw his dad take his "lucky charm" out of his pocket.

Oh, my god, he says to himself. I can't remember how long it's been. The detective said the ring was circling a finger on the corpse in the barrel. His father would never give that ring or his lucky charm to anyone.

Sitting down in his chair he realizes, hey, that might really be my father, but then who the hell has lived here and for how long? Twenty years? Thirty years? Forty years? He can't get his head around this.

He gets out of his chair and walks out of his office. "I am leaving for the day Millie, I'll see you Monday."

"Is everything OK, sir?"

Junior doesn't answer. He walks past her and out to his car.

On the drive home, he tries to put this new information into some sort of perspective, but it doesn't make any sense. His father has always been around. He hardly even took vacations, and the few times he did, he went somewhere with Junior. For most of his life, Junior has seen his dad almost every single day of his adult life.

Arriving home, he drives up the drive past the compost heap and the barn. Yellow crime scene tape still encircles both areas. He stops and looks at both areas. How could that be his father's body in the barrel? That would mean his dad has been in there at least ten years, maybe more. But he saw his dad every day; it seems impossible.

He'll just have to wait until the DNA test comes back. Maybe the test will confirm it isn't his dad after all. But then if that is true, then who was in the barrel, and why was he wearing his dad's ring? And why was his dad's lucky charm in there, too? His reasoning tells him that if the body iasn't his dad, then his dad must have put that body in the barrel, and that might indicate that his dad had killed someone and hidden the body there for all those years.

That made no sense to him either. His father was a pacifist. He didn't even have to go into the service because he got a deferment based on that fact. His dad didn't even hunt. The closest he got to hunting was skinning and preparing deer and other small game for him and their friends. He did that right there in that barn His dad never killed anything, and Junior knows he never could.

Junior knew it would be a long weekend waiting for the results of the DNA test. He also knew the news was not going to be good, no matter which alternative proved to be correct.

He drives up to his house, parks his car, and goes in to tell his wife what has just happened. He supposes he needs to call his brother and tell him, too. This whole thing, the boat blowing up, his father not being found in the lake, the body found in the barn, and now his father's rings and lucky coin showing up inside that barrel, it is all too crazy to be real.

37

Tom and Don arrive Saturday afternoon, the day after the State Police take a DNA swab from Junior. They drive to Billy's house and park next to his truck. Through his living room window Billy watches them arrive and get out of their car. He goes to the front door and opens it before they get to the front steps.

"Good to see you again," he extends his hand first to Don, then to Tom. "Come on in." The brothers walk in as Billy yells out toward the kitchen, "Diane…they're here."

Diane walks out into the living room, drying her hands on a kitchen towel. "Oh, how nice to see you two again. Billy's been pacing all day like a fox outside a hen house," she laughs.

"It's good to see you two as well," says Don.

"Would you guys like a beer, or something stronger?"

"I'd love a beer," Tom says. Don nods as well.

"Be right back," says Diane, who disappears into the kitchen.

"Sit down, sit down," Billy tell his guests. "I have a little more information for you."

Diane returns with the beers. Handing each of the brothers a beer, she excuses herself to the kitchen to continue making dinner. "I hope you're both hungry," she smiles.

"Always," Tom answers.

Once Diane leaves, Billy begins to update them on what has happened the last week.

"Nothing much since I spoke to you last. Junior comes into work every day, but I think he just does the minimum work. I think he's preoccupied with thoughts of his dad, and what's going on.

"I stopped by his house this morning to see how he's doing and we sat and talked for a while. He told me the state police had been there Friday to speak with him.

"He said they showed him some photos of items found in the

barrel, and that they took a DNA sample from him.

"When I asked why, he was at first hesitant to tell me, then said he would, but only if I promised not to tell anyone, so I am breaking my promise now with you too, please don't say anything? I didn't even tell Diane what I am about to tell you."

Both Don and Tom nod agreeing not to repeat anything he tells them now.

"Junior said they took the DNA swab to compare it to the body in the barrel. The pictures they showed him were of things owned by Junior's father, things he was never without. One was a pinky ring found on a hand bone from the body in the barrel. They think the body may be Emerson's."

"That's impossible," Don says. "How could that be? There must be hundreds of people that can attest to seeing Emerson up until the boat accident, and you said parts of the body looked mummified, right? That doesn't happen in a few months; that takes years."

"I know. Crazy, huh? Junior can't make any sense of it either. He said that if it's his dad inside that barrel, then who's been living here in Dexter all this time? If it isn't, then who put the body in the barrel, stuck his dad's ring on a finger, threw his father's lucky charm in there, too, then hoisted the barrel up to the loft in the barn, and all that, without anyone noticing?

"He says either possibility doesn't make any sense."

"He's right. Neither scenario makes sense." Don looks quizzically at Tom.

"There is one other explanation, one other possibility."

"What's that?" Billy asks.

"Before I say anything, we need to wait for the DNA results to come back. No sense opening up a new can of worms.

"But if what I am thinking might have happened, then this is a much bigger story than even Arthur Conan Doyle would have dared to make up.

"Let's wait for the DNA results. If they come back positive, then we need to talk first with Junior, and then we're going to have to talk with the state police. Until then, though, it's all a guessing game."

"Oh, boy. Here we go again with his ideas," Tom says. "He isn't going to tell us anything until those results are back. He does this all the time. Lures you into a situation, then leaves you hanging there. He's been doing this to me my whole life."

Billy laughs, and Don smiles.

"You mean we'll have to wait until Friday to hear what he's thinking," Billy asks. "Always with the mystery."

"Unless those results come in sooner, you won't be able to pry his mouth open," replies Tom.

"OK, then. It sounds like we sit and wait until the test results are back." Billy stands and signals them to follow him into the kitchen. "Let's see what she's cooking up tonight."

Tom and Don spend Saturday night and Sunday visiting with Billy and Diane. Sunday night, Billy leaves for work at the plant around 11:30 PM. He asks if the brothers will be meeting him at the Chicken and Cow for breakfast or if he should just come home. They opt for the restaurant and plan to meet around 8 AM.

Monday morning all three sit waiting for their breakfast to arrive. Laura, surprised to see the two brothers again, asks if they will be in town long, to which they reply they are not sure.

"What are your plans for the day," Billy asks Tom.

"We thought we might ride up to Magog and see what's been going on there since we left. We were wondering if Antoine has been seen up there recently. You would think that everyone up there would know about the boating accident by now and that someone would have spoken to Antoine about it.

"We're curious about his reaction to the news his friend is missing. And we're curious as to why he hasn't tried to contact the family if he and Emerson are such great friends."

"Will you be back tonight," Billy asks.

"We're not sure," Don answers. "If we come back tonight, we should be here by dinner time, but don't plan on dinner for us. We'll catch something out."

A little after 9 AM the three of them leave the restaurant.

Billy turns south to his house, and Don and Tom turn south and east toward Harmony Corners. They have plenty of time to kill before they can head north to Magog and the yacht club's marina. Frank, the bartender, won't be in until the afternoon, so they decide to ride down to Antoine's house to see if he might be there.

An hour later they ride down Devon Road in Harmony Corners, stopping at number 22. The first thing they notice is that there is actually mail in the box. It is not only full, but the door to the box isn't even able to close.

"Wow! Antoine has gone from getting no mail here to having his mail box stuffed to the gills with the stuff," Don says. He gets out of the car and walks around the house, not expecting to find anyone there or see anything out of place from the last time he was there. He returns to the car where Tom sits waiting.

"We need to take a ride to the post office," Don says.

A few minutes later Tom asks the postmaster about all the mail in Antoine's mailbox. He uses his shield to get the clerk to loosen up and talk to him.

"So, I notice his box is overflowing. Last time I checked a few months back, he had no mail going to that address at all." Tom says.

"Yeah. Strangest thing. The beginning of this month mail starts coming into his address again. That's the first time I've seen anything in years.

"But we had to stop delivering his mail because we can't just leave it on the side of the road, we have to put it in a box, and as you have seen, his box is full.

"I have a small box of mail for him here, so if you see him, let him know. We'll hold it for a while, but pretty soon, we'll start returning it as undeliverable."

"So, he hasn't been here or even notified you that he was going away, or anything like that, huh?"

"Nope. Never said when he came back, and never said when he left again. We asked his neighbors if they had seen him, and no one has. Seems kinda strange to me, but you know people, they do strange things."

Tom thanks him for his time and returns to the car. "No one has seen him and no one knows where he is," he says to Don. "Where to now?"

"Let's see what the mail drop place has to say."

They drive straight to the building where My Mail Address, Inc., is located in Burlington. Tom walks into the building this time, while Don waits in the car.

Walking into the offices of My Mail Address, Inc., he pulls out his shield and calls one of the staff over to him. Just before the kid can clearly see the shield, Tom flips his wallet shut.

"I need some information on one of your accounts," Tom says authoritatively.

"We can't divulge that information sir," the kids says.

"All I want to know is if a post box you administer is still receiving mail here. Don't make me go through the hassle of getting a warrant. If I have to do that, I could just as easily pull your name and see if there is anything I should know about you."

"Uh, what box number did you say it was?"

Tom tells him, and the kid disappears into a room on the other side of the office. He returns a couple of minutes later.

"That box number is no longer active. It was canceled starting this month."

"Now, who owned that box office number and where was the mail sent?"

"I really can't tell you that sir. I could get fired. They'd be pissed if they even knew I told you about the cancellation."

"How pissed off are they gonna be if I find something on you, let's say maybe a bust for a little marijuana or meth? You think they'll like hearing that?"

"Ok. But don't ask me anything more."

The kid rushes to the back room again and returns with a small index card onto which he has written the forwarding address, and who paid for the PO box.

"Thanks, kid. Your secrets are safe with me. Now, uh, you

better not mention this to anyone, understand. If I hear you did, well, use your imagination, ok?"

The kid nods and watches Tom walk out of the office. He doesn't see Tom chuckling to himself as he walks down the stairs to the car.

"Piece of cake," he says to Don as he gets in the car and hands Don the index card. "Here ya go."

"No surprise here," Don says as he reads the car. "Emerson Prescott paid the bill.

"The forwarding address, though, is a little surprising. It's another PO box, but it's not in Dexter or in Harmony Corners. It's in Irasburg, Vermont. Where the hell is that?"

Tom enters the name into the GPS unit in the car.

"Looks like it is about five or six miles south of Dexter. Guess we're going there now, right?" Tom pulls out of the parking space and they head back toward Dexter and Irasburg.

They arrive in Irasburg, a town even smaller than Dexter, in a little over an hour. Tom finds the post office located in the center of town. The town consists of a common square, which is a grassy park, and a wood frame building on one side that houses Pete's Mini-mart and the Irasburg Post Office.

Tom pulls into one of the five parking spaces outside of the building. The brothers look at each other and laugh.

"This place couldn't have been more rural," Tom says. "One building in the whole town. One building! And a park. And the park doesn't even have any benches. It's just open grass. This, is a small, small town."

"If it weren't for that hand painted sign on the porch post, you wouldn't even know there was a post office here. Never saw a post office building without a flagpole outside. They always have flag poles with a flag flying high. I thought it was a law or something."

Tom gets out of the car and enters the post office with the index card in his hand. Once inside he walks over to the counter and waits while the clerk gets up to help him.

Tom flips his wallet again, just before the clerk gets to the desk. "I have a couple of questions you might be able to answer," he says as he flips it closed again.

"What are those questions. I'll help if I can," says the clerk.

"I have a post office box number here that we believe is registered to Emerson Prescott from over in Dexter."

"Yeah. Heard about his accident couple months back. Actually, I happened to have seen him a day or so before his accident. He came up here to cancel out his PO box. Said he wasn't going to need it anymore. He picked up his remaining mail and said goodbye.

"He must have had that PO box for more than fifteen years, which is as long as I've worked here."

"Well, you just answered all my questions," Tom smiles. "thank you very much."

"Any time officer."

Tom opens the door and sits down in the car. "That was almost too easy. I didn't even get a chance to ask a question and he told me everything I needed to know."

"What did he tell you," Don asks.

"Seems that Emerson rented that PO box number for at least 15 years, and then suddenly canceled it a few days before his accident."

"Hmmm…that's odd. He cancels the mail drop, he cancels his secondary PO box, and all the mail that came to either of those addresses now seems to be delivered to Harmony Corners. It was as if he knew he was going away."

"It's starting to look like that, doesn't it?"

"Let get up to Magog and see what Frank has to say. He'll be in to work soon if he isn't there already."

Forty minutes later they walk into the bar at the Yacht Club and sit down at the bar. It is almost noon. They order lunch and a couple of beers and wait for Frank to show up.

38

It is nearly 2 PM when Frank walks through the doors of the Yacht Club's restaurant. He walks past Don and Tom, who he does not recognize. He says hello to the regulars at the bar, and ducks into the kitchen for a few moments before returning to his normal space behind the bar. The current bartender and Frank have a few words before he cashes out of the register. After checking the stock behind the bar and making sure everything is as he likes, Frank starts at the other end of the bar from the brothers, freshening drinks, taking orders, generally saying hello to everyone. Finally, Frank stands in front of Don and Tom.

"So, gentleman, can I get you anything," he says.

"Don't you remember me, Frank," Tom asks.

Frank studies him for a moment. "I picture your face, but the name and where I know you from eludes me. Help me out here."

"The name is Tom Winston. I was up here about a month and a half ago. We had a conversation about Antoine Beechen, your buddy."

"Oh, Yeah. Now I remember. How have you been? You were going to do some fishing as I recall. Ever get around to that?"

"No. I never had the opportunity. Business came up and I had to leave."

"Too, bad. You up here to try again? The season is just about over you know, maybe only a couple of weeks left, so you better do what you can, while you can."

"Actually, I am back on business this time."

"Too bad. It's nice out on the lake this time of year."

"I heard about that big accident on the lake last month. That must have been something."

"Yeah. That nice 38-foot boat we talked about caught fire and blew up. You remember I told you about the old guy that owned the boat, well, it seems he was on it when it blew and must have gone overboard. They still haven't found his body, poor guy. Probably won't be until the spring. That when lakes give up their dead."

"You seen his friend since then? What was his name? Andy, wasn't it?"

"You mean Antoine? Nope. Haven't seen him since a little before that accident. Maybe he won't be coming up this way anymore now that his friend is gone. I think I told you, he and I had a few good times up in Sherbrooke."

"So, he hasn't been around since then, huh? You would have thought if his friend died he would have come up to see what was going on."

Frank nodded. "Yeah. You'd think that, wouldn't you? But everyone is different, I guess. Maybe he's been down to Dexter rather than up here, seeing as that's where the old guy was from."

"Yeah. Maybe." Tom changes the subject to something more mundane, then tells Frank he and Don have to get going, that they have an appointment in an hour or so. He tells Frank he'll see him next time he's through this way.

Don and Tom leave the bar and walk down to the marina docks. Tom is thoughtful. "So, Antoine hasn't been here since before the accident. And no one has heard from him in Harmony Corners. He's not picking up his mail, and the forwarding service isn't forwarding his mail to Emerson anymore.

"This is a tough one to figure out, but it's beginning to sound like some kind of a conspiracy here."

"Maybe more than a conspiracy, Tom. They haven't found Emerson's body yet and now Antoine has disappeared. Do you think the accident could have been rigged? That the two of them have disappeared together? There's no body for Emerson, and Antoine is gone as well. Two brothers, like you and me, disappear at the same time. More coincidence? I don't think so."

"We'll, if your theory is correct, what's the motive? Emerson has lots of money, and Antoine has that little house in Harmony Corners, and neither seem to be in debt. Why not just continue doing things as they have been doing? What is there for them to gain?"

"That's a good question; but here's the real kicker. What if it turns out that the body in the barrel really is Emerson? How does that factor into everything?

"I didn't want to go over this in front of Billy, but what if Emerson was in that barrel for what, twenty or so years, then who has been making believe they were Emerson for all this time? There's only one logical person that could pull that off right?"

"Antoine? Are you saying Antoine somehow has taken Emerson's place for all these years?" Tom emits a low whistle. "Hmmmm...that's a good theory, bro. There's one little loophole in that theory, though. They've been spending days, and sometimes weeks together on the boat all these years. Explain that away."

"How many people have seen them together at the same time?"

Tom thinks for a moment. "You could be right. No one has ever really seen them together at the same time. It's always been Antoine's word that the old man was on the boat.

"If you're right, how do we prove it?"

"There's nothing we can do until the DNA tests come back. Before we try to tell the police everything we suspect, we have to tell Junior what we suspect. He deserves to know first before anyone else. We can do that tomorrow or the next day."

"Let's go back the other way around the lake. We have to kill some time before dinner. We can try to get back before Diane plans a meal for just the two of them," Don says.

"Yeah. She's a good cook. We should pick up a nice bottle of wine for tonight. And you know Billy will want to hear everything we found out today. He's probably up already, just waiting for us to get back to fill him in on everything."

Don and Tom roll into Billy's driveway around 4 PM. As Tom guessed, Billy is already up from sleeping all day, and waiting for them to come home.

He opens the door and walks out to meet them on his front lawn, three beers in his hands: one for him and one for each of them. They walk over to a picnic table under a maple tree off to the side of Billy's house and sit down.

"OK. Tell me what you found out today. You know me, I can't stand the waiting." They all laugh.

Don goes over everything including that part about Antoine not having been seen since before the accident. Then he tells Billy his theory. When Don finishes explaining it, Billy just stares in disbelief.

"As amazing as that sounds, my god, it all makes sense."

"We still need the DNA results, though. Trying to present this information to the state police will only make it all sound like the ridiculous ranting of two out of towners without the DNA to back up the theory." Don sips his beer. "We need to talk with Junior about this, too. Maybe tomorrow morning we can stop by his office. He's still going in isn't he?"

"I saw his car there this morning when I left work," Billy says, "so I assume he's going in."

"Good. We can do it in the morning then."

"What's Diane cooking tonight?" Don asks. "I'm getting hungry. And...I have two bottles of very good wine sitting in the back seat of that car with our names on it."

"Go get the wine," Billy laughs, "and bring it inside. We'll see what she's cooking up. You're lucky she ignored your instructions about not cooking for you tonight."

"Ummmm....I'll go get that wine."

The rest of the night is just friends spending time with friends until Billy has to go to work.

"I'll see you guys at the restaurant in the morning," Billy says, as he leaves for work.

Diane goes to bed right after Billy leaves. Don and Tom stay up talking some more before both admit they need their sleep, too.

The next morning Billy meets the brothers at the restaurant. Billy says he didn't see Junior's car yet, but now, Junior sometimes comes in a little after 9 AM. They eat a leisurely breakfast, staying off the subject that they will soon be discussing with Junior.

Don doesn't think Billy should be at the meeting, but Tom disagrees.

"Listen. Junior feels comfortable enough having Billy help him at the house cleaning out all that stuff, plus Billy was with Junior when they discovered the body. Don't forget, he told Billy about the photos and the police visit. My guess is Junior wants to share this all with a friend, and Billy has been placed in that position already.

"Let's take the chance. Billy can join the circle for real."

Don looks at Billy. "I guess you've earned the right to be in this all the way. We've trusted you with everything, as you've trusted us, so it's time for Junior to trust us all as a group. You're in, Billy."

Billy nods. "I won't say anything out of line. I feel part of all this now. Thanks."

Nine o'clock comes and the three of them walk over to the plant and see Junior's car in the lot. The walk to the office and up to Millie's desk.

"Hi Millie," Billy says. "We'd like to talk with Junior. It's important. Can you let him know we're here?"

"Sure, Billy. Let me tell him."

She opens Junior's office door and walks in. Then they hear Junior's voice, "Come on in guys."

The three of them enter his office as Millie leaves, closing the door behind her.

"Hi, Billy," Juniors says. "Don and Tom right? Have a seat everyone."

As they take their seats Don says, "We're sorry to hear about your dad's accident."

"Yes. It's been a shock not only to me, but to the community. He was well liked.

"What can I do for you today?"

"Remember those questions I asked your dad the last time I saw him?"

"I'll say. He was blazing mad at me for letting you into his house. He got over it though and everything was OK after that."

"Good. I would have felt bad if I had caused a family rift."

"No problem."

"Junior told us about the discovery of the body in the barrel on your farm, and about finding your dad's ring and lucky 50 cent piece in with the remains."

Junior looks at Billy. "Honest, Junior," Billy says, "they are the only people I said anything to about that. I know they are interested in all this and they asked me to keep them updated on what's been going on. They only want to help."

"Help? How can you help me, Don?"

"If you remember those questions I asked your dad, I'm guessing he never answered them, did he?"

"No. He told me to mind my own business."

"I would have guessed that. Would you like to have the answers to those questions now?"

Junior looks at him quizzically. "Do you have the answers? Why couldn't you have told me then?"

"I thought it more appropriate for him to tell you, but he apparently thought different. Now, with everything that's happened, I think you need to know everything I've discovered about your dad.

"Some of it, you won't believe, and I'm sure you've never heard most of it. It's going to take some time, but by the time I finish telling you what I know, I think you'll understand why I couldn't tell you before."

39

After Don finishes telling Junior everything he knows, and everything he suspects, Junior sits in disbelief. His whole world is turning upside down. He has an uncle he didn't know he had. His grandparents weren't really his grandparents. His father may have been leading a double life or his uncle and his father, who may be twins, may have committed arson and fraud and have now both disappeared. On top of that, his father's ring and lucky charm are attached to someone's body which has been found in a barrel on his father's farm.

"That is a lot to digest, Don. I guess we have to wait for the DNA result to come back don't we. I mean, if that is my father in the barrel, then who has been acting as my dad for all these years? This mysterious Antoine?"

"That may be the case," says Don. "But without the DNA, we have no proof."

"I'm going to share something with you that I received in the mail yesterday," Junior says. He reaches into his top desk drawer and pulls out an envelope. He unfolds the flap and removes two pieces of paper from the envelope.

"This is my father's bank statement for the time period just before he disappeared until two weeks ago." He pushes the paper toward Don, who picks it up and reads it.

Don whistles as he reads it, and then hands it to Tom.

"Did you contact the bank to make sure this is accurate," Don asks.

"Yes, I did. The bank manager confirms it and told me dad explicitly told him not to tell anyone about it."

Tom looks at Junior, then at Billy, then asks Junior, "Is it OK to mention this in front of Billy?"

"Billy…this stays in here, OK? I am trusting you."

"Absolutely," Billy says.

"According to this, all tolled, your dad withdrew from various accounts, almost a half million dollars in cashier checks, money transfers, and cash, a few days before he disappeared. Does that sound like him?"

"Not at all. Quite the contrary. Dad almost always only used credit cards to pay for things."

"What happened to the money?"

"The bank manager is tracing the trail of the cashier's checks. They weren't deposited in any local banks, he told me. Matter of fact, he's pretty sure they weren't even cashed in any banks in this country. He won't know for sure until they reenter the American system.

"He expects to know more by the end of today. All he can see is that they were deposited to an account, but it appears to be one of those offshore bank accounts identified only by a number, no name."

"A half a million dollars. That can keep you going for a long while, especially if you are out of this country. You can really live large on that kind of money."

"I think it may be time to bring the police in on everything you've told me. I have no idea about any of this. I don't know if my dad was in that barrel, or if he perished in an accident on that boat, or if he decided to take off with half a million dollars of his own money and faked his own death, or if his brother has been impersonating him for thirty or whatever years."

Junior looks on his desk for a card, and when he finds it, calls the number.

"Detective Goldstein, please....yes, tell him it is Emerson Prescott, Jr. calling...Yes...I'll hold.

"It's the detective that came to see me last week."

Everyone is silent for a couple of minutes as Junior waits for the detective to come on the phone.

"Detective Goldstein... Is this Mr. Prescott?"

"Yes, it is. I think you need to drive out here today. I may have some pertinent information regarding that body I found last week. I also have two gentlemen here that have a lot of information you are going to want to hear about....yes...this afternoon would be fine. We'll be available, thank you. See you then."

He hangs up then looks at Don, Tom, and Billy. "I hope you're wrong about all this. I hope it's not my dad in that barrel, and I hope if he took all that money, there was a good reason for it."

"We'll know soon enough," Tom says. "Once they start assembling the information, they'll be able to put into play a lot more resources than we have available to us as civilians."

"I have one more thing to tell you before the police arrive," Junior says, "and you're probably not going to like it either.

"You've been lying to us all this time, haven't you? Telling us you are just history buffs, interested in the stories hidden in small towns. It's all been a lie, though. You're a writer, right? I went on line and did a search on you last week. You befriended us just to get a story for a book."

Billy is the first to express disbelief and a little resentment.

"Actually, it all isn't a lie. I just left out the part about the book. Just to set your minds at ease, I am not writing a book about you nor about the town. I will not use Emerson's name, or this town's name, or even the region in the book. I only hoped to get some background for a premise for a book.

"Thing is, the more I learned about Emerson, this company, this town, the people here, the more intrigued I became in following all the threads I saw. One by one, bits of information lead me somewhere else.

"Tom can attest to the fact that three or four times I was just about to leave and let everything end, then something came up that turned me back into it, and I had to follow up. It's the inquisitive nature of a writer to do that.

"I never meant to offend you or take advantage of you. In fact, I've become concerned about what's happened here, and hope whatever I can contribute to the investigation will help solve this whole riddle."

Junior stares at Don. "You did take advantage of our friendship, but I understand why you did what you did. You even tried to help me get my dad, or whoever that was, to tell me about some of the things you had learned about him. Now, at least I'll finally know the truth about everything. So in that sense, I have to thank you, I guess."

"Let's try to concentrate on resolving this for you. Once I speak with the police and tell them what I know, if you want me out of all this, Junior, I'll be gone."

"No – without you, we might never have learned anything about my father's life."

Detective Goldstein and his partner arrive a little after noon and join the four others in Junior's office. As junior begins to tell him about what they have discovered, the detective pulls out a small voice recorder and begins recording everything.

"Does anyone have a problem with me recording this," he asks. Everyone agrees it's OK.

Two hours later, Don and Tom, who has disclosed to the detective that he is a former detective with the NYPD, complete telling the detectives everything they know about Emerson Prescott and Antoine Beechen.

At the end of the conversation, Goldstein turns to Junior. "I have something to tell you, but I wanted to wait until I heard what you had to tell me.

"I am sorry to tell you, but the man in the barrel was indeed Emerson Prescott. The DNA swab we took from you came back today, and it matches your DNA with a 99.9% certainty. Although, with this new information, I guess it is possible it could be your father's twin brother, we weren't looking for that possibility, but my guess is, it is your dad."

"So who died out on the lake?" Junior asks.

"My hunch is no one," says Tom. "I'd lay odds that the man you have known as your father for all these years is his brother, Antoine Beechen and that when he started feeling the squeeze Don put on him for information, well, he figured it was time to get out. So he faked his own death and has evaporated into who knows where?"

"I think we'll put out an APB for this Antoine Beechen fellow," Goldstein says. "My guess is he's using his credit card to purchase things, thinking we're not looking for him. After all, as far as he knows, no one knows he exists in connection with Emerson Prescott. They always make a mistake somewhere, and maybe that's where his mistake will be made."

Don says he has all that information on his computer and if the detective follows him outside, he'll bring it up for him. He'll also give him all the PO box information, as well as the high school pictures, and copies of birth certificates, etc.

Junior reaches into his desk drawer and pulls out a new thumb drive he always keeps handy in his desk and gives it to the detective.

"You can just transfer the files, it will be easier that way."

Goldstein thanks him and he tells Junior he'll be in touch. The two detectives and the Winston's leave, but Junior asks Billy to stay for a moment.

"Billy," Junior says, "don't be angry at them. Writers do things like that all the time, that's how they get their story ideas. Besides, if Don hadn't done all that investigating, all that fact checking, we'd have never known all this."

"I guess so," Billy says, "but he could have told us sooner."

"If they had, maybe none of us would have been so forthcoming with them about what we knew."

"You're right. I guess they did the right thing after all.

"I hope you find out exactly what happened to your dad and when. You deserve to know that."

"Me too, Billy. Me, too."

40

The next day the Vermont State Police, along with the New Hampshire State Police enter Antoine Beechen's house in Harmony Corners, New Hampshire. They remove items from the house for DNA testing, and they also retrieve his mail from the mailbox in front of his house, as well as from the post office.

The credit card company runs a report on all credit card charges to Antoine Beechen's credit card for the last year. The Vermont State police, in conjunction with the Sûreté du Québec (Quebec Provincial Police) locate and interview people that know Antoine in the town of Magog. The Vermont State Police forensic team, now armed with the theory that the fire on board Emerson's boat may have been deliberately set, review all the evidence they have on the fire. They contact the salvage company and luckily, they still have the boat and have not yet begun dismantling it or parting it out. The boat is revisited by the team to search for more evidence.

The local bank where the money was withdrawn from has received more information on the possible location of where the checks were cashed. A bank in the Cayman Islands. The state police put in a special request to release any pertinent information on who cashed the check and where they may now be residing.

Within a few days, Emerson's dentist is asked to provide dental records, but that dentist has only been working with Emerson for less than twenty years, so the police set about locating his former dentist since they are really interested in Emerson's dental records from before then. Emerson's previous dentist retired in 1989, but his son still has the records in his basement and provides the police with those records. Once the coroner has those records, identification of the body in the barrel is officially identified as that of Emerson Prescott.

Within two weeks, enough evidence is assembled to charge Antoine Beechen with at least bank fraud, impersonation, arson, falsifying a death, and a host of other small charges. The Vermont State attorney orders his arrest.

The big break comes when the credit card reports show

Antoine charging a plane ticket to Grand Cayman Island. Once the airline is identified, the date Antoine flew there is verified. Using that date, police request records from the airports in the Caymans to determine if and when he might have flown out of the country.

A small airport on Grand Cayman Island recorded that Antoine Beechen flew to Montego Bay, the day after he landed in the Caymans. Checking flights out of that Montego Bay airport reveal Antoine caught a flight to Sao Paulo, Brazil that same day.

The US consulate requests the Brazilian government assist in locating Antoine. It takes a few weeks to locate Antoine in his apartment on Av. Antonio Rodrigues, Sao Vicente, in the State of Sao Paula. He is relaxing in the afternoon sun on his balcony, overlooking the Baia de Sao Vicente when the knock comes at the door.

Within 48 hours his extradition papers are complete and he is on his way back to the Untied States, and the State of Vermont.

Once back in Vermont, Antoine is brought to Orleans County Courthouse for arraignment. He is held without bail since he is assumed to have financial resources available to flee the country, and is remanded to the Johnathon Bridges State Correctional Facility just outside of Dexter for trial.

The State begins piecing together the information they have and decide they have enough circumstantial evidence to charge Antoine with the murder of his brother, Emerson. Antoine is returned to court ten days later after a grand jury charges him with murder. He is remanded back to the correctional facility and held under 1,000,000 dollars bail, which he cannot post.

Though there is no death penalty in Vermont, but with the surety of a guilty verdict regarding the fraud and theft charges, which can carry up to 20 years if convicted, Antoine and his court-appointed lawyer succeed in having the murder charge reduced to involuntary manslaughter. Part of the deal is to have his time served in a federal facility. One of his charges is a federal count of crossing a state line to commit a felony since he lived in New Hampshire when he committed the manslaughter.

Three months later he is sentenced to 20 years for the manslaughter and five to ten years on each of the other counts.

Effectively, he will spend his remaining years in prison.

Before the trial, Junior asks that he be allowed to meet with his Uncle. He wants to find out exactly what happened and why before the trial starts.

Antoine agrees to meet with him. The meeting lasts for more than four hours as Antoine explains how it all happened.

Junior sits in the room with the man who impersonated his father for more than 25 years. He has so many questions but decides to let Antoine do all the talking.

"So tell me, Antoine, what happened that day you placed my dad in that barrel."

"I knew for a long time I was adopted. Apparently, my mother knew she was pregnant with one child and somehow arranged for him to be adopted by your grandmother and grandfather.

"She was surprised during labor when a second child was born. I was that second child. She didn't want to just give me away to just anyone, but my father wasn't coming back from the war and there was no way she could raise me on her own. My father's brother agreed to take me in and raise me as his own, so he and his wife soon formally adopted me. Of course, I didn't know anything about my real mom, until much later in life. I knew I was adopted, but my adoptive parents never told me anything about my birth mother.

"I spent years trying to find out who my mom was. During my mid-twenties, I discovered my then long deceased birth mother's identity, and I also learned I had a twin brother. I set out to locate my brother. I looked for so many years trying to determine who my brother's adoptive family was.

"I finally hired a private investigator to help me. The PI knew how to grease the wheels for information and one day the PI told me that he located the name of the family, Prescott, but he couldn't with any certainty know which of the more than 64 Prescott's, in New Hampshire alone, they might be. There wasn't even any information guaranteeing that my brother's family even lived in New Hampshire, but the adoption address on record was in Portsmouth, New Hampshire, so that was a start.

"Armed with this information, even though it was a long shot, I began to methodically search phone books, research local papers and even high school yearbooks in New Hampshire, then Maine, and then finally Vermont, in hopes of finding a Prescott around my age.

"One day I was reading an article in a local paper in a small town in New Hampshire, about an hour from where I lived then in Harmony Corners, New Hampshire, near the Little Moose reservoir on the Vermont-New Hampshire border. It was a story about an Emerson Prescott, a wealthy man who owned a grain processing plant. Looking at the accompanying photo in the article, I realized that the man looked just like me. Hoping he was my brother, I began to conduct more research on Emerson, tracking down where he lived, his family, his business life, and his financial status.

"At the time, I was really down on my luck. I had been drifting around for a few years, doing menial labor jobs. I had saved just enough to buy a little rundown shack in Harmony Corners that I began to call home. But I knew that was as far as I was going to go in life. And here, all of a sudden, I thought that if this man was my brother, he could help me out, maybe get me started in a business, or better yet, bring me into the family business.

"So I decided to contact him, thinking he might at least give me a little money. I drove into the town where Emerson lived. At the time, I wore my hair long and had a beard, and I doubt if anyone in town could see the resemblance. I stayed for a couple of days to see if I could locate him and figure out how I could contact him, and let him know I was his brother. I wasn't sure how Emerson would take discovering he had a brother and so I kept my beard and long hair until I at least had the chance to meet him.

"The first time I met him, it was a few years after he had the car accident where your mom died. I knew where he lived and one afternoon I drove up to the house and approached him, revealing to him that I was sure he was my brother. Well, of course, Emerson didn't believe me. He told me to get the hell away from him and to leave him alone.

"He was still recovering from the amnesia he had from the accident, and he later told me he decided he needed to check his birth certificate to see what it might say about a twin."

"I remember that. He asked me to help him find it. He never told me why he needed it, but he was really interested in finding it quickly," Junior says.

"You know, he didn't know he was adopted. They never told him. When we spoke again he told me he saw that he had an Amended Birth Certificate, but due to the amnesia, he had no idea why, then you told him it was because of an error about his date of birth that had needed to be corrected from the initial birth certificate.

"After seeing his Birth Certificate, I assume Emerson was sure I was trying to scam him. Then I returned one day a week later, this time clean shaven and with a haircut just like his. Even he admitted our resemblance to each other, but when I tried once more to assert we were brothers, Emerson tells me again to go away and stop making such false claims.

"Then he threatens to report me to the police as someone trying to shake him down. Not wanting to get the police involved, I left again.

"I returned a week or so later, late in the afternoon and I once again asked Emerson to admit we were brothers. I begged him to let me part of his family since I now had no family left.

"We got into a heated discussion and Emerson started to walk away from me after again ordering me off his property. He was screaming at me that he was going inside to call the authorities and tell them I was trying to shake him down.

"I grabbed your dad by the arm and a fight ensued. We didn't strike each other, we just grabbed at each other, but Emerson lost his balance and fell. He hit his head on the car bumper there in the driveway. He was knocked out cold; I tried to revive him, I couldn't.

"He wasn't breathing and I panicked. I knew he was dead. His head was bleeding from the gash and I didn't know what to do. Not wanting to hang around for the police who I knew wouldn't believe me, and seeing that no one else was around to see what happened, I made a quick decision - hide Emerson's body somewhere and then become Emerson Prescott. I knew I could do it. I would just pretend a clunk on my head caused me to have another bout of amnesia.

"I looked around the property and saw our run down two

story barn. I carried Emerson's body into the barn and looked around for something to put him in to hide the body. I saw a couple of old 55-gallon oil barrels, and one was empty.

"I found some rope and tied it around the empty barrel, then climbed up the ladder to the loft and hauled up the barrel. I placed it way in the back in that corner where you found it. I went back down, lifted Emerson up on my shoulder, and carried him up to the loft.

"I looked around the barn floor to see it there was anything I could add to the barrel to cover what I knew would soon be the smell of a rotting, decaying body and found a couple of bags of sand, and a couple of bags of fertilizer. I removed Emerson's clothing, dressed in them, and threw my clothes in the barrel. I lowered my brother into that barrel and poured first the sand, then the fertilizer in the barrel and over the body until it was covered. Then I locked the security ring on the barrel and hurried off the loft.

"I returned to the car and bending down, smashed my head as hard as I could trying to break the skin and make it bleed. I had to hit it so hard I almost knocked myself out. Then I sat down against the wheel of the car, blood running down my head and over my face, and waited till you came home. You finally did, and when you found me, you wanted me to go to the hospital, but I argued that I was OK and only needed to clean up.

"You called the doctor anyway, and when he came, he wanted me to go for some tests at the hospital, but I argued with both of you, and you finally agreed you would watch me overnight to make sure I didn't have a concussion.

"The next day I woke up in Emerson's clothes. I had a terrible headache, and believe me, I felt terrible about what I had done to Emerson. I had spent so many years trying to find my brother, and then I ended up killing him. I was afraid if I told anyone the truth, well, I'd end up in jail, or worse, maybe the death penalty back then.

"So I lived out the amnesia story, which everyone bought, and gradually, I returned to having a semi-normal life living as Emerson Prescott.

"I never meant to hurt you, Junior. I wanted more than anything back then to be an uncle to you. If only your father had let us be brothers, we wouldn't be here today. I am not blaming him for what I did, I am just saying it might have been so different.

"And just so you know, you were always so kind to me. I am sure you were like that to your dad, too. I know he had to be proud of both you and your brother, John. Please tell him what I told you, and let him know I am sorry I didn't get to know him better, but most of all I am sorry I caused your dad to die."

By now, Antoine is near tears. All the angst of the last 25 years has poured forth, and he feels drained. He realizes he lost his brother 25 years ago and has now lost the only family he cared about.

"Antoine," Junior says, "I can't tell you I feel no anger toward you. You killed my dad, you stuffed him in a barrel for 25 years, you lied to me about who you were, and in the end made me and John suffer the anguish of losing their father in what we believed was a fiery boat accident.

"We have suffered so many ways because of your actions, I can hardly count them. First, taking our dad away, second losing who we thought our dad was, and lastly, having to find my dad in a barrel in the loft of my barn. What a mess you've made.

"I am sorry for all you went through in life. I guess it just proves that old theory about nurture versus nature. Nurture can win out, even with exact twins, life can end up differently depending on how they are raised.

"At least you let John and me know why all this happened. It will provide some closure for us. And now I can at least give my dad a proper funeral and burial.

"I don't know if we'll ever see each other again, Antoine, but if we do, it won't be soon. I feel sorry for you. If you had just given it more time, you might have finally gotten through to your brother and you could have had the family you so desperately always wanted to have.

"Goodbye, Antoine. I wish you peace."

Junior gets up and walks out of the small visiting area as Antoine sits and watches his nephew walk away.

"I'm sorry too, Junior." Antoine says. "And Emerson, I'm sorry for you, too."

Epilogue

Don Winston sits in the studio of WFDS 97.9 in Wahsawswoon, North Dakota, about fifteen miles northwest of the capital city of Bismarck. He and Sherman Smyth, the host of "All The Things We Read", a local independent radio station cultural show, discuss Don's latest novel, "Two for the Price of One" published two months earlier.

"So, Don," Sherman asks, "you have said this is not a historical true-life novel. It is, though, based on true-life events that unfolded in large part to you, is that correct?"

"Aren't all novels based in part on truth? Wouldn't it ring untrue if everything in a book was created purely from the imagination?" Don answers cautiously. "To answer your question more completely, yes, the idea for this book came from events of which I had first-hand knowledge. That's all I am willing to reveal about that."

"The character in your book, Henry Dumstall, without giving too much of the story away, ends up spending years in prison for a very interesting type of murder. Was that a concept you conceived or did that really happen?"

"Reality and fiction, in this case, end up being very similar. The real Henry Dumstall was a much more sympathetic person, though. He was not an unlikeable man, whereas the Henry Dumstall in my book is a cold, calculated character."

"I know your brother is an ex-New York City Detective. I assume the main character in your books, Jeffrey Stamford, is based on him rather that upon yourself."

"Not completely. My brother Tom, and he won't mind me saying this, is not so reserved as Jeffrey Stamford. Jeffrey would rather sweet talk his way through things, whereas Tom goes straight to the heart of the matter. You'll note that in the book, Jeffrey often lets the other characters in the book volunteer the information needed to move the story along, rather than pull it out of them. Tom likes to dive into people and grab the information, and keeps pulling until he pulls it completely out of them."

"So, did Tom have to pull the information from Henry Dumstall's real life counterpart?"

"No – but he used techniques that as a detective worked well for him when interrogating suspects. I would guess that those he interrogated though may say different. He's a pretty tough interrogator."

The interview concludes 25 minutes later as Sherman thanks Don for participating on his show. Don thanks Sherman for the opportunity to promote his book, and then graciously departs for his hotel room in Bismarck.

These book junkets are tiring and they are especialy boring in smaller towns like Bismarck. It is not that the town is boring, it is that there is no time to explore when going from one town to the next.

As the car service takes him back to his hotel room he receives a text from Billy Shavers. He and Billy keep in touch and for the last year, while Don has been writing the book, Don would contact Billy if his memory needed a refresh on an aspect of the events that transpired regarding Emerson's death and Antoine's subsequent trial and incarceration.

Ever since Antoine pled guilty to the more minor indictments of arson, theft, obstruction of justice, impersonation, and a few other offenses, as well as the major indictment of manslaughter, Billy would email or text Don when something interesting occurred relating to the case.

Don looks down at his phone at the text message from Billy.

Don – some bad news from the prison this afternoon. Antoine is dead. He committed suicide at 1:30 PM Got the news from Junior. He left a note – "time to join my brother at last". I'll send you more news in an email.

So, that's that, Don says to himself. Antoine wasn't really such a bad guy. In the end, all he wanted was to have a brother.

About the Author

Stephen H. Lancelot grew up in Manhattan, New York City, NY.

He writes fiction, composes music and lyrics, is a performing musician, sails, gets lost on streams while fly fishing, and enjoys woodworking.

Stephen has a B.S. in Arts and Humanities, from the *College Of Saint Rose, Albany, NY,* an A.A.S. in Performing and Creative Arts, from *Staten Island Community College, CUNY, Staten Island, NY,* is a recipient of an American Poets Society Award, and was a Guest Poet at S.I.C.C.

Stephen served as a Quartermaster 3rd Class in the United States Navy on board an oil supply vessel.

Stephen lives in a log home in the town of Westerlo, New York, with his computer, his Prius, and a Martin D-28.

Other books by Stephen H. Lancelot

Strong Are The Strangers (2016)

Made in the USA
Middletown, DE
20 August 2017